DECENCY

A Novel of Men Who Fell from Grace

DECENCY

A Novel of Men Who Fell from Grace

Alex L. Tavares

SANTA FE

Sunstone books may be purchased for educational, business, or sales promotional use.
For information please write: Special Markets Department, Sunstone Press,
P.O. Box 2321, Santa Fe, New Mexico 87504-2321.

Book and Cover design › Vicki Ahl
Body typeface › Minion Pro
Printed on acid free paper

Library of Congress Cataloging-in-Publication Data

Tavares, Alex L.
  Decency : a novel of men who fell from grace / by Alex L. Tavares.
     p. cm.
  ISBN 978-0-86534-849-3 (softcover : alk. paper)
  I. Title.
  PS3620.A8956D33 2011
  813'.6--dc23

                    2011045582

WWW.SUNSTONEPRESS.COM
SUNSTONE PRESS / POST OFFICE BOX 2321 / SANTA FE, NM 87504-2321 /USA
(505) 988-4418 / ORDERS ONLY (800) 243-5644 / FAX (505) 988-1025

A man is fortunate to be blessed,
even when he may not deserve such grace.

For Susan, Paulette, Larissa, Hyacinth and Claire, the
women who have encouraged my countless blessings.

PART ONE
THE SACRIFICIAL SCAPEGOAT

1

Dank, deep-rooted wooden pews with stained-glass impressions stand in rows before God's son. Behind the pews, Lanier walks up to the burgundy-black curtains of a confessional, enters, pulls the curtain closed behind him and prays for a few moments before the Father slides open the partition grate. Father Hibbens has sleep in his bloodshot eyes and small shards of toast in the creases of his mouth, dry and cracked, as he stares blankly at the curtain in front of him.

"Bless me Father, for I have sinned," Lanier says as he pulls the headphones down from his ears and lets them rest around his neck. He kneels in front of the Father's profile and signs the Holy Trinity with his head bowed.

"How long since your last confession?" the Father asks.

Lanier looks up toward the priest's stone grey eyebrows, watches the man's face-forward stupor. A finch darts over the open booth, weaving through the rafters of the steepled roof. Lanier listens to the faintest sounds of passing cars. The creak of the swollen floorboards as a person walks down the corridor alongside the stained-glass portraits of Christ's death and resurrection. The hurricane rains, though relentless throughout the week, finally settled like the smoldering ashes of an epic fire; still the misgiving qualms and rumbles of the dying storm linger. "It's been about four years."

"That's quite a long time."

"Yes, father."

"Go on."

"I disobeyed my mother."

"Anything else?" the priest asks.

"Yes father, I've stole things."

"What did you steal?"

"I've stole so many different things."

"How old are you son?"

"About thirty," Lanier brings his hand up to his chest pocket. "Father?"

"Yes."

"May I read something to you?" Lanier unfolds a piece of paper, the soft crinkling, his delicate nature exposed.

"Is it a piece of scripture that concerns you?"

"No, it's something that I've written."

"Something you've written?"

"Yes Father. Sort of like a requiem, or a..." but Lanier sits there, confused, unable to think of the word he wants.

"Well go on," and Hibbens waits, hands together, chin up and eyes squinting.

"I am a liar and a thief, but otherwise I strive to be decent..." Lanier breathes in deeply through his nose and the breath shakes his whole body as it leaves him. The paper trembles and takes on moisture from his fingers.

"Of course my son, you seek forgiveness and the Lord shall cherish you."

Lanier reads on, quieting Hibbens, "Mother had an abortion a year before she had me. For her, I have sold drugs. I have sold drugs to schoolchildren and I have coveted your daughters." Lanier pauses again as to listen to Father's breathing; it is slightly louder, the air moving deeper into his chest. Then Lanier continues, "I have broken into your house, through the wide windows, under the cat-creases in your garage. I have cheated. I have mugged. I have beaten your adulterous wife and molested your dog, all in an attempt to be a decent man."

There is silence, eyes-closed silence, ears pounding at the faintest ruffle of polyester and cotton.

"Without consciousness or will, I grow facial hair that scratches at your lips and hips, and forms rashes and rashness. I have been on both sides of the gun, knife, and needle. I have seen both sides of masturbation and disease. I have sold parts of myself for things other than money. I had to watch my sister, without being able to help, as she was burned. Pleading, choking, crying through the smoke that circled her, around and around, until the smoke was her, like the cream in the coffee I can no longer drink. Father, forgive me. I am an addict, a jealous lover, a man without friends and I hate to be alone. I curse every lord and every religion, but in my struggle for decency I strive to please God. Because God gives me life and desire, and ability. Because God stimulates me and gives me the opportunity, every day; because God gives me throbbing blood and headaches and allows me to live even when I wish I were dead." A deep base tremors, echoes in his words, and then he releases and calmly says, "It is this sense of decency that saves me, Father. I only do what I believe the Lord wants, Amen." Then Lanier says it again after a moment of quiet, "Amen."

But Father Hibbens does not reciprocate, nor does he forgive him, damn him, or say anything.

Lanier begins to speak slowly, pausing between words and thoughts. He looks at the paper but stops reading from it. "I love all of your daughters..." he says softly, breathes in, then continues, "...just as I loved my sister. When the fire and smoke killed her. I tried...to stop it...but... it was my fault. I tried. It was so strong my eyes bled." Lanier stops for a moment, closes his eyes, "It was too thick to push through. I was so slow...but I'd rather not talk about it with you, Father." Lanier runs his fingers over his stubbled hair and then rests his hands down atop his lap. He has a pocketknife in his pants' pocket that he begins to feel through the fabric. He outlines it with his finger as he rocks, front to back, his molars clinching up. His jaw in taught knots. He opens his eyes and slightly pulls aside the curtain to see a lady at the pulpit, and he watches her slow and languid movements toward the front pews and the altar made of stone that appears to rise from the earth. He lets the curtain fall back. "When I was a kid, my mother had us stay with a man that looked a lot like Jesus. He did terrible things to people, people like my mother. He laughed at the things he did, laughed for a long time. Then he would stop laughing, and it would look like there was nothing behind his eyes. It's sort of hard to explain. It was just blank. Not tired or even angry, just blank." Lanier laughs through his nose. "Sometimes it was funny to watch what he did. I would hide in the closet. Quiet, trying not to laugh along. He eventually found me, and when he found me, he fucked me. He was tired of junkies, he said. He was tired of my mother, he said. He wanted something fresh, he said. Something new. Then he laughed. He left his seed inside of me, and it blossomed Father. Into disease. Then he fucked the disease with a broken broomstick, Father. Maybe mother gave it to him and he gave it to me, but it doesn't really matter now. Does it Father? God gave it to us. I don't want to give your daughters my diseases. Fucking junkies, god-damned disease carrying sparrows. That's all we are, that's all I am..." Lanier stops himself as he feels his voice is rising and leans back on his heels with a muffled chuckle deep in his chest. "My mother cleaned me with bleach when I told her what he did..."

Lanier's hand digs into his pocket, slowly, and feels the cold spine of the folded blade. "I was fine with that. I understood that I deserved it. And, you know, I still went back to the closet. I still watched him when my mother wasn't there, but when I saw him, on top my sister…his stomach pressing down on her back, her wrists cuffed to the metal bed. Her face swollen red. Her hair clumped in his hand… I knew I had to kill him. I was only a kid, but I knew. It was a remarkable feeling. Even when she tried to stop me, she couldn't. She couldn't move. And when I covered his body with gasoline…I couldn't stop." Lanier looks beyond the paper that is about to slip from his fingers. With a thin chin pointing towards the ground, Lanier closes his eyes and asks, "Father, are you still there?"

There is no reply.

Lanier opens his eyes to the open ceiling of the booth, clear to the ceiling of the church, swollen with mildew stains and water damage. "Sin came into the world by the fall of the first man. By this fall not only he himself, but also his natural offspring have lost the original knowledge, righteousness and holiness. All men are sinners by birth, dead in sins, inclined to all evil and subject to the wrath of God. Born in sin, I still try to be decent, Father. Amen. I'm sorry, Father." Lanier folds the paper and pulls aside the curtain of the booth. He lets the paper he had read from slip down near the Father's feet. "I will pray, Father. For both of us." He dabs his fingers in holy water, signs the cross and puts his hand back into his pocket, holding the knife as he walks head down out of the building.

Hibbens does not move as the young man leaves—deep breaths rattle behind his sternum. The curtain dances in front of him as the long-stalked electric fans hum slow and hang low. And the curtain continues to dance for some time, and it resembles a timid girl's trembling gown, waiting to be torn away. Hibbens had never heard such a voice, this voice in particular, such a soft tone bereaved. As the voice wanders, echoing in and out between his ears, Hibbens cannot help but imagine a small animal, opossum or raccoon, trucked down the middle and fixed to the road, desperate in its last few moments, a fatal attempt to claw itself to a soft place to die. Hibbens knew not to get close because injured animals are desperate and lash out at compassion or empathy, which they cannot understand. Hibbens does not move. His nose starts to water, and he lets it slowly trickle down the side of his mouth. He holds himself in his corner, as if the serpents of Asclepios were seeping through the heavily shaded partition grate. He listens to the children just outside of the church windows, splashing puddles and creating laughter in shrieks. A dog whinnies at the unsung thunder. Though he tries to concentrate on those sounds, in his mind he hears over and over the young man's whimpering—either whimpering or laughing through his nose.

And for a brief moment, a thought traipses into the midst of the psychotic laughing, and for that brief moment Hibbens questions his relation to God, with true meaning, for there is always that sense of uncertainty.

2

"I'm right here," Lanier whispered. His lips were slightly apart, and his eyes, though deep set, bulged from their pockets with intensity and desire and a certain amber glaze. He was tall, delicately structured, and his hair lay in bangs like a hammock across his forehead. Loose, foam padded headphones sat haphazardly above his ears. He stood at the back of the house, underneath the outstretched arms of the Japanese Plum tree. He leaned against the warped stucco that framed the little girl's bedroom window as the music sang into his ears, lyrics about how I can't take my eyes off of you, and how you'd be like heaven to touch. He knew how to tap-dance around the motion sensors in the darkest of night; there was a rhythm to it, swinging his shoulders back, bobbing right to left. No lights, no stars. He hadn't heard a car pass the front of the house in over an hour. It was late in the night and late into the fall when the poplars and oaks had begun to turn, and the pines greened sharply for winter. Around midnight the sky was the color of Muscari hyacinths, a deep bruised purple-black, the moon covered by thin clouds, and when he stopped the tape player, the sounds of night became amplified all around him.

"Sadie-baby," he whispered as he gently ran his fingers along the glass of her window. He watched her sleep, knowing that her mother was on the other side of the house. Her mother, the fat cow, he thought. Her mother, whom he had watched earlier brushing tangles from Sadie's hair until the poor girl hollered, her face wet with tears. Her mother, whom he couldn't watch as she paddled Sadie with the backside of the brush for crying, paddled until his sweet little girl moaned, her cries so deep that they were hollow and muted.

He also watched for the cats, the cats that watched him. He hated those cats for how close they got to her. Lanier wiped the sweat off his palms onto his pants; the dark sweater he wore closed in on his neck. Sadie's knees were always scraped, her hair bunched in soft red curls, her socks with little frills he wanted to chew up and swallow. It was impossible for Lanier to say how long he had been coming to watch her—more than a year, less than a year—

nights bled into mornings when poised like a sandhill crane and invigorated, deluded by coffee and crystal, suffering. His fingers shook like meter. Every sound, every leaf and blade of grass became muffled by the hammering in his lungs. And yet he could hardly breathe. He could see her; tangled in her sheets, one leg out of the covers, one little fist balled under her chin.

She runs in her sleep, he thought. Her ski-sled bed surrounded by glow lights for nighttime, little beacons that gave her soft, freckled cheeks radiance. He often imagines pinching, nibbling them; he wants her cries deep inside of him. A cat leaped onto the foot of the bed, the shimmer of the eyes, a livid and direct glare. He startled and pulled away from the window. The tabby rolled on its back, rubbed its ear onto the comforter and began to pat at the uncovered sock frills in a taunting, almost provocative manner.

"I'm right here Sadie-baby," Lanier whispered. The breath from his mouth turned to a dense fog in the night chill and brushed against her bedroom window, clouding then clearing, clouding then clearing. He pulled a piece of tinfoil from his pocket that had been folded neatly into a four-square. He unfolded it, and in the middle crevice he placed a crystal, clear ice, and lit it from underneath. He sucked the rising smoke through a short plastic straw and watched the ceiling fan in Sadie's room spin trails on a slow cycle. The fan's breeze skated one thick curl of hair back and forth over her cheek.

Hers was a flat house—almost identical to his house down the street; most of the homes on the street were practically the same—hidden safely in the community of picket fences and tall hedges. The spark of the lighter never disturbs her, the orange glow reflecting in the window like a deadening pulse.

3

She was lost, walking the corridors of Graceville Hills First Baptist, and had been looking for her father. That was all it took: her gray-blue eyes—somewhat translucent—covered in tears, her puffed cheeks, her thin shoulders shaking, trembling before him: all of it reminded him of his sister. It seemed as if God gave him another chance. He thanked God for the church. He thanked God for Sadie. He thanked God for another chance at forgetting the fire that killed his sister. Lanier even volunteered many of his afternoons as a Deacon. It seemed as if he had been at Sadie's window ever since. Waiting, watching, trembling. The smoke filled his lungs, the smoke that kept his eyes open, that kept him awake, endlessly awake as she slept. He believed that if he could keep his eyes open, then he wouldn't see what had happened, what he had done to the man who looked like Jesus, what he had done to his own sister. The sacrifices that he had made.

In the morning, around 3:00, Lanier left Sadie's window and began to follow a cat. The children in the pediatric ward would be waiting for him in a few hours, as he was the first person they saw every morning. But today, the cat drew him farther and farther, and many of the children were going to wake up alone, waiting and wanting to be carried or to sit on his lap even though they knew they were not allowed to do so. Lanier made kissing noises for the cat, trying to lure it. The cat slowed its pace and stood tall in the back; its tail fluttered, and Lanier followed the cat timidly, slowly closing the distance. He followed the cat to a bike path, under a dark canopy of hickory and live oak, shreds of lamplight stealing through from landscape fixtures and motion sensors.

"Here kitty, kitty, kitty," he rubbed his fingers together and crouched down low to the ground. The cat, its tail flicking at the air, stopped and turned back and stared its reflective, instigative glare. Lanier stayed low until the cat came to him, rubbed against the back of his open hand. The cat purred, arcing itself alongside his thigh and then in between his legs. Lanier placed his hand under the cat's midsection, and the cat maneuvered out of the hold and gingerly walked a few steps and looked back to Lanier. He approached again, with open and slow moving hands, and again attempted to carefully pick up the cat. Once he was allowed, he noticed a collar, a dangling gold identification under the nape of its neck, which he removed and dropped to the ground. It must have been one of Sadie's cats, he thought, even though the tag read otherwise. He cradled the bottom legs and the tail with one hand, and with the other he stroked its rising head as he walked deeper under the canopy, the foliage clogged with thick wigs of moss. Lanier lowered his face into the cat's fur and lifted as much scent as he could, and when the cat would smell no longer he clinched quickly to the back legs. Before the cat could lunge out, Lanier swung the body against the trunk of an oak, the legs snapping in his hands. The ribs and back cracked with a dull, reverberating thud. The noise that escaped from the cat was not what he expected. It was more of a wheeze than the bellowing cry, hiss, and howl that he knew cats to make.

The start of Lanier's shift at the hospital passed as he sat under the canopy playing with the dead animal until nearly dawn. He then dug a hole and buried the carcass that he had dissected with his pocketknife.

Now, he came home and shaved, showered, scrubbed his rather hairless physique instead of doping up until going to the church, which is what he contemplated doing as he walked home with the cat's heart in his hand. This morning he considered eating the heart for breakfast, in between two pieces of buttered toast, but he could only take a couple of bites. It was much harder to chew than he thought it would be, so he wrapped it in tinfoil and put in the freezer where he kept the coffee.

He usually brought a tumbler of coffee to Sadie's mother around nine-thirty on the days he didn't work. It was almost ten. He hadn't bothered to knock in weeks. The front doors to the houses were all the same, unlocked and covered with lengthy ovate windows, and as he opened the front door he imagined what he might say to her when he came to her bedroom door.

Hey Beautiful. Coffee?

So-phi-a, rise and shine.

How's Sadie-baby feeling today?

Now promise you won't get mad, I think I killed one of your cats.
You don't deserve her. If you hit her again, I'll kill you.
You're a gift from God.

He passed the dining area and came through her kitchen. The dark of the hallway was behind him and he appeared to be glowing white in her bedroom doorway.

"Why are you so good to me?" Sophia asked him before he could say anything. Her large frame lay supine on her bed, surrounded and seeping into pillows, her breasts and stomach large and soft-skinned where the fat took little form. He turned his squint towards a few blurred splinters of light breaking through the blinds. A soft heat like smoke suffocated the bedroom, intensified by the smell of a woman's musk that made its way into his mouth and sat in the back of his throat.

"Just trying to help out, like the Lord intended. You know that—now just go ahead and relax a bit. It's still early." He made sure, though, to get caught staring at Sophia's cleavage as he poured her coffee into a mug and turned away slowly to crack open the window near her bed. Her comforter was pulled up to, and yet fully underneath the section of her nightgown that loosely covered her breasts. "Didn't see you at church last night, that's two Sundays now. Everything's all right?" Lanier asked.

"Everything's all right. It's just..." she smacked her tongue against the roof of her mouth. She tucked her hair behind her ears, and there seemed to be a thin mask of foundation and blush that stopped where her cheek met her ear. "You know I just haven't felt up to it. And Sadie is just a terror about it. She does not want to go, will not go, it's like pulling Jesus from the cross trying to get her out the front door."

Lanier laughed through his nose, short like a heavy wind, and he looked over to the corner where a crucifix hung above the bed lamp. The t-shadow slanted up the wall and onto the ceiling.

"And the worst thing is that she probably blames God or the church and not her father, who she should." Sophia had an inward gaze for a moment. "I shouldn't say that."

"Well that's what we are taught to do."

"What?"

"Blame God, blame society, blame the president, blame music and movies, blame, blame, blame. Nobody is willing to take responsibility," he said. The bedroom window allowed for a late morning chill to circle through the room. She pulled her comforter close and moaned deeply. Two books lay on her bedside, one on self-realization and the other a joke book. He could feel her eyes watching him as he glanced over at the books.

She coyly smiled and said, "What two things in the air can get a girl pregnant?"

"I don't know. What?" He poured himself a cup and put the tumbler down on her bed stand.

"Her legs." Sadie's mother threw her head back into the pillows with one quick laugh like a duck squawk. Her face was soft and light-skinned, almost a dying yellow-gold, though at one time she was gorgeous, and she kept that thought around the room in the pictures of her younger figure. "Want to hear another one?"

"Not really."

"You didn't think that was funny?"

"I did."

"You didn't laugh?"

"I did, inside."

"Do you think I'm getting fat?" she asked.

He shook his head. "Where did that come from?"

"It's just, I feel like I spend so much time in bed. I never exercise anymore. I used to be so active."

While she went on explaining her weight, Lanier sat down beside her and nodded along. Just being in the house, being so close to Sadie, being able to smell the lip gloss, the sweat, the smell like sour candies. Sophia must have trusted him; he felt it sincere. His interests in Sadie were bound, gagged, hidden and tucked deeply behind flattery and a sense of decency. Sadie's small feet, her blotchy pale skin, the nape of her slender neck where thin strawberry-blonde hairs swirled together. He didn't really want to eat her, but he would be lying to himself if he denied the thoughts that jogged through his mind. These were thoughts he never had with any other girl. The thoughts curdled in his stomach, but he couldn't really stop them. Thoughts of eating her. Not all of her, no—just pieces. The skin of her elbow dried out like jerky, her big toes braised like short ribs, her earlobes hard-candied so that he could suck on them for hours…"Fat? You can't possibly mean that. And I'll tell you the truth if you want to hear it. Do you want to hear it?" Lanier asked.

"Not really."

"Well I'm going to tell you. You are beautiful, and you know you're beautiful."

"That's sweet, but you're just saying that."

"Thou shall not lie." He brushed two of the cats off the bed with the back of his hand. "I mean really? You just need to get up and go."

"Go where," she asked with an upturned nose, "church?"

"No. I don't know, go anywhere. Get active. Do what you got to do. Don't just sit around. Do something you've never done before."

"Like what?"

"I don't know. Take a risk; go after a dream or some kind of fantasy."

For only a moment Sophia nibbled at her bottom lip, and the age that lined out near her eyes seemed to smooth. She adjusted her lower back to sit up a bit and pulled the comforter up over her stiffened nipples. "Don't be a tease," she said.

Lanier reached out and held one of her hands. He watched her as she pulled it against herself, softly. Her eyes darted from his eyes, to his waist, to the doorway, back to his eyes; her skin flushed a blotchy-radiant heat. She moved her hand from under his, and he felt her turbulent heartbeat. Her pulse began a sprint as she fingered his lower abdomen and the buckle of his belt. With a puckered smile, she pulled away the comforter and sheets, a vacancy left in her stare. He backed away with his belt loosened and repositioned her legs slightly apart.

"God," she said, long and drawn out, "I need this," and pulled aside her cotton underwear. He lowered his face down between her perspiring thighs, a scent, a hanging odor like the air over the stagnant, humid gulf. She pulled back at the thick hair and Lanier tasted her child, her birth, her beginning. What a beautiful child, he thought. He nibbled, and she giggled; he moaned, and with one hand she clawed at the sheets. With the other hand, she held his head in place with the tips of her nails. A tabby cat with tired eyes leapt back on the bed, only a foot from his head, and lay there licking the pad of its paw. The cat stared at Lanier crouched over with his knees on the cold tile, and it yawned as the door to the bedroom slowly creaked open.

"Sadie Baby, is that you?" her mother's voice cracked towards the doorway. She pulled the sheet over her bare midsection, covering Lanier's head, his hair still wrapped taut in her fingers; she held him completely still. He could only look forward, just above the soft rounds of her stomach to her lifted eyebrows and indented cheeks, the terror of surprise painted what he could see of her face.

"Mommy, what are you doing?" Sadie rubbed her eyes from sleep, yawned after she spoke. The girl was tall for seven, the sleeping shirt she wore stopped above her knees.

He wanted to look at her, but didn't move.

"Doctor Lanier had to come by and..." her mother's voice was shattered, then after a deep breath, "...make a special visit, because mommy's not feeling so well."

Lanier's face was in lock. He didn't move back from her thighs, yet it was hard for him to not let her pull the hair from his scalp in order to look at Sadie. "Go in the kitchen and get a popsicle. Mommy will be out in a minute to watch some cartoons. Okay baby?"

Sadie partially closed the door behind her, and her mother loosened her grip but did not let go. "Now, you were almost done," she whispered. Her body eventually tightened up and shuddered a bit, and Lanier pressed harder, gripping her thighs. He hadn't unzipped his pants, hadn't gotten erect; he made a sound that was almost a laugh. She ran her fingers through the wetness, and her eyes closed before she pulled her underwear back into place.

4

Graceville is a town very close to where all three states—Florida, Alabama and Georgia—meet. The way into Graceville, the northern gateway, is similar to that of any rural backcountry town, full of timberland, red clay roads, and small feed mills. Along either side of the highway are crape myrtle and wild roses flanking the road, pale pink and coral blooms in the heat of summer dividing fields of row crops. In this small town, a gated community sits between Holmes and Little Creek, full of Flowering Dogwood, Horsesugar and Hawthorne trees, and Sweetbay Magnolia that stretch out near ponds and marshland of dense copse. Redbuds and Royal Palms, Sweetgums and Saw Palmetto, and rain—the most glorious rainstorms in the country. Golf links interlace around tennis and shuffleboard courts, plastic coated playgrounds, softball and soccer fields. The entry drive, River Hills, is two and a half miles deep into the slash pine forests of Graceville Hills and empties into the parking lot of a renovated civil war mansion which serves as the clubhouse. The road picks up again and circles the contained countryside, passes the community grocer and dry-cleaner, the hunter's lodge, the church and elementary school. Set aside and private, it is a place where privileged families come with little children and wait for them to grow and leave so the husband and wife can separate, divorce, panic, move on with another step towards death and a new breath for life.

Four boys, instead of playing outside all day like the other kids on Thanksgiving break, sat at the empty bar of the Clubhouse. Their ages ranged from thirteen to fifteen. The two Leavitt boys, Corey and Abe Jr., had moved up from Punta Gorda two summers ago after their mother had died. They both were wide-chested and dawdling, their hair and sleepy brown eyes as dark as mud; Jarvis, whom the boys called Fatty, constantly looked flushed from high blood pressure; and Francis Drake, the painter's son, sat on the edge of his seat with his foot tapping against the wall of the bar. A voice on the radio came from the kitchen and could be heard through the service window:

"…after the category three last month, we thought we had had enough, yet emergency responders are preparing once again for another tropical storm threatening Florida's Panhandle…"

The two brothers argued as Drake and Fatty sat quietly on either end flicking a piece of paper, folded neatly into a triangle, back and forth across the glossy wood grain of the bar top. Elderly couples began to arrive for their early afternoon dinner reservations. Lonely old southern women pulled up to their seats in the dining room with the help of electric walkers, wheelchairs, or the pressed sleeve of colored boys in plaid vests and dark bowties. Gentlemen courted their cigars or ornate canes in the lobby, a sweating highball or julep clenched in arthritic fists. The bar overlooked it all, lavish with mahogany and a deep green and gilded trim. Large bay windows surrounded the clubhouse and looked out onto the tee-off area where small groups of white-pantsed men clapped out their spikes and sheathed their clubs.

"Dad says that I am not supposed to pray to the mother of god."

"God damn it, AJ, you fucking Jew, what does it matter who you pray to?" Corey back handed the side of his little brother's arm. Not only short and rotund, Corey also had his father's thick black eyebrows that seemed to darken his entire face, already speckled with moles.

"You're a fucking Jew, too," AJ muffled his voice and spoke down to his shirt.

"I am not going to ask again, boys—check the language, or I'm going to call your parents." The reprimand came coarse from behind a newspaper that the bartender was reading. He sat on a stool tucked away in the corner. The four boys glowered at the newspaper.

"See if I fucking care," Corey said, just loud enough for the three other boys to hear.

Even though AJ was the little brother, he was a foot taller and his shoulders were twice as wide as any of the boys. "Yeah, see if I fucking care," echoed Abe Jr. in a full bravado.

"That's it. You boys are out." The barman stood from his stool, winced at his side, quick-folded the paper and slapped it on the table.

"Damn it AJ, you fucking idiot." Corey cuffed his brother on the back of the shoulder.

The man picked up the phone, "You better get. I don't need to call the security too?" He looked down over his reading specs, his chin sat on the tuft that puffed from his chest. His silver hair was almost blue, and it was greased into one central curl. The uniform-vest that he wore was small, limiting movement and threatening to split at any overdrawn motion, so he bent down towards the phone not able to bring it up to his ear.

"Since when do you think that you give the fucking orders around here, old man? You're the frigging help. Our parents pay your weak-ass salary." Drake's voice wavered a bit behind his crooked smile, his vulture's face, pointed and sharp. "Seems to me that you're on the wrong side of the bar; all you need to worry about is whether I have enough cherries in my Sprite." The boys didn't move from their seats, nor did the barman start to dial. They waited, hands on the bar, as Otis Redding sang out through the service window.

"You goddamned good for nothing little shits," the barman whispered through clenched teeth. Veins highlighted purple on his cheeks and nose popped out like fireworks. "You think I give a horse's fuck about this job? I been to war, I could spin your little chicken necks. You know that?" The loose skin hanging from his jawline shook with fervent hate.

"Fuck this old prick. Let's just go see if Lenny's back from church yet," Corey turned to leave.

"No, I want more cherries in my sprite. This asshole needs to give me more cherries."

"Come on," Corey said.

"No, I want to see this asshole's supervisor," Drake said, putting a hand out and holding Corey's arm, keeping him from leaving. "We leave and this fucker wins. He can't threaten us, this fucking cocksucker. Where's your supervisor?" Drake demanded.

The old man lifted his middle finger, turned and walked through the swinging doors that led to the back area and the kitchen. "Now we can go," Drake said.

They walked to the north end of Graceville Hills, tucked into the backfields of the golf courses, in between juvenile longleaf pines and thick-thorn blackberry patches. "If he just tried anything, I would have stabbed him in the fucking hand, right to the phone," Corey said.

"Yeah, I would have broke my glass over the bar and shoved into his saggy old face." Drake came off spitting.

"I could've took my bar stool and thrown it at his head," AJ said.

"I wuh-would of...I would of..." Fatty couldn't think of anything.

"You would have fucking sat on him, Fatty," Corey said. "That's all you'd have to do," and the three boys laughed as Fatty dug in his pockets, rambling stuttered profanities.

"Yeah, r-r-real fa-f-fucking f-funny, can't anyone tha-think of a-anything else to s-sa s-s-sasay to the fat kid. Fa-ffuck you," said Fatty.

When the boys cleared from the clubhouse, Fatty pulled out the last of their dope and split a dollar cigar lengthwise. He dumped the cigar's insides on the ground and ran his shoe over the tobacco log until it blended into the dead leaves, twigs and pecan husks.

"Let me see what's left," Drake took the bag of pot. "We should've got in touch with Lenny already. Who knows if he's gonna be there? After this we're pretty much out, and this ain't shit. He better be there."

Fatty laid the cigar-skin between his thumb and forefinger and lined it with a couple of grams of crushed up dope.

"He'll be there." Corey flipped out a pocketknife that was worn smooth at the hinges and cut slices at the low branches. He stripped off a branch and whittled a flimsy point on a green stem, his down strokes close to his brother's arm. Overhead, branches fingered together, braided with Spanish moss, and white sunbeams pierced through like confetti.

Fatty slobbered the skin of the cigar and smoothed it over tightly. He took the bag back from Drake and tucked it into a pocket of his low-hanging shorts and dug around until he found a lighter. "Ha-have you ever sas-seen how much La-l-l-lenny's got?"

"Light that shit and let's go," Drake said.

"He's always got plenty," Corey said nonchalantly, a self-satisfied smirk. The others always had to stay at the kiddy park, a block away, while he went inside Lanier's house. Lanier had made Corey swear to never tell anyone about him, but the first thing Corey did was tell AJ and Drake, who inevitably told Fatty.

A little more than a year ago, Corey was shortcutting through the backyards of a few homes, heatedly coming back from the park where a few girls had called him a fat kyke and told him to get lost. He had walked slowly, wiping the wetness from his eyes, kicking and crushing whatever came in his path. He spooked a little when he had heard something large rustling through bushes at the side of a house. When he saw that it was a man, Corey tried to keep walking, looked the opposite direction, but Lanier had stopped him. "You all right kid?"

Corey wiped his face dry.

"What are you doing?" Lanier asked as he came up to him.

"Nothing."

"You're obviously doing something."

"Nothing, really," Corey looked back at the side of the house where the man came from. "What were you doing?"

"I lost something, and I was trying to find it."

"It's the middle of the night."

"What's your point?" Lanier said and then changed the subject. "What's your name?"

"Corey."

"Where you headed Corey?"

"Nowhere."

"You smoke?" Lanier had asked.

Corey shrugged his shoulders.

"Come on."

Corey followed. "You ain't gay, are you? 'Cause I ain't no fag," Corey had said.

Lanier laughed and when they got to his house, he sat Corey down and placed a pillowcase of pot on his lap. They smoked and ate ice cream and Lanier told him about SeaWorld, how he had always wanted to go to SeaWorld. "You ever been to SeaWorld?" he had asked.

Corey shook his head.

"When I was a kid, my mother always said that she would take us to SeaWorld, but then my sister died and my mother lost her shit," Lanier had said, and he didn't say anything else for the rest of the night.

Corey told him about his mother and how she had died, and Lanier nodded. He told him that he couldn't stand the woman that his father married, and Lanier nodded. He told him that this hick town was nothing compared to down south, and Lanier nodded. Corey told him about the girls at the park. "The stupid bitches," he had said, and Lanier nodded. When Corey had nothing else to say, Lanier nodded and put the television on and let Corey fall asleep on his couch. Lanier woke him up a few hours later and before Corey started out the door to go home he had asked, "Can I come back here?"

"Whenever you want."

"What's your name?"

Lanier sort of stared back for a moment, before he had answered, "Lenny."

Corey came back to Lenny's the next day for more pot.

The four boys turned down a pecan trail that led towards the wedding gazebo at the lake point, and they stayed behind the brush. Drake turned around at every sound, every crackling branch, twig and leaf.

"Wah-what's the m-ma-m-most you seen in there?" asked Fatty.

"Plenty," Corey said.

"How m-m-ma'amuch is plenty?" asked Fatty.

"Yeah, what's the most you ever seen in there?" asked AJ.

"I don't know—a garbage bag full? One of them big black ones I guess." Corey stepped ahead and walked faster as AJ and Fatty let out gasps of amazement even though they had heard this all before, many, many times. He left thick blue-smoke trails. "That's nothing. He's got all sorts of crazy shit in there. He's got dope plants tall as me, and he's got some crazy chemistry set in his bathtub." Smoke filed out as Corey spoke back to the other boys. "He collects all these knives. He has all sizes, long and skinny blades and short curved ones. Gave me this one here, said it was bust. It still cuts fine." Corey handed the smoke back to his brother. AJ still didn't inhale all the way, and Corey called him on it every time. "Hold that shit in," he said and then punched him in the chest. "Hit it again, and hold that shit in."

"All right. Sorry. God," AJ talked down, blew the ashes off of the coal and sucked on the thinned cigar again. "Jeeze-Louise, give me a fucking break."

It was after six by the time the boys got to the kiddy park. Drake and Fatty sat under a picnic overhang away from the light drizzle that had started and shared a menthol cigarette while AJ stood on one of the swing seats as the mist speckled down on him, his head tilted back and his mouth open, slowing dampening his shoulders and matting his hair. Corey was already halfway down the block before he disappeared from the sidewalk. He came up the bike path that ran behind a line of houses, completely covered by canopy, and noticed that Lenny's back door was yawning. He gave a slight knock and looked down the hallway, "Lenny, you home?"

Corey took off his shoes and opened the door a little wider and stepped inside. He peeked around the entryway to the living room, "Lenny, you here?" The lights were off, but the television was on and the screen reflected colors onto the dark walls and window shades. The coffee table held three full ashtrays, and the smell of wet cigarette ash filled the room. Corey took off his hat and ran his fingers through the thick hair he kept tucked away. He walked towards the end of the hallway, looking into each doorway that was opened. There were no lights other than from the television, no other voices or movement. The bathroom door was only slightly opened, and as Corey passed he turned his head away from the stench that wafted out from the bathroom, rotten fumes of burnt hair, vomit, and drying feces seeping and mingling out into the hallway. Corey hurried his pace, though quiet on the balls of his feet; he took deep breaths and kept watch out of the corner of his eyes. The bedroom door was wide open and he peeked inside. He gave another slight knock, "Lenny, you around?" The smell of pot in the bedroom was wet and fresh like a mowed lawn. Dark blue medical scrubs were scattered over the floor, bunched and wrinkled. The windows were covered with stapled black sheets and the desk across the room was covered with coffee stained maps and opened envelopes, knives and pictures. Corey went straight for the bottom drawer and started to fill his pockets, front and back; he took two ounces from a half pound bag before he found a bigger bag with much better pot in the corner. On the desk was a deli sandwich sleeve that he filled, tied off and stuck under his shirt. He tucked his shirt into his jeans.

Corey tried to keep the cellophane bag quiet under his shirt, sweat beginning to drip from his armpits to his sides. Leaving the bedroom and coming back down the hallway, he caught a glimpse of Lenny's feet on the bathroom floor. He stopped still, frozen, his calf muscles tightened to knots. Corey came right up to the door and looked through the thin opening. Pulling the neck of his shirt over his nose and mouth, he tried to block the stench that made his eyes water. He saw that Lanier was shirtless with his cheek and one arm rested on the toilet seat, his other arm hung idly at his side. Lanier's eyes twitched behind his closed eyelids. "Lenny? You all right," Corey whispered and then remembered that he had just stolen pot and wished he hadn't said anything. But Lanier lay there still, rather lifeless. Lanier's bare shoulder shuddered and relapsed; the arm was speckled in vomit as was the back of the toilet and the side of the bowl. Corey looked deeper, his cotton-covered nose almost breached through the doorway, and noticed Lanier was breathing and completely naked. His bare and bony knees were covered in filth, splattered on the walls behind him. A few blue bottlenose flies had found their way in, landing and taking flight around his haunches. Corey's stomach seemed to roll inside of him, and he removed himself and cautiously continued down the hall towards the backdoor.

Corey slipped on his shoes and took long strides out into the now heavy drizzle, little bits of green dropping from his pockets. On the bike path he broke out, adrenaline that started in his lower back took over and coursed throughout his body for release. The bag under his shirt stuck to his sides from the sweat. His pockets packed, he ran past the kiddy park where the others waited under the picnic nook. They saw that Corey was running, saw that he wasn't going to stop, and they looked past him for someone chasing; no one came. They followed for a few blocks and knew where they were going, and Fatty slowed down to a panting halt. His face was red as his slicker, his hair in unkempt waves. His cheeks went straight into his collar. "Slow d-dadown. You fa-fa-ffuckers . . ." They didn't slow down and by the time Fatty got to the new lots, he had to listen carefully for his friends. It was dark out and the street lamps were up but not running. The houses were bare cinderblock with open spaces where windows would be fitted and black slat roofs waiting to be shingled; cement-slab floors and two-by-fours stood like the skeletons of rooms. PVC and copper pipes jutted up from the solid ground. Fatty walked towards a spark of a lighter inside one of the houses, but it was just a firefly. Fatty shook the rainwater out of his hair and zipped his slicker up to his collar. He was turning sharp and walking backwards, he looked from side to side. "You g-guys?" He stumbled over a caulk gun and kicked an empty bucket.

5

Lanier checked his watch. It was a little past four in the morning. He had slept on the bathroom tiles fourteen hours in his own mess before he woke up brittle, pale, and shaking for a push. Images of Sophia and the sounds of Sadie's voice all rambled and meshed incoherently in his mind as he tried to remember coming home. He had pulled out the picture of Sadie at the beach and put on plastic gloves. He had licked the fresh meth powder; he could still taste the bitter alkaline residues that lined his gums, but he did not remember becoming sick. "Lord, watch over me." The picture of Sadie and her mother still sat on the sill of the bathtub, creased down the middle and worn on the corners. In the picture, Sadie is about to cry, her mother holding her. St. George's sand dunes are behind them blurred with the sway of tall, gray alligator weeds and dried out sea oats. Lanier began to suffer chills and arrhythmias. His naked frame that he scrubbed clean at the sink was pink and practically hairless in front of the mirror. Lanier's back was long and arced over the sink, and his boyish ass cheeks were like two knots at the bottom.

He turned and bent over the tub, only wearing a medical mask and vinyl gloves. Sometimes the crystal cooked clear like glass shards, and other times it yellowed and became chalky. With a good batch, Lenny stayed up on three-day binges and wouldn't wear too thin. He kept baggies full of generic meds from the hospital that could put a prison to sleep—noctec, rivotril, libritabs, lorazepan intensol—though he seldom used the downers. The bathroom exhaust hummed from above and a large window unit pushed fumes out and obscured any view in. He carefully set aside a Pyrex bubble beaker of anhydrous ammonia next to a smaller beaker of extracted ephedrine, to which he added a pinch of salt and measured in a dash of paint thinner. He stripped lithium from batteries and red phosphorous from the side strips of matchboxes and combined iodine. He turned the electric skillet to high and watched as the coils turned tangerine.

He stood up, holding the warmth to himself with his arms across his chest and left the bathroom as the double boiler began to heat. He closed the bathroom door behind him and pulled down the medical mask, but he kept on the gloves and walked down the dark hallway to the kitchen. He sat on a barstool with his ankles crossed and ate peanut butter on a frozen waffle. Crumbs fell to his midsection, and he stared forward but at nothing as he listened to the messages on his answering machine.

"Hey Lenny? Pastor Deene here…It's just a little after six. Was wondering if you were stopping by the rec-hall this afternoon; also wanted to check with you about the youth Bible study group that starts this Wednesday after the five o'clock service. Well, hope all is well. I guess I'll talk at you later. Okay, b-bye now, God bless." There was a pause, click and beep.

"Butchie," it was a woman's voice, burned out and muffled by street traffic. "I'm coming down. I'll be there in a few days." Lanier put the waffle down on the countertop, stopped chewing, and let the food just sit in his mouth. He listened: pause, click and beep.

"Hey *Doctor* Lanier, it's me. I know it's late, I thought I could catch you before you were out for the night. I needed to ask a favor, last minute. Can you pick up Sadie from school tomorrow and watch her for a few hours? I want to meet up with a few friends for happy hour down in Marianna, and I'd really appreciate it. Give me a call in the morning if you can. Thanks." Pause, click and beep.

"Hey Lenny, it's Schmidd. It's like six-forty-five, where you at? We need you down here in maternity, like-stat. Two other orderlies didn't show this morning, and one volunteer called it quits in the middle of the shift. " Pause, click and beep.

He started to walk back to the bathroom and slowed as the last message played. "Lanier man, it's Schmiddy again. The supervisor's gonna write you up, man. It's after eight-thirty; you're more than two hours late. This shit ain't like you, man. Give us a call, let us know everything's all right."

He went and put on a pair of shorts and a shirt that were balled on the floor. He pulled the thin mask back over his nose and mouth and returned to the bathroom. Lanier turned the double boiler down to a simmer and placed the ephedrine beaker gently into the rumbling water.

6

The four boys generally stayed together at the Leavitt's guest home. The living room was an opium den of large floor pillows and low set couches as wide as Buicks. Six or seven furnished bedrooms remained vacant throughout the year, each with a personal bath and glossy walnut floors. Large paintings from the streets of Barcelona and Madrid, two fireplaces, three lofts. They woke up to a mound of marijuana on the living room table and Fatty exhaling thick clouds of charcoal smoke in their sleeping faces.

Corey sat up, rubbed his eyes and tossed a pillow at his brother. "Dude, you'll never get laid if you keep jacking your dick all the time," Corey said. AJ had his knee up under his blanket, and there was movement, then no movement. "Damn it AJ, at least go private if you're gonna jack your dick."

"Dude, I wasn't jacking my dick."

"Dude, your never gonna get laid."

"Dude, I wasn't jacking my dick. I was repositioning."

"Whatever man, you're still never gonna get any trim," Corey said.

"You weren't laid when you were thirteen," AJ peered back at his older brother, nostrils dilated, fluster building in his cheeks.

"Shit if I wasn't," Corey said. "You got to be joking me," Corey laughed as he took the smoke from Fatty. "Dude, we got to get you a hooker. It's the only way you're gonna get wet."

"I don't want a hooker," AJ said.

"Why da-don't you wha-w-wwant a hooker?" Fatty asked.

"I don't know—I just don't," AJ spoke inwardly, then turned to Fatty, "why don't you get the hooker, fat ass. You're gonna need her 'fore I do."

"F-fafuck you, AJ."

"Both of ya'll shut up," Corey said.

"We sha-sh-should all get ha-ha-hookers," Fatty leaned back into the sofa cushions.

Corey shook Drake awake, "Dude we're all gonna get some hookers, you down?"

Drake nodded with his eyes still closed. "What fucking time is it?"

"I don't know, nine in the morning."

Drake put out his middle finger and rolled back over, burrowing his face into the couch pillow.

"Wha-where are we ga-g-g-gonna get ha-h ha-hookers?" Fatty asked.

"Yeah, where are you gonna find any hookers?" AJ echoed.

"I'll just ask Lenny. He said he could get me anything I wanted."

Fatty took a deep breath and swallowed hard, "*Anything*?"

"He told me *anything*."

"You b-ba-believe him?"

"Of course I fucking believe him, why shouldn't I?"

"Aren't you afraid of going back there, what if he knows you took all his pot?" AJ asked.

"I'm gonna have to find out one way or another, besides there's so much he couldn't tell none was missing." Corey began to divvy up the dope into three piles: one large pile for stashing, a purse for carrying, and a pile for smoking. The coffee table was granite with glass inlays, ashes and stems buried in the creases. The living area had the space of a small home, and windows looked out onto one of the community's largest black lakes surrounded by purple buddle pickerel weeds and lily pads. "I'm telling you guys, Lenny was out cold."

"How do you know he was even alive? Maybe he was really sick, maybe we should have called an ambulance or something," AJ said to his brother.

"Then he would have found out it was us, you idiot."

"Us? You st-sta st-stole the shit, na-n-nobody asked you to," Fatty said.

"You're smoking it though, ain't you? Well ain't you, Fatty?" Corey laid the blunt stub into the tray to die out as thin trails of belly-dancing smoke curled upwards.

With his eyes still closed Drake asked, "What if he had cameras?" His voice muffled by the couch pillows. He sat up, rolled around the thick taste in his mouth and opened one eye wider than the other. "What if he had cameras set up?"

"If he does—I never seen'um."

"It's not hard to hide them. I've got three of them in me and my sister's room. They hook up to my computer and I can get a live feed any time of the day."

"Why d-d-do you have ke-k-kacamera's hidden in your ra-rr-room?" Fatty was splitting another dollar cigar, tearing the thin tobacco skin with his two thumbs.

"So my sister will go to sleep."

"Why won't your sister go to sleep?" AJ asked.

"None of your fucking business."

"I can't believe you share a room with your little sister," Corey said.

"Yeah, I can't believe you gotta share a room with your sister," echoed AJ.

"I practically live here. Besides, not everyone is rich as shit," Drake said. His family lived in one of the small two bedroom apartments on the outskirts of the community. His father was a painter hired by the home owner's association in exchange for a commissioned rent, and he was also one of the few electricians. He had gray eyes, much like Drake's, but his were underlined by bags of sinking skin. Before Drake's mother left, they grew up handing out flowers, pamphlets and children's bibles. His sister never felt safe. She woke up to sweat and terror a few nights a week, screaming, piercing like a snared dog. Her father had to drink more to be able to sleep through it, and Drake found other places to stay.

"So you gag-got any ff-fa-f-footage? You na-nen-know?" Fatty lit the re-rolled cigar and bounced his eyebrows. "Anything of your s-ssister, you know, maybe n-nak-kked or in the sha-sh-shower?"

"Dude, she's like *ta-ta-ta* twelve, you fat, stuttering bastard," Corey said.

"Yeah, but she's a fa-ffull ta-tatwelve. Hubba-hub," Fatty said.

"Unless you want to get your ass beat, I'd stop talking about his sister, you fat fuck."

"What? He kna-knows I'm just ff-f-fafucking around. Don't you Da-dadrake?" Fatty looked over. "Da-ddude, I was just mm-ma-messing around," Fatty pleaded as Drake sat tilted back, the muscles in his jaw tightening. "Dude, I was just ke-kake-kidding around," Fatty said again. "Ba-bbut honestly, I would p-papay a pretty p-pp-pa-penny for some hot v-video action."

"You're gonna have to save your money to bang a hooker. Fat asses pay triple," Corey said as he laced his fingers together and put them behind his head. "Rules of the hookerdom." He waited and watched the confusion cover Fatty's face like lemon juice curdling milk. "What, you didn't know that? Yeah, sucks for you, huh," then the three boys laughed at the fat kid's solemn, internal grimace and pudgy clenched fists.

7

Around ten in the morning, the rain had started, quick bloomed like a dark tulip, and water cascaded from the corner of the roof where the shutters met. Lanier heard a few dogs howling, and then they were gone. His lungs ached; the blood seemed to stop in his veins. He sat on the edge of the toilet seat and tried to look through the falling stream of water.

The world he saw wasn't washed—it was being carried along with all the dirt. It was too wet in the air to keep the window open, powder was clumping. The days of his youth, as Lanier looked back on them with his eyes closed, seemed to flutter away like leaves in a gutter. He had tried to be practical and paid young girls to suffice his questionable cravings. He discussed original sin with social workers and sat evenings with loose-jawed veterans under the overhangs of bus stops and drank from plastic fifths for dinner. The girl from his past—his sister, crying, trapped in the smoke—now becoming faceless as a ghostly dream, abject and lonesome. Lanier could see her through a stream of water, dancing in a smoky blur, choking on the smoke he had created, trying to say something, trying to scream. She was a lovely child, quite a few years younger and from a different father, and she smelled of sweet biscuits. She was misery and courage and strong, afraid of not being satisfied. They had run away together many times, over the train tracks, away from the campgrounds to a desolate stretch of pasture where they had dropped to her knees and tasted the salt on each other's lips. She had left him with an opened sore, and twenty years later the love had not matured, the wound he had inflicted upon himself had not healed. He opened his eyes and prayed for forgiveness.

"Sin came into the world by the fall of the first man," he prayed. "By this fall not only he himself, but also his natural offspring have lost the original knowledge, righteousness and holiness, and thus all men are sinners by birth, dead in sins, inclined to all evil and subject to the wrath of God. Amen."

Lanier said the prayer twice more and stood to leave the bathroom.

Behind closed eyes, the faceless girl waited for him to listen to her cries, looking up with red curls falling around her face. He rubbed at his temples as he walked down the hallway. In the kitchen, he held the phone to his ear with his shoulder as he looked into his refrigerator. There was a quart of spoilt milk, a liquid vitamin supplement, a pullout drawer full of batteries, a few condiments.

"You sure it's not a problem?" Sophia asked. "Now it will only be for a couple of hours, I should be back by six or seven. Now you're sure?"

"Of course I'm sure, it'll be fun. Sadie'll be waiting for me, three-fifteen at the playground near the school. And you'll be back around seven. And she knows I am coming to get her?"

"I already told her you might."

"What did she say when you told her I was going to pick her up?"

"Not much. She's been a real moody molly lately. Now you're sure it's okay?"

"It's no problem, but you got to do something for me," Lanier closed the refrigerator door.

"Name it."

"I want you and Sadie to accompany me to the Wednesday night service. Will you do that for me?"

"I had something else in mind, but we can definitely do that."

"What did you think I was going to ask for?"

"I'll tell you later."

"You thought I was going to ask for something kinky, didn't you?"

"So what if I did," she said playfully.

"You got a filthy mind."

Sophia scoffed in a sarcastic way and said, "God made me that way."

"He makes all kinds," Lanier smiled, said that he would talk to her a little later, hung up the phone and went into his room. He put away the crinkled picture in his desk. He pulled off the medical gloves and the paper mask that sat around his neck and put both in one of the biohazard bags that he had stolen from the hospital. Thick gusts of wind rattled the window screens. In the mirror above his desk, his reflection looked sickly, his skin pale as pool water, his eyes sunk back in black pockets. He needed solid food. He pulled out a pouch of shag tobacco and mixed in some pot and powder from on top of his desk. He rolled up a smoke two papers long, lit it and laid himself out on the floor of his bedroom. He stretched apart his toes and straightened his back. Lanier spent much of the morning in that position and by noon the clouds separated and the day grew warm, drying out the puddles.

The first girl was loud, obnoxious. Maybe ten or eleven. But she had this unmistakable laugh, a laugh he could never forget, and he was very confused by how it sounded so much like his sister's. Only thirteen or fourteen himself. She said that her father hit her almost every night. He told her there was a place she could go if she needed to hide. They had to cross a fallen tree that stood over the river's surface. He followed her and nudged her along when she became scared. They were more than an hour into the backwoods.

He didn't know what to do with the body. He dug in the wet dirt the entire night. Using his pocketknife and bare hands. It was a very shallow grave. He stripped tinder from palm trunks and found armfuls of dried twigs. He started the fire and was amazed that she wouldn't burn.

On early November afternoons, the main road is empty, nothing moves, not even the baby palm fronds—there are no children, no young lovers picnicking, only decent people who were at work in town already set about their business with their lunch pails or briefcases. Lanier put on his headphones and walked his bicycle out of the garage and down the driveway. He rode away from his house, strict to the side of the road, his exposed hair flipping about. He chopped through small puddles, licked his lips, and shouted, "Buenos dias," towards the landscapers.

He leaned his bike up against the wall outside the grocer's, and as he entered the store, the cold air pressed against his face. He left his headphones on as he walked the vacant aisles, listening to "I'm Free" by Kenny Loggins over and over again—*Looking into your eyes, I know I'm right…Nothing I want is out of my reach…Heaven helps the man who fights his fear…Running away will never make me free…But I want to hold you now…I'm free.* Lanier's stomach was dry and entirely deflated. He wasn't hungry, but his stomach garbled when he picked up a red onion. He then grabbed a couple of tomatoes, a bulb of garlic, some sweet cornbread, chicken hindquarters, gherkins pickles, and some colorful candies for Sadie. With a full basket, he made his way towards the only man working a register, not the teenage girl who Lanier thought to be stringy and oily, and somewhat repulsive. He was an older man, mid fifties, who looked eagerly into Lanier's eyes. He had short arms with sagging skin that hung down over his elbows. His glasses hung on a beaded string that wrapped around the back of his neck.

"You're the young Pastor at First Baptist, right?" he asked as he weighed in the tomatoes and then bagged them.

Lanier pulled the headphones down from his ears.

"You're the young Pastor at First Baptist, right?" he asked again.

Lanier nodded.

"You ain't looking so good Pastor, you feeling all right?"

"Little under the weather—ain't been able to sleep so well," Lanier replied.

"Need to eat more eggs."

"I'll try to remember that."

The man lifted the glasses and rested them on the end of his nose. He held the jar of pickles, studying and turning it. "Can I ast you something, just 'tween you and me?"

Lanier looked away from the periodicals and tabloids, over to the man's nametag, WALT, and then up to the man's face. Little grey hairs stood out from his ears and curled from his nostrils. A jingle that played in the store stopped for a moment and then started again.

"I think my little girl is starting to question her faith, and I don't know what to do."

"Really?" Lanier asked, his interests piqued. "How old is she?"

"She's about ten."

"Ten? Really, I wouldn't have guessed at your age."

Walt looked down at the groceries, his eyes following what was said.

Lanier cleared his throat. "I didn't mean for that to come off as rude as it sounded, sorry."

"No offense taken."

Lanier breathed in deeply and dug his fingers into his pockets, "You think she is starting to question God?"

"It's just that my oldest boy left the faith when he went off for college. Now he's got himself a good paying job and an apartment, and all these lady-friends bothering him at all hours. He's got such a disrespectful sense about religion and calls me ignant for my beliefs. I can't even relate to him no more; but it's my goal to love him and keep the door of God open to him."

Lanier reassured the man, "That's good. That's really all any of us can do."

"Yeah, well my youngest, she looks up to her older brother an awful lot, and it's got me fearing for her faith."

Lanier cleared his throat. "Your son's irreverence is no threat to God. Nothing he says or does can harm our sovereign Lord." This line he had memorized, but never knew why.

Walt nodded, but it was clear he was having trouble understanding what Lanier had said.

"Some people feel any joking about our faith, or even doubting, is a sacrilege." Lanier began to explain, "I've often told people that I think a sense of humor is a divine gift—and at times we all need a bit more *religious* of a sense of humor. So I guess, just try and lighten up a little; I'm sure your son is dealing with God in his own way. We all do. And you don't have to be quiet about your faith, especially around your little girl, but at the same time try to relate to your son's sense, try to understand why he feels the way he does. Try to really understand. You know, put yourself in his shoes."

Walt finished putting the last of the groceries in the bag and held out his hand and Lanier shook it. "That'll be fi'teen-eighty-two."

Lanier nodded, pulled out his wallet and paid, then put the change in a receptacle for Rescued Restavek Children from Haiti. "And if you want, I could have a personal chat with your little girl for you; see if I can stoke that spiritual flame."

"I'd like that very much. That'd be very godly of you." Walt held out his hand again, and Lanier shook it again.

Once outside of the store, Lanier straddled back onto his bicycle and a smile surfaced. Sometimes we all have to laugh at God, he thought, He sure as hell laughs at us. And sometimes we have to cry to God because He cries to us, and sometimes we have to smite God because in all fairness God smites us. And he rode back to his house, sweat soaking his arched back as these thoughts circled about his mind like a flushing toilet until they settled in his stomach.

Lanier's kitchen was clean in the dim lighting, it was mostly unused, spare a few crumbs and peanut-buttered knives near the toaster. The smell of stale gas lifted as he clicked on the stove top. A pointed blue flame climbed after the gas, then settled. He browned the chicken in a pot with sesame oil, added crushed garlic, roughly chopped onion and tomatoes and doused the pot with an apple brandy that took on a hissing blue flame. He stood back and lit a cigarette waiting for the alcohol to cook out as he sipped from the bottle of Calvados. His face was finding color with his eyelids half-closed and his mouth partly opened. He looked about the room at the scuffed cabinets and the stained countertops as the flame in the pot struggled and died. Lanier added a bottle of chili sauce to the pot, then the can of tomato paste and the juice from the sweet pickles, a few spoonfuls of mustard, and just let the molasses slide in until the color was right. He dashed in random amounts of dried spices and herbs, then salted and stirred. He brought the sauce to a slow simmer and let the chicken cook through.

Lanier closed his eyes and said a short prayer, "Please god. I am so tired. Amen." He stared at the blank face on the black innersides of his eyelids, ghastly white surrounded by red curls. His skin paled again, and his large empty hands became clammy. Lanier held his hair back off his forehead. Sweat that had moistened his neck and the center of his back was beginning to dry. His throat ached with every swallow, and with every swallow came the tinge of fresh vomit.

When the food finished cooking, he was no longer hungry. Lanier picked at a small chicken thigh and a chunk of the dry cornbread with a plastic fork and knife, delicately. The remaining sauce continued to reduce on the stove.

Sadie had her curls pinned right above her temples. She picked at a small cat scratch on her cheek. She dug her hands in her sweater pockets and walked directly behind the chaperone in a baby-duck line of four or five children. Lanier watched as they walked along the side of the road, from the school down to the playground and once they arrived Sadie sat alone, tranquil on a low swing. The after-school chaperone occasionally glanced up from the book she read, and of the few kids corralled within the playground's fencing, two of the boys ran circles around her and shot their pointer fingers like guns. Lanier stood at a distance for ten minutes watching Sadie stare towards the ground, toeing circles in the sand. As he approached her she did not look up, nor did she smile. Her knees came together, and she tucked the few long bangs of hair behind her ear that weren't already bobby-pinned.

"Hello Sadie," Lanier said. He crouched down, bent at the knees, and tried to look into her eyes. For a second they gaped back at him, bold round grey-blue, centered and scared like a doll. "You want'a swing?" he asked. He moved to step behind her, and she tightened up on the chains and slowly shook her head. "Is everything okay?" he asked.

She nodded, slowly, but didn't look up. Sadie's father had left her at the church and hadn't returned since. Lanier merely found her crying, turning in circles. *Daddy*, coming out of her mouth in drawn out sobs, crying out that choking sound. *Daddy*, she had been standing near the Statue of Mary breastfeeding Baby Jesus, right outside of the chapel's double doors. Lanier had walked Sadie around the church three times until he found out who her mother was and where she lived. He had tried to hold her hand but she wouldn't let him. She just followed in tears. He had immediately wanted to hold her, to take her away, to pet the hair from her face, to put his lips to her teary eyes, her neck. But she wouldn't let him. She'd just followed in tears.

"Do you want anything? Some candies? I got you some candies."

"I want my mom to come get me," she said and started a dry cry, just the scrunched face, the voice, the wincing eyes. He pulled her back on the swing, high up to his chest and breathed in the faint smell of the sweet child, like salt water, glue sticks and sticky candy.

"That's too bad. We could have had a lot of fun together."

The sounds of her dry cries were short, soft shrieks.

"Why don't you want to be my friend?" he asked, holding her up to his chest. He could feel the warmth of his breath bouncing off the back of her head. "I am only here to make you happy," Lanier said.

"I want my mom."

"Yeah well, I want my sister. You always can't have what you want. Your mother can't always be there for you," he whispered into the back of her hair.

She clinched the swing chains until the tips of her fingers were maroon. He held her back up to his face for a few seconds, breathed in deeply, then let her slip between his fingers. A tear dripped down her cheek. "Stop," she demanded.

The chaperone had her back turned. She reprimanded one of the two boys, the one who had kicked the other in the groin. She was bent over shaking her book at him. Lanier caught Sadie by the chains on her return, held her again back up to his face and then pushed her off, and then again. She was biting back a tantrum. Then he caught her, held her in a deep hug with his arms wrapped around her. She squirmed in his chest, kicked her heels back at him, an enraged dimple buried deep in her blotchy cheek.

"Shhh," he cooed.

"No," she whined. "Stop it, just leave me alone."

"Well, if you don't want to hang out with me, we can just walk you home, and you can sit in your room and wait for your mother to get back," Lanier said in an animated voice and Sadie softened her sniveling. "You want me to take you home?"

She nodded slowly with her lips pressed tightly together.

"Okay, but you have to hold my hand. Okay?"

She nodded.

"Let's get you back home then," he said and gently lowered her to the ground.

8

A breezeway led from the Leavitt's guest home to the library of the primary estate. The library looked out onto the private tennis court, beyond that the black lake. Corey and AJ's stepmother was on the court with her personal instructor. She was bent over in front of the man, warming her hamstrings. Fatty walked on through the passing hall into the kitchen as Corey turned from the window and went through the desk drawers for cash.

"Her p-pap-purse is in here," Fatty hollered, his mouth already chipmunked with ham and challah bread he had found in the fridge. AJ followed Corey into the kitchen as Drake flipped open a book and sat down on the chaise. His eyes skimmed over sentences as he flipped pages back and forth, eventually letting the book lie open on his chest, and he put his hands behind his head, a rich funk like stale cheese rising from his armpits. He sighed deeply and his stomach set off on a low rumble. He startled awake shortly to Corey yelling at his stepmother, "Don't be such a cunt. Come on, just give me some money."

The tennis pro stood there, his white shorts tight on his thick thighs, a little gator embroidered on the peck of his shirt. He cleared his throat, "Excuse me son, don't call your mother that."

"Get fucked, you cocksucker. She's not my mother," Corey said.

"Scott," she said and hesitated. "It's probably better that you go now." She wiped the sweat from her brow with the back of her wrist and finished the water in her glass. "He's only going to try and show off from here." She took the glass from Scott and nodded him towards the front door.

"Yeah Scott, fuck off."

"You're just going to let him talk like that?" he asked.

"I'll see you next week, Scott," she said and physically turned him towards the door.

"You're honestly going to let him talk like that? If he was my son, he wouldn't be able to sit or speak for a week."

"If he was my son, I would have aborted him," she whispered. She had a dainty, stringy frame, a defeated smile that sagged, and burnt blonde hair, yet her voice was youthfully calm. After the main doors closed and the alarm beeped secure, she walked back to the kitchen, heading towards Corey. Her thin-lined eyebrows clinched together, as did her thin lips, and her voice matched the livid vigor in her eyes, "Just wait 'til your father gets home." Her hands were trembling before his face. "He'll handle you."

"Yeah, when's he coming home? I haven't talked to my dad in a week. Jesus Christ, just give me some fucking money."

"I'm not giving you anymore money. You get an allowance."

"I spent it."

"Well that's just too bad, now isn't it?"

"Yeah well…when I do see my dad, I'll just go ahead and tell him I saw you sucking off the tennis pro, you fucking whore. Think he won't believe me?"

"Corey James Leavitt!" She smacked the boy across the face.

AJ stood in the corner laughing.

"You want some money! Fine. Take it. Here. Here's my purse."

"It's my father's money anyways. I have more right to it than you," Corey screamed back at her. Fatty stood there with his mouth slowly moving around the gourmet food he had stuffed into his cheeks. Drake lay in the library with a turned head that Corey could see partially peeking at the end of the hallway.

"Stop eating all my food you fat little shit," she snatched the platter of finger sandwiches that Fatty had been holding and slapped it down on the kitchen counter. "They're for a party!" she yelled, her white tennis skirt bounced above deep red gravel marks on the back of her hamstrings.

"Dude, your sta-st-step mom is fa-fucking hot. I'd fa-fuck the sha-sh-sh-shit out of her."

"She's a dumb bitch," Corey said as he dug around the purse until he found some money.

"She laced you up good," Drake said as he made his way into the kitchen, "look at the fingerprints on his face."

"She is a dumb bitch," AJ said.

"I'd still fa-ff-fuck her."

9

"Butchie," was all that Lanier heard as he lowered the headphones from his ears and pushed his front door open. It wasn't fully closed, and he distinctly remembered closing it. He craned his neck through the doorway and peered into the living room area. He heard the grinding flicker of a lighter, and in the corner a dull orange glow lit up deep shadows in his mother's face. She was lighting left-over foil squares and sucking up the chalky lavender of meth resin. She held a short straw between her lips. Only sixteen years older than Lanier, her face was broken down and weathered like an old catcher's mitt. She had a raincoat zipped up to a dingy and marked sports bra. Gym shorts revealed anemic bruises and spider veins. She did not have shoes on her feet, only calluses. On the ground next to her was a purse with a broken strap tied in a knot and sandals with black grimed imprints of her heels, toes and the arcs of her feet.

"Butchie, come give a kiss." Smoke billowed from her nostrils. She had a sore, split-dry on her bottom lip, and she scratched at her elbows and bare ribs leaving red streams.

"You said a couple days."

"What's wrong baby, you're not happy to see me?"

"Don't..." He looked at her only for a moment before he turned. "You can't stay here. I want you out of my place."

"You shouldn't talk to me like that."

"Don't start. You could really fuck things up for me." The room smelled of urinal cakes and unused semen.

"It smells good in here. You been cooking?" she asked.

"You're hungry? You look spun out of your fucking head."

"Not really," his mother started to shiver and held herself tightly. She closed her eyes as a deep cough tore through phlegm, followed by another and then another. She hunched over with her arms crossed trying to catch her breath and once she filled her lungs without coughing, she leaned back and began pulling crinkled and folded bills from her bra and jacket pockets, and then from the crotch of her shorts, piling it on the table in front of her. "What?" she asked. The corners of his mouth were down in disgust. "You came from down there too. What's done there raised you."

Lanier raised his eyebrows and nodded, stopped, then slowly shook his head. "I want you out tonight, before tonight!" He walked back to his room and brought out two large bags of crystal and a bag of pills and dropped them on the table in front of her. He took the money and straightened it, all the faces in the same direction, and put it with the stacks of bills he kept in the freezer. "I told you, I don't need the money. You can keep it."

"I am keeping it. I'm just keeping it here. I'll get it if I need it. What pills are these?" she asked.

He didn't answer her.

"They downs or ups?" When he didn't answer again, she put two of them in her mouth and forced them down. "Doesn't matter."

The money was piled up in the freezer, all small bills, and he just stared at it, the cold air circling towards his face and tickling down the back of his arms. He closed the freezer door and grabbed the bottle of brandy off of the counter, unscrewed the lid and swallowed three times before he pulled it away from his lips, his chin wet. He carried the bottle out to the living room. One bag of crystal was opened with her hand in it. Dirt lined her fingernails and smudged the bag of chalky white. As he watched her shuffle through, he picked an empty coffee cup off of the table and blew out the ashes that had settled inside, poured a drink and set it in front of her.

"When you gonna stop all of this shit?"

"I guess when it kills me," she said.

"By the looks of it, you ain't that far off."

"Sometimes I wish I weren't."

Lanier nodded as he watched his mother light a fresh piece of foil, her eyes coming together over the smoke and then rolling back. He took the bottle back up and finished what was left. He pulled off his shirt and wiped his mouth with it, dropped it to the ground and pulled out a cigarette. He offered the pack.

"I'm real proud."

"Of what?"

"Of the way you turned out. Could've been much worse."

"Couldn't be much worse."

"I'm just real proud."

Lanier nodded.

"You still working up at the hospital?"

"How do you think I got those pills?"

"Working with the children?"

Lanier nodded.

"Always so good with them kids," she spoke as she exhaled.

Lanier walked away, his fists clenched, and as he reached the end of the hallway he heard a faint knocking at the back door. He took his time walking to the back and waited by the door and listened. The knock came again, slightly harder than before.

"Who is it?" he asked.

"It's Corey."

Then Lanier door opened enough to peek out.

"What's up Lenny?"

"I can't really help you out right now, sort of tied up. Page me later tonight," Lanier pulled back and started to close the door.

"Just wanted to ask about something."

He peered back out, "What?"

Corey swallowed hard and wrapped his fingers up, "We was sort of wondering…"

"Spit it out, let's go."

"Well, we was wondering if you could get us some hookers."

"Who's the fuck's *we*? You been telling people about me?"

"Naw, my little brother and a couple of friends. They don't know nothing about you."

"You tell them about me?"

"Naw man, I haven't told them anything about you."

Hookers, Lanier thought. His eyes darted around. He turned and looked back down the hallway and heard the lighter striking. He popped his head back out. "I can probably work something out. Where are you gonna be? Where do you all want her?"

"I didn't think about that," and after a moment he told Lanier the number to his parent's guest house.

"I'll have her call you. That work?"

"Yeah," Corey hesitated. "Yeah, yeah, I guess that'll be good. You think tonight?"

"Probably..." Lanier turned back inside. "Hold on a sec." He walked into his room and crushed a few Viagra pills and mixed it with meth powder.

Corey was standing on the back porch with his hands together looking inside the cracked door when Lanier returned. He handed the boy a nickel bag of the bluish-white powder and a couple of condoms. "Take a pinch of this and put it under your tongue about fifteen minutes before. Trust me." He started to close the door.

"How much do I owe you?"

"I'm not a pimp."

"For this," and Corey held the little baggie.

"My treat."

"How much will *she* cost?" Corey asked.

"Cheap," was all that tapered out of the closing door.

Lanier herded his mother out into the garage. She stood there as he walked around pulling the cover off of the sedan, the dented brown sides and khakied ragtop. Lanier's mother still had a perk to her frame, standing there with a hand on her hip. He pulled up the garage door. Her face read tired; her eyes dark, slippery as eel skin. Revered at trucker stops and dives all along I-10, from Jacksonville to Birmingham, she worked back doors and glory holes, not because she liked to and not because she despised it, she simply worked at what she had experience in. The ones that knew her called her Crystal because she always had meth, and as she became older, she sold more pep than herself. Lanier used to pray for his mother, but now he sees her only as disease, spreading at an accelerated pace. She is dying and there was no use for fruitless attempts of redemption. She opened the door and sat still in Lanier's car, a cigarette seesawing between her fingers.

"Try to get someone young for these kids," he said before he started the engine.

"Kids? How old are they?"

"I don't know? Fifteen maybe, what does it matter?"

"They're just babies," she said.

"What do you care," Lanier said softly and turned his head back to reverse from his driveway. "How old were you when you had me?"

"That's different, I didn't grow up with no doctors and lawyers for parents. I did everything I had to."

"As long as you survived, right?"

"What's that supposed to mean?"

"You know goddamn well what that means," he came to a stop and turned to look at his mother. "Not all of us survived."

She didn't speak, took long drags on her cigarette, looked out the window at the passing streetlamps, her right leg bouncing a nervous rhythm. She finished the cigarette and lit another. "What the fuck could I do? I didn't know what to do. He supported us."

"No. He kept you stoned. He fucked me. That's not support."

"And now you keep me stoned."

"No. I keep you from spreading more disease than you have to. I keep you from fucking scum for dope cut-up with rat poison. And I'd like to keep you at a distance. You smell like hell, roll down the window."

"I should have just aborted you and your sister, like the others."

"You always said it, wish you done it."

They passed under the streetlights, shadows running back and forth through the car. She looked out of her window as Lanier stared straight down the road. The center strips ticked by like a metronome. Only one car passed, and Lanier avoided eye contact by holding the side of his head in his hand, thin strands of brown hair spilled out between his fingers. Tall horseweeds stood in clumps between the roadside and a bordering creek, the moon belly-danced on the water's surface, and the night was thick with low curdling clouds like octopus ink. When Lanier came to the brick driveway under the shadows of a tall oak, he turned into the corner without hesitation and parked. Lanier's mother questioningly pointed towards the Leavitt's estate and Lanier nodded. The main house was enormous, looming over the trees like a black beast sitting Indian-style in the night. She held her little bag of belongings on her lap, the number and address on top.

"I'm guessing the guest house is the smaller one, over to the right?" she asked.

Lanier flicked his lights back on and pulled away.

When Lanier was two miles outside of the community, he pulled the car into a gas station and Crystal opened the door and stepped out.

"Just make sure she's young…" he said, leaning over the passenger seat and looking up to his mother outside of the car, "…and clean." She turned and walked to the payphone.

10

It was a little after eight when Corey met back with the other guys at the playground. He held the little baggie of meth powder in his coat pocket, inside of his clammy palm, and walked slowly watching his shadow stretch under the streetlamps. He laughed to himself as he walked up, a queer inward laugh. His little brother stopped dangling from the monkey bars, and Drake pulled out the little flask he carried and turned it upwards. He offered the flask around.

"What kind of pussy shit is this, mint schnapps?" Corey said after he took a hard swallow, and then closed both eyes and skewered his face.

"I think it was called Sambucca. Something like that. It's all your parents had left at the bar."

"It don't te-tetaste like mm-ma-mmint, more like black ja-j-j-jelly b-beans."

"You would be the one to know what it tastes like, fat ass. It's fucking gross."

"I kind of like it," AJ said.

"Whatever, who cares?" Drake grabbed back the flask. "So, what's the deal? Did he know that you took his shit?" He pulled out his menthols and lit two, and they all passed them around. They sat huddled around their bench, and Corey started to laugh to himself again.

"Not a clue. And you guys are never going to believe it—"

What, they all echoed.

"You're never gonna fucking believe it," Corey said again.

What, tell us, what, come on, the other boys said simultaneously, rather chorus-like.

"We got one calling the house tonight."

"Wh-wha-what, we ga-g-got a hahooker? Are you s-ss-serious?" Fatty asked.

"I'm dead serious. Lenny said he could work it out and he's never let me down before."

"How m-mm-much?"

"Cheap."

"She's coming to the house?" AJ asked.

"It's either that or the playground."

"What if we get caught?" AJ asked.

"By who?"

"Mom and Dad."

"Don't call her that."

"Whatever. What if they catch us?"

"Then they'll have to pay for their own turn."

She scratched at her elbows as she walked along the entryway. Foot lamps spread a golden border for the manicured landscaping. Lime green fluorescents shot up into the arms of large sycamores. The grass was the same grass as on the fairway, short and better kept than any bed she had ever slept in. She glanced around sharply, perhaps for dogs or groundskeepers, and held her bag tightly to herself in case she had to sprint. When she came up to the front door of the guest home, she gazed at her ethereal reflection in the glass, dreary and slouched. She finger-combed her hair back, ripping through snags and rats. She began by knocking gently.

The boys were in the den, their pupils like black saucers. AJ was rearranging the pillows on the floor, and Fatty was trying to do sit-ups swearing that he could lose all his weight tonight. Drake rambled incoherently, paranoia-stricken sentences, "Did you hear that? Did you fucking hear that? I heard it again. Did you hear that? It sounded like," he paused, swung his head back and forth and then got up and met Corey where he was pacing with a cigarette and a joint and a toothbrush and the half empty little nickel bag of meth. "You got any more of that?" Drake asked Corey. "Hey, you got any more of that?" He tapped incessantly on Corey's arm. "Hey, hey give me some more of that. What do you think it is? Come on, give me some more," and then he stopped completely. "Oh shit, did you feel that? I think someone we know just died somewhere. Did you feel that? It's like being in warm water. God damn it that feels good."

Corey paced with a vacant stare. "She said she would be here by now. Where is she?" The knocking grew louder, and then the doorbell chimed.

"Did you fucking hear that, somebody's here. Somebody, somebody found out. We got to get…" Drake could not stop rambling.

"She's here!" Corey ran over the floor pillows and tripped. He got up and fell again, and stayed down in rolling laughter. AJ turned and looked over to his brother with a wide smile and even wider eyes, the whites glossy and marbled with thin bloodshot veins.

"Who's here?" Drake asked.

"The hooker you twats, the hooker's here. And I got first dibs."

Fatty followed Corey down the stairs to the front door, and they swung the door open. Their mouths opened slightly, their bottom lips drooping down. She was a real hooker. Corey half expected a woman like the ones in the magazines his father had given him, but this woman looked as if she slept in bus stations, shelters, YMCA's, and smelled as if she let people piss on her for five dollar bills. When Corey imagined a hooker, he pictured large, fake breasts, thick blonde hair, pouty red lips, long eyelashes. When he imagined a heroin addict, he pictured what was now in front of him. AJ and Drake scoped down from the top of the stairs to the dimly lit front area.

"So?" Crystal asked and pushed between Corey and Fatty, looked down, up and around, and walked to a dark corner away from the entry light. "Fancy stuff," she said as she ran her fingers along the tall end tables and bent down to look at the titles of the books in the low-laying, room-bordering bookshelf. "You got anything to drink in here?"

Across the entry room was a brick-lined firebox as tall as a person, above it hung the head of a twelve-point buck. Crystal found her way towards the empty crystal decanters atop a rolling bar that hadn't been stocked in years. AJ leapt down two stairs a step with Drake's flask; still at the top of the stairs, Drake continued to ramble but not loud enough to be clear.

"It's Sambucca," AJ said.

She slowly unscrewed the lid, one eyebrow higher than the other. She brought her nose to the flask and took a glass from the bar. She poured herself a drink, sophisticated pinky drawn. Her athletic warm-up jacket was zipped to the top of her sports bra and she downed two fingers of schnapps before she asked, "What do you call this shit again?"

"I told you guys," Corey said.

Fatty stood back near the front door, his mouth still a bit open, showing his bottom teeth. He blinked sporadically, looked down at her bare and blackened feet, then back up to her calloused knees and bruised thighs.

"It's Sam-buc-ca," AJ sounded out the word's syllables.

"You got nothing else to drink? I thought ya'll was some naughty boys."

"Hey Drake?" Corey hollered up the stairs. "Drake?"

"How many is here?"

"Just four, ma'am," AJ said.

"Drake, go get that bottle I got under the couch. You hearing me?"

"Yeah. Yeah, I got it. I'll go get it." Drake rattled off.

"He's the shy one?" she asked.

"I guess so," AJ said.

"All right, first and fo'most, I'm a have to see some money up front. Seventy-five to start. Then once we're done with whatever you all got planned for the evening, I'll tally the rest of the bill. Sound good?"

Fatty held his shirt down and stuck his chest out. He started to say something and hesitated, then collected the saliva bubbles that accumulated at the sides of his mouth. "Mu-mm-ma'am, do I have to pa-ppay te-te-triple?"

"Why would you have to pay triple?"

"Because I'm f-ffe-fat," Fatty said while he looked at the ground, biting the corner of his lip trying to keep it from turning.

"Now who told you something that stupid? You believe that?" Crystal asked.

"Ka-keka-corey, you're an asshole," Fatty said.

Corey pulled out a hundred dollar bill from his wallet and handed it to her.

"You boys got a ladies' room I can use?"

She loosened her hold on her bag and slowly followed Corey up the stairs. AJ and Fatty kept right behind her. Corey picked up pillows from the ground so that she wouldn't step on them. Her bare feet left grimed imprints on the walnut floors. Her eyes bounced from painting to tall window to painting, to all the colorful and large pillows that covered the floor. Corey opened the first door in the upstairs hallway and turned on the light.

"You got one with a shower in it? I mean it ain't that necessary, but you boys should get your money's worth."

Corey turned off the light and walked her to the third door down, opened it and turned that light on. Fatty and AJ followed at her heels.

"Ke-ka-kk-can I watch ya-yyou sha-shishower?" Fatty asked.

"Yeah, yeah, can we watch you shower?" AJ said.

"I'm all yours tonight boys. You can do whatever you want. Just give me a couple of minutes. Then I'll open up the door and whoever wants to watch can just come on in." She winked at AJ and then blew a kiss at Fatty before closing and locking the door behind her.

Corey pulled his brother and Fatty from the closed door they stared at. It was dark in the hallway; only the thin line of white light seeped out from the bottom of the door. "Let's go, come on."

"What, where are we ga-gg-going? She's ga-g-good to g-go," Fatty insisted.

"Come on, we got to talk about this," and Corey pulled the two boys to the den. Drake had curled up on the couch sucking on the corner of a pillow. He rocked gently and turned his head sharply towards any noise.

Crystal took off her jacket. She dragged her fingers over hundreds of thin, short scars that ran from her ribs to her pelvis. They were faded and razor thin, wounds that she had inflicted at a young age. Before Lanier was born, she stared into the sun, picked scabs, swallowed batteries so they would break down inside of her. She would pinch a grip of skin and slit, slit, slit, slit, slit, slit, slit, purge.

She opened her bag and took out a sock that held her glass pipe, burnt black at the stem. From a baggie of three or four glass shards of meth, Crystal took the smallest one out and pushed it in the screened bowl, gently put the pipe down on the sink top and turned on the exhaust fan and the shower to full heat. She pulled the knob to let the water come and took off her sports bra and shorts, dropping them in the sink and turning on the water. Standing naked and scrubbing the fabrics together with hand soap, she rubbed out weeks of hers and other's sweat and then dried her hands as she looked at herself in the fogging mirror, holding her breasts up and stretching her stomach taut. She pulled her lighter from her bag and turned up the adjustable flame, plugged one end of the black glass pipe with the fire and put her mouth to the other end. Smoke filled the glass slowly at first, but then thick curls came together in a cloud and she cleared the chamber of smoke into her lungs. As that bluish-yellow chemical smoke curled back out of her nose, she brought her face close to the mirror and stretched the skin near her eyes, pulled down on her cheeks, and ran her finger over the sore on her lip. She didn't pick at the sore; instead, she finished the crystal and put the thin glass tube back into the sock. Fumbling around through all the cabinets of the bathroom and the two drawers, she found shaving razors and some hair conditioner and some toilet cleaning products that she bagged. She unlocked the door, opened it slightly, and stayed on her filthy toes as she stepped into the tub. Little black prints marked the tub floor, one by one, until the entire basin was murky with charcoaled water. And then the water eventually became clear, soapy with thick clumps of shaving cream. Matted hair fell from her crotch and her underarms, a thin trickle of blood streamed down her inner thigh.

"Did you see that sore on her lip? That can't be good." Corey said.

"So wuh-wuh-whawhat, she has a ke-kecold s-s-sore," Fatty said and looked down the hall trying to listen to what she was doing. "My ma' g-gg-ggets'em all the time."

"That's probably gonorrhea or herpes, or some shit," Corey said.

"Whatever, the-th-that's what ke-kk-kecondoms are ffa-ff-for," Fatty said, and then a look of confusion plagued his face. "Do we have any kek-ke-kk-kecondoms?"

Drake sprang up, a deep panic in his gaze, "Where's that powder at?"

"Fuck that pp-papowder, I na-nne-need ke-kecondoms." Fatty swallowed hard and took a deep breath, "Where are the ke-condoms at?"

"Where did you put that powder? Corey," Drake stood and walked over to Corey, "Corey, where'd you put it?"

"Calm the fuck down," Corey said.

AJ just sat there looking from person to person, "I don't think I need anymore," he said. "I think she's pretty. Do you guys think she's pretty?"

"Dude, she's a hooker. What are you falling in love?" Corey said and cuffed his brother on the back of his head.

"I'm not in love. But I want to see her in the shower."

"Yeah, so do I, what's ra-rawrong with that?" Fatty asked.

"Go ahead, I just think that she's gross. But whatever man—just don't kiss her. I'm telling you that shit on her lip'll spread, and it probably lasts forever." Corey folded his arms and jerked his elbow out of Drake's hand. "Just saying, I'm telling you."

"Let me get another pinch of that powder, Corey." Drake whispered. Then said it again a little louder, and then again. "Where's the little baggy?" he yelled.

"It's right here. Jesus Christ," Corey spun around to face Drake. "Would you calm the fuck down, there's plenty. We're all gonna take another pinch, but we should put it away after that." Corey dipped a key in the little baggie and pulled out a little pile and dropped the powder under his tongue and let it dissolve. His body didn't want to swallow, but slowly the pinch of methamphetamines dissipated into his moist flesh.

"I don't want anymore," AJ said.

"We're all gonna take another pinch," Corey grabbed his brother by the arm and spoke from his chest, "All right."

"Dude," Drake said, "If he doesn't want it, I'll take his share."

"Fuck that, he's doing it. Open your mouth. Open it," he yelled up to his little brother, grabbing his jaw. Corey squeezed until AJ reluctantly opened his mouth. "Lift up your tongue," and he did. Corey gave his little brother a small pile and then a large push for Drake and Fatty.

"D-dd-daDude, she op-pp-pened the door," Fatty said. "I'm going to wh-wuhwatch, you keke-coming AJ?"

"Fuck yeah."

11

*F*ather Hibbens sits in his chair. Short Sago Palms whip against his window. He sips cold soup from a coffee mug as the television plays a series of infomercials at a very low volume. A dim light behind his chair casts his shadow on the ground in front of him. He places the coffee mug on the table stand next to his chair, his eyelids shutting, fluttering.

Father Hibbens looks at the staircase that leads to his bedroom. During evening Mass, he had merely stumbled along through the scriptures and skipped sections. That voice, that young voice was nowhere to be found amongst the elderly amens of his patrons. It wasn't hiding behind their unnatural wigs and bald heads, loose skin, eyelids and lips that had recessed, bulbous noses covered with deep set pores and thin veins, swollen arthritic fingers held together in prayer. He opens the bottle of scotch at his side and lets the liquor slowly sift into his mouth and down his throat. His sunken eyelids expose bloodshot whites, his bottom lip protrudes in a wet pout, and Father Hibbens raises the bottle to the TV and sings.

"Hark! The loud celestial hymn,
Angel choirs above are raising.
Cherubim and seraphim
In unceasing chorus praising,
Fill the heavens with sweet accord.
Holy, holy, holy, Lord."

He takes another slow pull on the bottle and dribble rolls down his chin. He drinks again, finishing what is left. It is good scotch that leaves a sweet acid taste in the back of the mouth, which he rolls around and then swallows. He stands, walks in a stiff way towards the kitchen, holding his lower back and not bending much at all at the knees. The falling cracks of lightning coming through the window over the kitchen sink meet him at the doorway. He squints as he turns on the light. The kitchen tile is cold on his bare feet. Hibbens opens one cupboard, then another. He knocks over boxes of cereal and dry noodles. He picks up can after can of English peas and Cannellini beans, reads the label and tosses them farther back into the cupboard. As he finishes searching one cupboard he leaves the door open and starts on the next. He pulls out a can of cling peaches, turning it in his hand. With a fingernail he digs at the tab on the top of the can and it snaps off, leaving only a small gouge. He slurps the thick nectar from the jagged aluminum as he stares at the phone sitting on the counter. An aggravated tic plays under his right eyelid. Hibbens, with the tin can in his hand, his head bobbling above his shoulders, pulls out the drawer next to him and slams it shut. He takes a paring knife from the sink and begins to pry into the can for the peaches.

A sober, calm voice echoes in his mind, pedantically, arbitrarily, against all emotion. He can't hear it very clearly. Help him, it might have said. Once he pries open the can of peaches, he sees that they had turned; no longer slippery soft gold segments but broken down and the syrup had browned. He pours the can down the drain and turns to leave the room but stops before passing through the kitchen doorway to take the loaf of bread and another bottle from above his fridge. He walks back to his sofa and places the bottle on the floor near his feet. While he sits, he tears out the white insides of the bread and balls it up. He pulls a blanket around his shoulders and eats the dough balls one by one. He lets them sit in his cheek, chewing very slowly.

He falls asleep with the half-hollowed loaf at his side, the bottle at his feet, and his head lulled back as if he kept his closed eyes on God. As he sleeps he shakes his head, his shoulders jerk, and his nose flares. He wakes up a few hours later on his sofa in much of the same position. He looks towards his watch but can not make out the hands in the dim light. He rubs his neck, looks at the clock on the wall above the television. It is just before midnight, and he watches the minute hand as it touches the hour hand, held in prayer he thinks, before he stands up. Hibbens combs through his hair with his stubby fingers and fastens his belt. He puts on his shoes and a coat and walks towards the door quietly, not letting the heels of his shoes clickety-clack down. Sister Anita, in the quarters adjacent, if she knew where he went in the night, he thinks, she would be appalled. Father Hibbens puts his hand on the doorknob, turning it slowly to quiet the mechanics and straightening himself as he walks outside; he smoothes out the wrinkles on the front of his shirt and zips up his coat with the young man's letter in the inside pocket. After walking a block east of the church, he turns right and heads towards Wallace Community Library, passing Napier Field by a few blocks before he juts left and crosses the train tracks. He quickly passes through the commons, littered with cigarette stubs and scraps of trash; he notices a few colored boys standing in clumps under various breezeways. He drags his heels as he walks, his fists balled inside his coat pockets, his eyes on the ground, his chin doubled-up, tucked into his collar.

After crossing Dothan Green and the track, and after walking alongside the parking chains until there were no more, he steps off of the grass onto the sidewalk along Montgomery heading towards the business district of North Dothan. He begins to sober along the walk, the cool air of the night running around his face. His feet become heavy, ligaments in his right knee popping and clicking with each step. He walks for an hour before he reaches the main street, West Main, and follows it towards the statue of Our Lady of the Peace. Closely spaced red-brick store fronts, intricate street lamps, wide walking lanes and long abandoned businesses with ivy bordering the windows seem to enclose upon him. The cafes, the speakeasy, the hardware depot, the wholesalers, the tailor and taxidermist, all but the attorneys had boarded their windows. The town had flourished when Hibbens was a boy, when peanuts had replaced cotton, but now it was a shadow, a dark and fermenting exhale of the past. Father Hibbens pulls at his belt and walks past the two old men sitting on the stoop of the theatre. They have short, curly grey beards, thick moustaches only slightly golden above the lip. One of them has a bottle that weighs down the pocket of his coat, and the other man—with a very dark complexion and dry eyes that seemed to say they would have loved to have cried just once—digs his sullied thumb into his tobacco pipe. He presses down on the coal and puffs the thick molasses smoke into the air. Even with the streetlamps, the night is dark as currants and thick currents of wind run through the sugarsweet magnolia. Nothing to be heard but the crackle of burning tobacco, breath, and the wind that makes the leaves sing, sway, march, clap and shush.

Hibbens opens the side door of the theatre, after hours a juke, and an explosion of colors and voices work together. With a closed mouth, he burps up a thick, acidy peach sugar scotch bile that he swallows back down the side of his throat. Two large-bottomed women, both dressed in yawning red are followed up the stairs by men in tweed coats and then out of sight. Hibbens walks right by the dark sneers of a few young people who are sitting in the lobby with iced drinks and stubby cigars, black button down shirts half unbuttoned and product in their hair that slicked the curls straight. He walks directly to the back counter, hands still balled in his pockets.

Little candles line the countertop and two large ashtrays sit on either end. It takes a few minutes, but eventually a short and round woman comes from behind a curtained doorway. Thin black hairs curl slightly at the corners of her mouth and Hibbens stares at them as he drinks from the watered-down scotch that she brings him without ordering; opens a pack of Dorals that somebody has left on the bar; drinks until the room eventually clears out.

12

While AJ and Fatty each took two turns in the bedroom, Corey and Drake were balled up in the den finishing off the meth powder. Drake mumbled that he missed his mom and loved his father. Corey said he missed his dad and had loved his mother. They sat there, only a foot apart from each other and Drake cooed and cried, "He used to hit us, but I know he loves me. I want him to love me."

Corey looked over his shoulder to his friend. Drake had his forehead cradled in his hands. Corey stretched out his arm to put his hand on his shoulder, but pulled back and rubbed the wetness from his own face.

"He hasn't hit us for close to a year," Drake said. "A few months ago," he snorted back, "...a few months ago, he came in our room in the middle of the night and took off his pants. He just stood there, yelling at her. I didn't know what to do. Then he pissed on the floor."

Corey—with a reluctant open mouth, blurry red eyes that stared vacantly just past Drake, and hands glossed over in sweat—couldn't keep his thoughts contained. With his eyes closed, the thoughts bumping and swerving into each other; breaking away, twisting, one after the other, the same ideas over and over; he knew what thought would come next but had no control, just had to wait for it. Corey quivered and held himself from outright trembling.

Drake still mumbled, his forehead rubbing against the butt of his palms, he sobbed and gasped. Tears mixed with snot on his face, "I want to go see my father. Tell him I love him." He sat up straight and cocked his head back, wiping his red-marked face with the bottom of his shirt. "What time is it?"

"What?" Corey jarred back.

"What fucking time is it?"

"It's after three in the morning."

"I need to go see my father. I have to talk to him."

"Dude, you're fucked up. You should just chill the fuck out."

Drake put his head back down, "You think Lenny'll have more of that shit, if we wanted it?"

"I don't know," Corey said. He pulled the empty nickel bag out of his pocket and shoved it into an empty soda can. "God, I hope not. This stuff is too much. It's feels like a rollercoaster took a shit in my head."

It took a second, but then laughter rushed from both of them.

Corey slid off of the couch and kneeled in front of the center table and split a cigar with his pocketknife.

AJ came swaggering from the dark of the hallway, his belt and button of his jeans undone, his shirt inside out. A smile broke into every part of his face and demeanor. "Who's got a smoke?" He came and sat next to his older brother. He threw an arm over his shoulder, laughed into his ear.

"You didn't kiss her?" Corey asked as he lit two cigarettes and passed one to AJ.

"I kissed her boobies," he said with the cigarette clenched in between his teeth. He rolled back onto the large pillows surrounding him, laughed until he coughed and burped smoke. His face paled, his smile vanished, and he stood up in a quick dash and vomited down his shirt before he could open the door to the patio. He fell to his knees and dry heaved until his tongue was purple.

"Dude, what the fuck?" Corey hollered over.

"I don't feel so good," AJ whimpered while trying to catch air in his lungs. "Corey?"

"I told you not to kiss her. Now look, you went and got gonorrhea, or some shit."

"He doesn't have gonorrhea," Drake said plainly, his head still resting in his palms.

"How do you know?" Corey asked.

"Because I know what gonorrhea is, you dumb shit." Drake said.

"Fuck you."

Drake lifted his head. He turned to look back where AJ was hunched over, "I'm sure he's fine if he used the condom."

AJ didn't say anything; he coughed a wet cough and spit on the floor.

"You used a condom right?" Corey said more directly.

AJ still didn't say anything. He caught his breath and pulled off his soiled shirt. His chest was wide and sunken in, a few curls of black hair stood in the center crevice and around his nipples. His back was wide like a harp, and when he stood up his abdomen stretched taut and knotted.

"Tell me you used a fucking condom." Corey stubbed his cigarette and started to walk over to his little brother, leaving the pile of dope and the cigar skin on the table.

"Just leave me alone," AJ said.

"What did you do?" Corey demanded.

"Leave me alone!"

"AJ, tell me what the fuck happened."

"The condoms you had didn't fit."

"What?" Corey said in a hushed way. He tried to look up into AJ's eyes.

"They didn't fit."

"What do you mean they didn't fit?"

"I couldn't get it on," AJ whispered back.

"What?"

"They were too small. I couldn't get it on."

"So you didn't fuck her?" Drake asked.

AJ looked down to his groin, but didn't say anything.

"What did you do, AJ?" Corey put a hand on his brother's shoulder, squeezed to get the boy to look at him.

"I don't know," AJ said and turned to look through the glass patio doors, but the night was so black that the only thing to be seen in the glass was their reflection. "She put it in her mouth. I never felt anything so good. Then it was over real fast."

"And that was it?" Corey asked.

AJ shook his head. "After Fatty went in for a second time, I wanted to go in for a second time. And I kissed her boobies. She got right on top of me. I thought you were going be proud of me."

The three of them turned their attention to Fatty who walked into the room with his chin up. The smooth skin of his face was blotched with blushed-red patches, his eyes seemed crossed. He walked over to the table to break up the small pile of pot that Corey had started. He searched around for another dollar cigar. "Wuh-where're all the 'ga-ggagars? This one's all dried out."

"Where's Crystal?" AJ asked Fatty.

"Crystal?" Corey asked, obviously taken aback at learning that the hooker had a name, and even more so at his brother saying it so endearingly.

"Her," AJ wagged his head towards the hallway Fatty had just come from.

"Said she'll ba-b-be out in a ma-ma'aminute," Fatty said as he licked the split cigar leaf and paper. "Said she ke-kacould use a ra-rarride to the gate, if wah-we're all di-di-dddone w-with her." He turned to Corey and Drake and asked, "Why di-didon't ya'll have a ga-gga-go? Wuh-whahat ya'll sk-ke-ke-scared of?"

"Shut up fat ass. I ain't gonna fuck no old skank, specially not *after* ya'll. And sure as hell ain't paying for it. How much ya'll owe her?" Corey asked with his arms crossed.

"I ain't got no money Corey," AJ said.

"Yeah, I ain't gg-ga-got no muh-ma-money, either," said Fatty.

When Crystal came from out of the darkness, she had her bag over her shoulder, an unlit cigarette dangling from her lips, and her jacket unzipped showing her breasts riddled with hickies like fresh lesions. "You mind if I have that drink now?" she asked and lit her cigarette. "What's that smell, somebody get sick?"

Corey dropped to one knee and fished under the sofa for the half empty bottle of Cognac that Drake never got. When he handed her the fifth, he told her that he got too wasted and had thrown up before he could get to the patio. When he asked how much they owed her for the night, AJ partially smiled behind his brother. They settled on another hundred; Corey had three-fifty if she demanded it all, and she would have left with what she had already been given if that was all they had, but they settled on the two one-hundred dollar bills. "I can give you a ride about fifty yards from the gate, but you have to walk out from there."

"Sure you're okay to drive," Crystal turned the bottle to her lips before she handed it back. "That shit's sure rich."

Corey nodded. "Take it, we don't like it," he said and then led her down the stairs, and AJ wiped his mouth with his balled shirt, dropped it and followed. They went into the garage and pressed a button to bring the door up. Corey pointed towards one of the golf-carts but didn't say a word. He simply went and sat down, turned the key and waited for her to join him. AJ jumped on the back of the cart as they started to drive away, and Corey put the pedal down and sped out of his driveway and around River Hills Drive— sharp on the corners, the wind a bitter spike in their faces. AJ stood on the back platform and held on tight to the roofing posts. His chest, elbows and knees went to jittering. AJ sucked his upper lip into his mouth, and Crystal clasped tightly to the arm railing with a cool, clenched-jaw expression. Once Corey went as far as he was going to go, he floored the brake, and AJ slammed into the back of the roof, knocking the wind out of his lungs, and he rolled off the cart onto the ground. Crystal was able to hold strong to her seat. She pulled out another cigarette, offering one to Corey. She lit the fresh one from the stub of her last smoke and put the pack back in her bag. "This is where I get off," she said.

Corey reached out and grabbed her wrist. "You got AIDS?" he asked.

She shook her head, though unconvincingly.

Corey looked into her eyes and said nothing. He let go, looked ahead, and as she started to walk away AJ got up from the ground and followed her. "AJ," Corey called after him. "AJ, what the fuck are you doing?" and when AJ didn't turn back, Corey pulled away and drove back to the house alone.

When AJ stopped her, he spoke to the back of her head. "Am I ever gonna see you again?" She was standing under a streetlamp. When she turned to face him, it was the first time he was given the chance to see her in bright yellow light. Still, he would not look at her directly for more than a moment. He looked down to the ground, instead of at the creases that split out and surrounded her eyes, or at the gums that black-lined her teeth like mascara. "Probably not, huh," he said before she answered him. "For what it's worth, that was my first," AJ paused, then continued, "time."

She reached up to his face with a calloused thumb to feel the line of his cheekbone. They stood there like that for some time. She pulled a pen out of her bag and wrote down a number onto his hand. "You just gotta page me when you want me to come back down."

AJ smiled and looked to her eyes. The morning was starting to climb up his backside. "I think there's a bus stop a ways down on the right," he said, and she turned and walked away.

Drake was in one of the bedrooms, the lights off, and he was trying to masturbate.

Fatty had gone downstairs and outside through the breezeway to the primary estate; he slipped into the kitchen through the sliding glass doors and quietly opened the fridge.

Corey pulled the cart back into the garage and pushed the button for the door to roll down. He walked upstairs and picked up the flask of Sambucca and finished what was left, about three or four hearty swallows. He lit a cigarette and as he came up the stairs he noticed that the den was vacant. He called out for Fatty, and then he called for Drake, neither yielded a response. Corey walked down the hallway, and only one door was closed. He started to knock, then just opened the door and flicked on the light. He turned the light back off almost immediately when he saw his friend hurry to cover himself, but Corey didn't leave the room.

"Dude," Drake said. "What the fuck? Get out."

Then there was silence, only the scratch of the comforter and sheets, the hum of the air conditioning. Drake sat like a photograph; the light had caught him just right. Corey hesitated, listening to his friend scurry under the comforter, an erection of his own mounting, thumping against his leg, confusing him. With his hand still on the door handle, Corey ultimately decided to move back out of the room.

AJ and Fatty had finally fallen asleep. The rising sun bleached the windows. Corey hadn't told the others what he had walked in on; he hadn't said anything to them. Corey sat there, the erection still warm against his inner thigh, still pulsing, starting to ache. He remembered that he had put the empty baggie in the soda can on the table, and he pulled out his knife and cut into the aluminum. He pulled out the baggy and licked it clear. He stood quietly from the sofa, his brother nestled between two large pillows, Fatty snoring. Corey opened the door quietly, walked towards the bed, towards his friend, towards a decision that terrified him. Corey's soft toe-steps in the direction of the bed went unheard. He pulled the covers back, "Drake, you awake?" he whispered.

Drake was still naked and his limp penis coiled back at the cold air. Corey stood over him and pulled down his pants without undoing them and lightly caressed himself. Before he could climax, Drake sprang up, pushed Corey to the ground and left the room.

13

Groups of people congregated outside of the double doors before ushers sounded the welcome. Even then, the mAJority of the people waited for the initial waves to dissolve through the doors before they considered entering. They stood in slouched clumps with loose ties and rolling midsections, and many of them talked of football or housewives portrayed on television. They skated around political hearsay and regurgitation; nobody asked questions but merely nodded with blank smiles. The fire captain and his daughters with their long ears and short teeth stood with Mr. Drake, the portly town painter, and his portly little daughter. Dr. Jacobs and Dr. Parkson and Dr. Tylor and Dr. Berry and Dr. Brien wore the same clothes and contempt that they wore to the office and talked the same derisive chatter about young tail—in roundabout ways, of course—their menopausal wives just out of earshot. Children skipped and skirted around the plots of grass, rolled around in their argyle sweaters and khaki slacks, snickered and pointed in groups of petite floral dresses. Whole families spun off of each other, conversationally square-dancing around the one tall oak. A copper-headed woman held her little orange son in tow, his attention buried in the last pages of a book. He was dragged through the sanctuary doors, in between slow moving herds of shuffle boarders and bridge groups trying to mount the stairs with someone much younger bracing at the elbow; frail old ladies carried pocketbooks and weathered Bibles, streamers between the pages, held close to their midsections; little orthopedic shoes shuffled towards the statue of Jesus crucified.

Lanier wasn't ushering, but he stood by the door as if he were. He had a suit coat that loosely fit his slender frame, and he held a few youth group pamphlets in his veined grip. He was in a bit of abdominal pain as he looked over the oncoming crowd, a slight sweat forming over the back of his neck and dripping down his sides. And even when everyone had finally entered for the sermon, Lanier stood sentry as the collective prayers echoed through the closed doors in a soft hum that crawled up and down his spine. His eyes closed.

The second girl was thirteen. She lived in the same building as Lanier. Lanier would hold her hand some nights and they would share cigarettes that she stole. Her hand. It was her hands, the feel of them, the shortness of her fingers, the tightness of her grip.

It later turned out that she was being raped regularly by her stepfather. He was often drunk, loud and out of work, and therefore the first suspect. Lanier didn't know this until afterwards, though now he feels as if he had always known. She wanted to "do it" with Lanier, that's what she had said. When she went to undo his pants behind the apartment homes, she scoffed at the size of his penis. He pushed her. She got up and said that she was going to tell. He pleaded for her to forgive him. She said that she wouldn't and went back to her home. He wasn't sure whether she wouldn't tell or she wouldn't forgive.

Over the following weeks, he began to follow her. It made him feel good that she didn't seem to notice. He liked watching her. When she was coming back from the convenience store one night, it was late and along an unlit road; he came from out of the ditch holding a brick and chased her. She was fast, but he was faster. Once he was close enough, he struck her in the back of the head. He watched as she lied there with her face in the muck, and hit her twice more. He pulled her into the ditch and pulled out his knife. He stood over her body.

When he saw headlights far down the road, he ran. He ran until his legs gave out from under him. Until his feet bled through his socks. The stepfather was arrested once they found his semen inside of her. It was a long, drawn out process. Lanier watched when they put him in the backseat, his hands cuffed behind his back.

Sophia walked with a hurried step and ruffled hair. She hollered back for Sadie who was lagging behind, "Let's go Sadie Baby, the Lord don't like the late."

"Why do we have to go?" Sadie dragged her little black maryjanes. She wore a white laced skirt and plucked at a rosemary cardigan buttoned tight to her ribs. "I don't wanna."

She turned back and pinched the little arm of her daughter, "If we aren't living for the Lord, we aren't living for nothing. If I told you once," her mother said and continued on. Lanier appeared to have fallen asleep standing against the burnt blood bricks of the building. His head was bobbing, his hair falling over his closed and darkened eyelids. "Well, would you look at that, Sadie Baby? Dr. Lanier must have fallen asleep waiting for us. Look at him, he's about to tumble over." Sadie's mother laughed at the tall man wavering above a short flight of stairs, and as she laughed her joyous figure seemed to radiate warmth. Sadie rubbed the part of her arm that was pinched, yet her eyes ran over Lanier's face, his thin lips and pointed chin and thin curved nose. Her mother's gaze passed the chin, further down his torso and she bit the inside of her lip as she said, "Should we wake him?"

Sadie looked up at the desire in her mother's brazen smile and peered into her glistening eyes and puckering nostrils. Sadie's eyes intently watched how her mother clasped her hands together, how she held her purse to her chest and shimmied side to side, which let the dress that bunched above her hips fall straight. Sadie held onto a piece of the dress fabric like a blind child and followed right behind.

"Rise and shine. It's supper time," Sophia said with a hand reaching out for Lanier's arm. With her head slightly to one side, Sophia tapped Lanier on the arm, at first delicately, but he did not wake until he was shook with two hands, and even then he did not startle awake but remained dreary for minutes afterward.

"I have to admit, I haven't been sleeping as well I should be," he said. They stood by the doors while Lanier rubbed at his eyes and held his hair back from his face. He stretched out his long arms like a palm in the wind. He smiled first at her mother and then down to Sadie who looked away in return. The pamphlets he held had fallen to the ground, and as he bent down to pick them up he looked into her eyes, "I was wondering if Sadie would like to go and meet some of the other children her age after the sermon." Bent at the knees, he asked her directly, "Would you like that?" Lanier then peered back up at Sophia, "If you think that would be good for her, I could take her with me to Bible study?"

Her mother asked—with a firm hand on her shoulder, the thumb pressing on her exposed collar bone—as to what she would like, and Sadie smacked her tongue against the roof of her mouth and then sighed, which was something that Lanier figured she had learned from her mother. Sophia turned back to Lanier and said, "Getting to meet some of the other girls would just be perfect for her, might get her to see the fun side of church."

"Definitely, and I think it's only an hour or so. I can just run her back afterwards." He opened the door, and Sadie's mother gave a slight curtsy before she entered. As Sadie followed, Lanier gently placed his hand on the top of her head and she stepped ahead of his gesture. He followed Sadie and her mother through the sanctuary doors quietly, with yawning, blurry eyes and numb fingers feeling for his seat.

They were more than ten minutes late and the congregation was standing, singing a hymn. As they reached an open row, they sidled in and Lanier began to sing the final verse, a deep confidence, a baritone lurching from within. It wasn't long before the sermon had momentum. Pastor Deene's finger pointed up into the heavens as his tremulous voice called out over the congregation, "And after the torrential downpours," he preached, "I never cease to be amazed by the mystery and splendor of fall colors. I find it particularly ironic that the reason those autumn leaves are so beautiful is because they are dead. The life-giving nutrients that flowed into those leaves to keep them moist and green and alive have been sealed off. Would anyone ever imagine that death could be so delightful?"

Lanier and Sophia sat on either side of Sadie, the occasionally echoing "amen" circling around them, and she gently tapped at the back of the pew in front of her with the toe of her shoe. Lanier let his shoulders relax and felt the motion of her swinging leg rasp against his, and it made his stomach pain subside. He breathed in deeply the smell of her, sour apples, sweat and vanilla, her hair had been perfumed. Was it for him? he wondered. And before the man in the row directly in front of her could turn around, Lanier put his hand fatherly onto her knee and held her still for a moment, again gently. It felt soft. He was afraid to close his eyes, to see the face staring back at him, taunting him. When she wriggled her knee free, he smiled over at Sophia with a kind-hearted wink.

Lanier pulled from his coat pocket a rolled-up brown paper bag of sharp-tasting, orange, fuzzy little Japanese plums that he had taken from the tree outside Sadie's window. He kept the bag of loquats hidden to his right side and pulled out a short stem that bore three of the ovals. The bright-colored yield made Sophia peer out of the corner of her eye. Bringing his hand up to his mouth, as if he were covering a cough, Lanier popped one of the fruits into his mouth. His tongue tore through the thin peach-like skin and carved the ripe and mature ovary from the slippery seeds that he then pushed back out into a cave made with his fist. He opened his hand and showed Sadie the three brown pits, smooth like river stones. She reached out to touch one and his fist clammed up. "Forbidden fruit," he leaned over and whispered. She grabbed at his hand and began to pry between his fingers, but Lanier kept his hand firmly closed and began to act like she was not there, like he was alone, attentive only to the Lord's words.

"An old adage goes, 'Plant vineyards for your children, olive trees for your grandchildren.' I'll say it again: Plant vineyards for your children and plant olive trees for your grandchildren." Pastor Deene paused, his palms facing the sky. "Olive trees take many, many years to mature and even longer to fruit. Long before Christ, the golden oils were considered godly. Olive oil was dripped onto to the foreheads of entombed kings and pagan martyrs. Olive branches and wreaths, as many of you may already know, have been age-old emblems of kingdoms, deities, peace and war. A certain olive garden in the Bible has the name 'Geth-se-mane,'" Pastor Deene sounded out the phonetics, "…which comes directly from the Hebrew words 'oil' and 'pillar press.' Gethsemane," he said again with a contemplative glance at the surrounding crowd. "In the Hebrew tradition, Kings David and Solomon guarded these gardens and groves that bordered on the Mediterranean. And on the Mount of Olives, the Garden of Gethsemane became a place of worship for our Savior. It was a place where He took notice of every branch, rock, and blade of grass that met tenderly with His words of grace and compassion. And now, we have arrived at the gate of Gethsemane, and now we shall enter much as He did. We must be willing to be betrayed and taken to suffering and to death, in obedience with the will of God.

"Gethsemane was the place that Jesus awaited the traitorous kiss of his beloved brother, Judas. And it was also in this place, the place that He enjoyed most, that inevitably He knew to be the place where He would ultimately be called upon to suffer most. And in light of the Garden of Eden, where Adam's self indulgence borne all men unto sin, we can only conceive that in the Garden of Gethsemane that the son of God's purity and compassion should be able to pardon us. So it was here He boldly went—where He would be expected—it was here in Gethsemane that both his disciples and his prosecutors knew they could find him."

Pastor Deene removed his kerchief, dabbed his brow and methodically refolded the thin cloth and tucked it away. He placed both hands on the podium and oscillated a smile over the crowd. "And so on the eve of His crucifixion, following the final supper, Jesus walked into the Garden of Gethsemane to pray with Peter, James, and John. And in adopting all of the sin of man, God's sacrificial lamb is put to death without resistance, and yet we are compelled by His sense of grief, witnessing His suffering in Gethsemane. Here, our Savior endures absolute heartache and anguish for the first time, and in this grief, our Lord Jesus Christ becomes a man of sorrow, saying, 'Peace I leave with you, My peace I give unto you.' The grief he endured was balanced by purity, the calm fellowship of God, and benevolence." Pastor Deene took a sip from a glass of water and placed the glass back on the pedestal, his swallow amplified by the microphone pointing up at him.

Amens echoed from around the pews, a few hands raised towards the ceiling.

"He then received the weight of the world, stripped of His essence and of His purity. And with the persecution of Christ our Savior, Gethsemane has come to symbolize this sense of grief and suffering that comes from salvation and sanctuary. So, in grief, you will find salvation, and in suffering you shall find sanctuary. And yet it is suffering that gets our attention, it gets our notice. *We're watching Lord*, we're saying, *we're watching*. Suffering makes *us* look at one another; it forces *us* to question our abilities and roles in life; it forces *us* to eventually turn inward toward God and seek sanctuary. Even if it is to express displeasure and our despair, we turn to Him, and in pleas for forgiveness and empathy we display our faith unto Him as our Savior." And almost every time the pastor said "Him" he pointed upwards.

Lanier could feel Sadie's breathing stare, her thin ribs expanding and contracting; her sharp shoulder piercing into his side; it was as if soldered thorns were wrapped tightly around, splitting his head, a spear between his ribs. He looked over to Sadie. She blushed and turned her glare, but she did not smile. He offered a loquat to her. "Delicious," he leaned down and whispered, though still facing the sermon. She cautiously took the fruit from his fingers, held it for a while, rubbed at the thin hairs that covered the little orange plum and nibbled at the skin that peeled back where the stem was snapped away. When the tart flesh broke down to a juice that stood on her lips, she licked away the sticky residue and her eyes widened. Sadie used her front teeth to pull back and down a strand of the fruit's skin, which was slightly freckled from the sun. She saw the pale orange, granular flesh and tasted the mild acidity.

After the sermon, Sophia gave a moaning yawn and checked her watch as they were corralled into the aisle and out into the rectory. "That was pretty powerful," she said once they had distanced themselves from the emerging crowd.

"Pastor Deene is a strong speaker," Lanier replied as they slowly dawdled towards an open space, his hand hovering over the crescent of her backside, where only warmth could be felt in the small space between his hand and the fabric of her dress.

"I was a little lost for a minute."

"What about?" Lanier asked.

"The olives, the garden."

"What about them?"

"What do they mean?"

"I guess it depends on who's listening."

"But, what do the olives and the garden show me—what am I simply supposed to take from that?"

"Well…" Lanier paused and handed Sadie another plum, "to make olive oil, you have to squeeze the life out of the olive."

"Okay, and?"

"Well then, the weight of everyone's sins pressed the essence from our

Savior in the same way pure oil is pressed from the olive. In that purity, we are supposed to be able to see God through man, through His suffering and His grief."

"That sort of makes sense."

"In the garden that the pastor was talking about, Jesus, a man without sin, decides to take the blame for all the sins of man. He is sacrificed to save all those He loves, all those who love Him. And in death, He is placed between God and man, sort of blocking God's view."

"But, and this is going to make me sound stupid, but it's something I could never really understand, how does Jesus being killed on the cross free us from our sins?"

"Well, it's no different from any other sacrifice. People've always killed what they loved or what they needed so that they could show appreciation to some form of god. All civilizations, from nomads to Romans, they all sacrificed for one reason or another. Up until Christ, mostly livestock were sacrificed because it's harder for someone to kill something you've tamed and cared for, something that you otherwise may need to survive."

"Tamed?" she asked.

"Domesticated."

"No, I understand that, but why?"

"Why what?"

"Why animals?"

"You've heard someone use the word 'scapegoat', right? This is where it comes from. Jews would place the sins of the people on the head of the goat and send it out into the wilderness. But, over time, they started to kill the goat."

"That's terrible. Why kill a helpless animal."

"Animals seem so simple and pure. We don't believe that animals knowingly commit sin. So, the idea is that if you kill, for the sake of God, something that lives without sin, something that could otherwise be used, then the sins that you had committed will be forgiven with the sacrifice. So, to be free of your sins, you have to kill something that does not sin. So, that's essentially what happened to Christ."

"I'm sorry, but that's sounds ridiculous to me."

"Ridiculous?" Lanier laughed. "In the Old Testament, God demanded sacrifices. Abraham was asked to kill his son, Cain slew his brother, Noah's sacrificed from his herd, and many others killed for something they wanted from God or as an apology to God, or even just for a day dedicated to God."

"So Jesus was sacrificed like an animal?"

"Not really, He was crucified like a criminal. Only criminals were put on crosses. Animals were sacrificed on an altar. The idea's the same though."

"I've always had such a hard time wrapping my mind around this. It sounds so barbaric," she said, resting her hand on his sleeve.

"I've always thought that it's sort of like hitting a dog with a stick and blaming a bird that lives in the tree that the stick came from. Then to get away from the guilt of hitting the dog, you catch the bird and give it to the dog."

"I just don't think that I'll ever understand."

"That is why we have the word *Faith*. Sometimes it's okay to just believe and not understand."

"I guess so."

"Sometimes it takes a little sacrificial wine to really get into the right state of mind," said Lanier with muted notes of sarcasm.

"Maybe after the Bible group?" she asked.

"Can't see why not."

"I think I'm going to go home and lay down for a little while. After the Bible study, maybe we can all go down to the clubhouse for dinner?"

"I want to go home too," Sadie said but was ignored by her mother.

"There's supposed to be a pretty big storm that might hit tonight, we might need to bunker down," Lanier said to Sophia with a coy smile and a raised brow.

"Everyone says that it's going past," she replied without the same sense of innuendo. "Oh, but we'll do whatever we have to do," she smoothed her dress out on her hips, slowly, accentuating her curves.

"We sure will," he said and nibbled his bottom lip. The thought of her naked frame against his own made him want to cringe, but he fought to keep a smile. The image of her stretched areolas, her windflap breasts, the sandbag belly and buttocks.

"I don't wanna go," Sadie said.

"Baby, what did I tell you?" Sophia said sternly, almost with a hint of violence.

Lanier bent down at the knees and put his hand on Sadie's shoulder, "I guarantee Bible study'll be fun. I promise." He looked up to her mother and told her to drive safely; then she blended away into the dresses and slacks of all the people who brusquely passed by, the people who were wrinkled from the constant standing and sitting, sitting and standing; drab ties were already removed and stuffed into trouser pockets like dead speckled trout. A small group of boys who were running backwards and pushing off of each other bounced into Lanier. He fell on his backside and feigned injury. "Son of a bitch," he murmured under his breath, and Sadie smiled at Lanier for the first time. His pale face turned grapefruit pink, his lips like pig blood. "You like that..." he said, "...you like to hear me say dirty words?"

Sadie shook her head.

"Then what, you like to see me get hurt?" he asked.

She didn't say anything, but she didn't shake her head no again. The boys jollied off apologies on their way to the parking lot.

Lanier stood up and brushed himself off, "Shall we? I think we're over in one of those rooms."

She kept to herself, her arms remained crossed and hands tucked into her little armpits. One of her little black-toed shoes played in the grass. She wouldn't say anything, and as she stared down at the ground, her curls of red hair protected her face.

"It's okay to be nervous; I'm a tad nervous myself. I've never done this before neither you know? It's all new to me."

Still, she looked towards her feet with her toes pointed in and continued to mush her lips together.

"We just got to make the best out of the situation and get inside before it starts to rain." He looked around at the buildings, located the right one, and started to walk in that direction. He walked slowly and buttoned his suit coat. He pulled the plum seeds from his pocket and tossed them towards the bushes. Sadie stood still for maybe ten of his paces before she held herself tighter, smacked her tongue against the roof of her mouth and resigned to follow.

14

Fatty had been sent home when Mr. Leavitt came upstairs. Drake had left much earlier, abrupt in the gray mist of morning. AJ woke up to the deep baritone holler of his father. He held clenched fistfuls of blanket and flinched at the voice narrowing closer, deeper, sharper—until it cut through the door that kept him safe—until it tore the comforter and sheets from his body, shredding them to the floor—until it pierced into his ear and he was pulled out of bed and down the hallway. What he saw was water-coated and quick-glimpsed. Corey already sat in the den with his arms crossed, hugging a pillow the size of his midsection.

"When did it become okay to speak to your mother that way?" their father asked.

Corey and AJ were shoulder to shoulder on the couch. "She's not our mother," Corey said.

"Yeah, she's not our mother," AJ seconded.

"That's enough. She's all you've got now."

"Well, we don't need her. We never asked for another mother," Corey complained.

"Has it ever occurred to you that I may need her? Does that not matter to you two?"

"All she wants is money."

"I have plenty," Mr. Leavitt yelled back. He wiped his mouth, pulled at his jaw. "She makes me happy." He turned his back to the boys and walked a few steps.

"She makes a lot of men happy," Corey spoke down to his chest, elbowing his brother in the ribs before he could repeat what was said.

All three of the Leavitt men had blood-flushed necks and a little tuft of black hair poking from the collar of their shirts, though AJ's was just a few sprouts. Mr. Leavitt was shorter than both of his boys, "I just don't know what to do with you two? Tell me what I am supposed to do. Should I send one of you to military school, the other to boarding school?" Air ran through his dime-sized nostrils, quick and short. Then his eyes stopped, pointing in a way. "What is that? That better not be what I think it is," Mr. Leavitt came over and pushed the boys' legs apart. He pulled out the crystal ashtray that Corey had partially tucked under the couch the night before. Mr. Leavitt set it on the coffee table then went back to the couch. "Get up."

The boys sat there.

"Get. Up!"

They did as they were told.

Their father lifted the couch onto its back legs. There was nothing else. He put the couch back and searched the pillows and turned back to the ashtray. "What did I tell you about smoking? If you want to smoke your little lungs black, go right ahead. God gave you free will and there is nothing I can do about that. But I will not. Will. Not. Allow you to smoke in my house. Take this shit and dump it outside." He handed AJ the ashtray and headed for the stairs. "I swear to god, you guys are single-handedly going to tear down the value of this house. How am I going to get the smell of smoke out of the walls, huh?"

Corey stared absently. He could hear his father moving down to the bottom of the stairs. He hollered, "Dad?"

"What?" he snapped back, the agitation in his voice as rough as a gravel road.

"Me and AJ need to get tested," Corey hollered.

"What'd you say?" He took a few steps back up the stairs.

"Tested. We need to get tested."

"Tested for what?" AJ asked his brother.

"What kind of test are we talking about?" Their father asked after he came back up the flight of stairs.

"The only kind that means a damn," Corey said. "We need to get checked out, you know, for STD's and whatnot."

"You didn't even do anything," AJ said to his brother.

"Shut up AJ, I've done plenty. We need a check up, just to make sure we're all good."

"What the hell is going on around here?"

"We went to a party last night and AJ hooked up with a girl he shouldn't have. I told him not to," Corey said.

"What?"

"You know, he went all the way and didn't use a condom. Just to be safe he should get checked out," Corey was speaking towards AJ, though telling his father.

AJ, shoving his brother, said, "Dude, what the fuck?"

Corey went to say something and nothing came out of his mouth.

"AJ! Don't say the f-word!" Mr. Leavitt said and then turned to his older son.

"It's for your own good," Corey said.

Mr. Leavitt spoke with a calm anger in his voice, "Now everybody just wait one damn minute. Somebody needs to explain what the hell is going on?"

"Nothing happened," AJ insisted.

"Yeah right, AJ slept with a hooker last night. You need to be checked out."

"Don't call her that!" AJ grabbed his older brother by the hair and hooked a forearm around his neck.

Corey dug his chin into his little brother's stomach and in a panic bit down on whatever flesh was near his mouth, and AJ yelped and let go. Their brows seemed to perk out with shadows that shaded over their eyes.

"We paid her to sleep with you. That makes her a whore," Corey said.

AJ ducked right as Corey dashed to the left, and AJ took two steps and lunged at his brother's nose. The fist landed right behind the ear, dropping Corey to the floor like a waiter's tray.

Mr. Leavitt tossed aside AJ, yelling, "Sit down! Now! You might have really hurt him. Damn it AJ! You don't know your own strength!" He dropped down to one knee and kept Corey's neck stable watching intently as he opened one eye and then the other. He put his fingers to the back of his son's head, felt for swelling or blood, and there was neither, his fingers fondling a dry scalp. Corey stood up slowly with his father there to brace him, "Goddamn it AJ!" his father yelled.

"I'm fine," Corey said, his hand holding the back of his head. "It's AJ you should be worried about."

15

In the Bible study classroom, the children could use round-tipped scissors and plastic rulers. Mrs. Awlfors, the Bible leader for the seven to nine year olds, was huddled in the corner trying to start a Bunsen burner. She had piles of crayons assorted by color and plastic molds from a craft store lined out on a table. Her own thin skin was mottled with liver spots; her hands, wrists, and ankles swollen and discolored. She had a simple smile that slightly bared the tops of her front teeth and allowed white saliva to bubble in the corners of her mouth. Hers was not a sincere smile.

Awlfors used both hands to push in the ignition and the click clicked. Stale fumes filed towards the ceiling. She pressed the ignition again, and again. She picked up the little burner and closely inspected the canister. She put the hiss of gas next to her ear.

Lanier shuddered away as he watched, his eyebrows coming together as if trying to touch tips like little bent black fingers. Lanier could only think about taking Sadie. Violent images ran through his head, of his own persecution, of sacrifice. The churches he grew up around were full of martyred souls, lingering in purgatorial hatred and resignation. He wanted a push. His chest quaked. He was jealous of the children, their simple antics, how they were allowed to touch and tease each other; it burned in his chest. He walked around the room and studied the uprooted Berber carpet in the corners, the slightly different shades of eggshell on the four walls, the silk plant that looked dead from dust. He circled over the children as they diligently cut red construction paper into snowflakes. He tried to distract himself from the thoughts that toured through his mind, thoughts he had no control over: his sister choking, still choking in his mind, the smoke covering her face, the strength in her neck not willing to hold up her head. Before tears started to well, Lanier sat down next to Sadie on one of the little children's seats and took up a piece of paper and a scissor, a piece of purple construction paper.

He began to gingerly cut a silhouette of the Eiffel Tower. His knees were tucked up to his chest because of the low seat, and the long arc of his back went unsupported as it bowed over. Cackles broke through the children's mouths and cheeks, but Lanier didn't hear them. He looked towards the paper and the round-edged scissors with the tip of his tongue peeking out of his mouth, his sister's death and meth circling around his mind, and one eye terribly squinting as he cut little slits and snips and snaggers and turned the paper back and forth.

"Pastor Lanier," Awlfors called towards him as he sat at the corner of the table, "could you give me a hand?" He was cutting his paper and sipping a juice box, and by the time Lanier was almost finished, Awlfors had finally turned down the gas and was able to produce a flame from the burner. "Now everyone finish their cut-outs and write your name on the back. Come get a tack and pin it on the wall. After that I want you all to come and line up near the bookshelf." She set up a small Pyrex dish and turned the flame down and watched as, one by one, the children pinned their snowflakes to various spots all over the walls, and she explained, with the hoarse coarseness of a frayed rope, that in a few months the walls would be covered with the art of God's pupils.

Awlfors turned up the heat on the burner and allowed the children to pick four crayon colors. She scolded the boys and sneered at the girls and wouldn't let any of them near the pointed flame. They all wanted to help melt the crayons into colorful creatures, but they could only watch. And as Awlfors melted the crayons into a metal tray with shapes of seahorses and turtles, Lanier still sat on the toadstool with his knees into his chest, finishing his paper cut-out. With his last few snips, he unfolded and unveiled his construction only to see that it was bent, crooked, and he couldn't understand how. The little crayon animals were set aside to cool, the children pointing at the ones that would belong to them. Awlfors suggested that Lanier start the day's lesson before splitting into groups, to which he replied, "That's all right." He wanted to take Sadie's hand and leave and keep moving against the rain. He wanted to pull his sister from the smoke. He wanted to keep breathing in the smoke. He looked lost into her face and then turned back to his paper.

All of the students huddled around their teacher who stood in front of the eraser board. They sat on the ground, the boys and girls for the most part separated already, and Lanier crumpled up his tower and put it into his pant's pocket and sat down amongst the children with his legs crossed. The curls of her hair in front of him made his fingers ache like a thirsty palate, his cold fingers.

"I want you all to define sin." Awlfors had fatigued mannerisms—leaving no room for disruption as her jowls trembled. "One by one, I want you to come up to the board and write your definition. Now who is gonna be first? Maybe you could start us off Pastor?"

"Ma'am?" he asked.

"Would you come start us off?"

"With what?"

All of the children but Sadie giggled.

"Just come on up here to the board and write a definition of the word 'sin' for us, would you?"

"Yes ma'am." Lanier stood and walked around the circle of students, picked up the marker and paused with the green tip against the board. He thought about what to write.

The Babylonian god of the moon.

The 21st letter of the Hebrew alphabet.

Depravity of man.

Ill-desert.

Any want or conformity against the personal lawgiver and moral governor who vindicates his law with just penalties.

Then he wrote, A deliberate disobedience to the known will of God. "Is that good?" he asked as she stood facing the class. You ragged hag, he thought to himself. Lanier walked back to where he had been sitting before. Then the children stood and formed a line in an angle directly across from Lanier, half the room's distance. And the first child wrote—sin is taking something that is not yours. The next child scribbled—sin is hurting somebody. One after the next, the children wrote their conceptions of sin: stealing, lying, cheating, and coveting, in so many words what they were raised against, and what Lanier was raised within. Lanier's accelerated pulse began to drum through his shirt. His throat had dried out; his lungs ached for a cold, sweet chemical push. Then it was Sadie's turn, and she wrote pretending, just the word pretending.

"What do you mean *pretending*," asked Awlfors.

Sadie shrugged her shoulders.

"Do you mean lying?"

Sadie shrugged her shoulders again, "I don't know."

"Well, try to explain what you mean."

Sadie stood there, her hands poking in at her sides, an uncomfortable look on her face, a dimple in her chin. "Pretending…pretending to care about someone. My mother said that my father pretended to love her, and me. Isn't that a sin?"

Lanier stood up, excused himself and walked out of the classroom alongside the wall, away from the gutters sending water splashing down into puddles. He drank from a fountain that moaned and then hummed; the water that smelled of rust and rotten eggs slowly filled his mouth, and just as it entered, it streamed right back out into the reservoir. He eventually swallowed some and stood up straight, wiping his chin on the sleeve of his coat. "I hope this storm lasts," he said softly, speaking up to the clouds.

After letting the water build around his shoes, tapping puddles, and rambling incoherencies, he pulled a capsule from his pocket, opened it and snorted a jab before he came back to the classroom. As the meth circled into his bloodstream, he could feel weight lifted from the center of his back and chest, an orgasmic tingle starting in his toes and crawling through his feet, and the pumping of blood running through his body left him with a woodsplitting feeling filling his groin, thumping warmly against his inner thigh. Awlfors had already sectioned the boys from the girls by the time he came back to the classroom. "It's about time," she said to him. "Hurry up and take the boys into that room and us girls'll stay out here. You have your lesson plan?"

"Of course," he searched his pockets and pulled out the pamphlets that the pastor had given him that afternoon.

Awlfors pointed towards the adjoined room. "Young cherubs," she said and placed a hand on her hip, "Well go on then, with Pastor Lanier," and the boys followed Lanier into the room of only a few chairs, a marker board, and the same eggshell walls. Lanier stood in the corner of the room with his back to the boys and shuffled the few papers that he had and told the boys to sit down. There were only four of them and they sat directly on the carpet, not saying but a few words as Lanier mumbled to himself, "Straight. Straight from here."

The murmur of the air conditioner over the boys' silence grew louder. Lanier faced them, took off his coat and folded it over the back of a chair, which he stood in front of blocking the moving bulge in his pants. He rolled up his sleeves and cleared his throat, then shuffled the chair in front of him. "Today's lesson plan is masturbation." He looked down at the boys' faces. "What is Masturbation? Anybody? Does anyone here know what that word means?"

The boys looked blankly back at Lanier, four little pink faces, pink in the cheeks and the chin.

"It's a sin, plain and simple. Pleasuring yourself, touching your penis..."

Two of the boys giggled at the word, "penis".

"You think that's funny?" Lanier asked. "Do you think it's funny that God hates you? Do you think it's funny that every time you masturbate, you are killing thousands of babies?"

The boys looked down at the carpet.

"You'd be better cutting your penis right off..." he pointed towards his own crotch, "Is that funny? No? I didn't think so. You know why you should cut it off? Because you're going to commit this sin if you don't. Not only will God hate you more if you touch yourself, masturbation also leads to depression, pornographic materials, mental and physical illness, and, most importantly, masturbation will lead you straight to hell. You become addicted to pleasing yourself, and it will be the only thing that you can think about. When you touch yourself, you are being selfish in the eyes of God, and the more you do it, the more God despises you."

One boy dug at a staple that had been wrapped up in the threads of the carpet, but the other boys looked terrified.

"Did you all know that every time you touch yourself, God gives someone cancer."

One of the boys raised his hand. When Lanier looked to him, the boy said, "My dad says smoking causes cancer."

Lanier snapped back at the child, "Now that's just stupid! God gives you cancer only if you deserve it? God! God gives you cancer. And do you know why? Justification. Because people are ungrateful sinners. And we don't want to be ungrateful, do we?"

Fraught with apprehension, the boys shook their heads, petrified by the low tone of Lanier's voice, and they didn't make a noise for the remainder of the class. Lanier simply lectured about the various effects of masturbation, constantly repeating and contradicting himself, until Awlfors knocked on the door. As she opened it, Lanier stopped mid sentence, and Awlfors informed him that the time had expired, and that the little girl he had brought was sitting alone in the main room. Lanier nodded, looked towards the group of boys and said, "God loves you all, God bless."

The rain clouds bloomed and loomed above like larks covering the sky. Whether it was two in the afternoon or two the morning, the sky wouldn't tell. It was black, curdling and coursing, bubbling and taking over the last of the light. Children scurried from the overhangs outside of their church classrooms as their parents waited near their sport utilities and minivans under ponchos like tents. Outstretched hands waved them to come to the cars they recognized. Lanier held his coat above Sadie and held her shoulder close to his leg as they walked to his car, and when he was inside he shook out his hair like a dog, "Put on your seatbelt."

"I'm hungry," Sadie buckled her seatbelt. Her toes kissed the floor mats. "I'm not allowed to have milk before I go in the car or on an airplane because I get sick."

"Well if you're hungry you shouldn't get sick then, sort of a counterbalance in the stomach. We'll get some food soon." Stuck in the exiting traffic, Lanier drove and stopped, drove a few feet and stopped. His windshield wipers tossed back and forth sheets of water. Through the fogged glass, the red halo of tail lights pulsed in front of him. He felt down to his waist, and with the tip of his finger turned off his pager and turned it back on, making the little black box beep and vibrate. He pulled it up to the steering wheel and turned to her, "We have to make one quick stop at the hospital before we can go home."

Sadie let out a deep sigh, another trait Lanier could tell was something that she had learned from her mother. These tics made him wonder how pure she was still was and he suspiciously watched her from the corner of his eye as she put a loose string that hung from a button of her shirt cuff into her mouth and snipped it off between her front teeth.

"How was your class with Ms. Awlfors?"

"She's not very nice."

"No she isn't, is she? What did she talk about with you girls?"

"Can't tell," Sadie turned to look at the rain drops running down the window, racing at a slant. She trailed one with her fingertip, her nail chewed down.

"Why not?"

Sadie didn't answer him and kept trailing the drips of rain running along the window.

"I'll tell you what the boys talked about if you tell what the girls said." Lanier put on his turn signal and drove away from the community.

"Nope, she said boys can't be trusted," Sadie raised her hands to cover her mouth and nose as she sneezed.

He turned left and drove north. "Gesundheit," Lanier said with a pass of his wrist. "Awlfors is the one that can't be trusted," Lanier paused for a moment, slowed the car through a large puddle in the road sending an arc of water over the bordering cross vine, limbs of the red buckeye slashing in the wind, the water on the ground drowning the fallen leaves and flowers. "You know she killed her old man. Cut him in pieces, and we tried to put him back together but it would have taken all the king's men and most of them were on holiday at the time." He laughed. "And besides, I'm not a boy, I'm a young man." Lanier turned left on Ross Clark and headed towards Flowers Hospital, taking the curve along the backside of the hospital where the construction of the new wing was unfinished. He parked beside a large trash dumpster. He opened his door slightly and popped out his umbrella. "You're not going to tell me? Fine," he said and he got out of the car. "Stay put," he said before he closed the door back. The rain pelted the tight nylon skin of the umbrella as it opened wide and the shaft clicked. He walked around to his trunk and pulled out three yellow biohazard bags, then tossed them into the open mouth of the dumpster. He walked back to the car and opened the driver's door a crack and told Sadie that he would just be a minute. Her arms were crossed and she looked down her nose and towards the ground. "It'll be worth your while.

Soda, candies, or both?" he asked

"Soda candies?"

In the hospital, he took the elevator to the fourth floor and walked straight out into the pediatric ward. Flowers and butterflies the size of children had been painted along the ground and up the walls and even on the circulation desk. A receptionist was sitting behind the desk. "Hold on just a sec," she said into the phone and then put her hand over the mouthpiece. She pulled out one of the desk drawers and turned to face Lanier, "Here for your check?"

Lanier nodded and took the envelope, folded it and stuck it in his front pocket.

"Treat yourself to something nice. You look beat up."

"I'll try," Lanier put up a couple of fingers and waved as he turned to leave. "Have a nice afternoon. God Bless," he said and walked around the reception desk and down the main corridor. Through the few opened doorways, fat-bellied bees painted on the walls flew in spirals, drunk on nectar. Paled children lay in beds or sat in wheelchairs, parked unattended. One room at the end of the floor, RESERVED FOR PHYSICIANS read the placard on the door, had a large television, sofas, recliners, a refrigerator stocked with sodas and sandwiches, and a countertop teeming with platters of bagels, fruits and boxed-chocolates. An orderlies' room was on the first floor with Jell-O and juice but Lanier walked directly into the physician's quarters and took three cherry sodas and two cups. He opened a box of the chocolates, took all of his sister's favorite foil-covered cherry cordials and left the way he came.

Outside, construction of the new wing had been postponed by the storm and the area had been sectioned off with hazard tape. Scaffolds with rusted edges stood against the walls and warped wooden planks and sheets of plywood were stacked on the wet ground. He glanced around and ducked behind fresh sheets of drywall and hanging sheets of plastic. He opened a can of soda and poured out two plastic cups. He dug deep in his pocket and pulled out a pocketknife and five pills. He swallowed the biggest pill, a Libritab, and crushed the other four together, Noctecs and an Ativan. He put the mixed powder in each of the soda cups.

Lanier walked over and picked up his umbrella, which was sitting cup up under the scaffolding that he had left it under. He quickly rounded one large puddle, and Sadie sat up in her seat. He opened the door and handed her the sodas before he sat down. He closed his umbrella and pulled the chocolates from his pocket and tossed them onto her lap. She handed him back one of the cups once he was situated in the car, and he sipped from it. "You like Cherry?" he asked.

She held her cup with both hands as the carbonation climbed up through the dark soda and popped at the surface near her nose. She chewed at the innerside corner of her mouth with a little white incisor that peeked through. He stuck the key in the ignition, watching her peripherally, and turned it, just enough for the starter to grind, but not enough to actually start the car. He did this again. He pounded on the steering wheel and then the dash. He turned the key once more, but again not far enough to actually start the car. "It won't start. I'm gonna have to go back in and call your mom, tell her we'll be a little late coming back. I'll be real quick." Sadie breathed out deeply, warm, sticky and sweet. Her thick curls were tangled and frizzed from the humidity; two hung at the side of her face. It was a shield he wanted to pull aside, tangle in his fingers, cut away. "I'll be real quick, I promise," he said as he leaned to the back and searched around with his hand. He got out, opened the umbrella back up, and walked to the front where he could pop open the hood of the car so that she couldn't watch what he was doing. He then walked to the back of the car and opened the trunk and pulled out a screwdriver. He unscrewed the license plate and shoved it halfway down the front of his pants and pulled his shirt over it. He came back to the front of the car and lowered the hood and held up a finger, motioning to Sadie that he would just be a minute. He watched her sigh and simply smiled at her. He headed off towards the construction area, away from where she could possibly see him, and then walked over to where other cars were parked. He still had the screwdriver in his hand, and he was looking for anyone around before he unscrewed another car's license plate and replaced it with his. He walked back to the construction area to watch her. He lit one cigarette after another as he huddled under the scaffolding for about twenty-five minutes staring into the car windows. He turned for only a moment to throw out a cigarette stub, but when he had looked back, he could not see her in the car.

As he approached the passenger side, he noticed that Sadie had unbuckled her seat belt and sprawled across the front seat with two chocolate smudged wrappers crinkled in her loosened grip, an empty cup on the floor, a sweet dark smear at the corner of her mouth. He returned to the trunk and put on the stolen license plate.

The third girl was only four or five. Lanier found her at the Mississippi state fair walking aimlessly among the carnival games where he was working as a ball toss attendant. Her chin and hands were lined with dried chocolate and ice cream. He had pulled down a stuffed teddy bear and approached her. He asked her where her parents were. She didn't know. He handed her the bear and took her hand. As he walked her around, he asked her many times if she saw her parents anywhere. She held the bear close to her chest. He walked her to the parking lot and asked if her parents had a truck or a car. She said a truck. He asked if she knew which truck was hers. She said that she didn't see it. He put her in his car and they drove around. He asked again and again as they circled the premises. Her smell filled the car, soft like baby powder and sweat, like strawberry gum and sour milk.

He kept her locked in his trailer home for days, brought her a new stuffed animal each evening, each one larger than the last. Whenever she cried, he was usually able to calm her with a silly face or dance, with news of finding her parents. When he couldn't stop her from crying he would crush up sleeping pills and mix them in Kool-Aid. He didn't mean to kill her. He wanted to keep her. Even after she was dead, he kept her.

He was taking classes in nursing at the community college and spent most of his time studying medical books and used her as his own personal cadaver. He operated and stitched, field dressed and amputated. Until the body became too coarse and his little home reeked of rot. He had kept a few small pieces as mementos, either dried out or kept in a preserving liquid, but then deposited the different parts in different places, each in a different county. In a well in Holmes. In a dumpster behind a Waffle House in Lafayette. In a retention pond in Franklin. In an abandoned motel in Lincoln. In the trunk of a Buick in a salvation yard in Pike. In the bushes near a hunting camp in Calhoun. In a reservoir near the waste management plant in Attala.

When he drove back to his street, he parked two blocks down from his house and left Sadie asleep in the running car. He ran up the bike trail behind the houses, causing the neighbors' dogs to bark, their noses pressed to the glass of sliding glass doors and windows. Lanier was drenched as he walked up the steps to his back door. Once he was inside, he locked the door—he pulled back at his hair and wrenched the knot out of his tie. Lanier took off his coat, balled it up and threw it on the foot of his bed. He ripped open the drawers of his desk. He cursed himself as he hurried to his closet and pulled down a duffle bag and started to fill it. He stuffed in clothes, papers, bills; a few pictures were put aside. He filled the duffle with bags of crystal, pills, and pot. He grabbed a raincoat and put it on. He went from room to room tracking water, dragging the duffle, his shoes squeaking on the tiles of the hallway, his hair soaked and matted back from his face.

In the bathroom, he carefully poured out and accidentally broke a few of the vials and beakers as he let the liquids, powders, and residues leak down the tub drain followed by the stream of the shower. He sat down on the toilet seat, lightheaded, and looked for a lighter in his pocket. He started to smoke a shard of meth in a foil square. When his eyes tweaked and his neck stiffened, he continued to blindly rummage through his belongings and found a bottle of cough medicine, some band-aids and rubbing alcohol, and toe-nail clippers. Then he stopped packing, the meth straw still hanging from his lips, and began looking through cracks in the window blinds but at nothing directly—the hazel-grey globes of his eyes, darting, twitching left to right, glared back at him reflectively. He patted his pockets and walked down the short hallway that led into the kitchen. From there Lanier took his roll of foil and tucked a box of straws under his arm. He looked at the cutlery hanging on the wall and fingered the knife handles. He opened and closed cabinets and pantry doors. He grabbed a grill lighter, a box of strike anywhere matches, the stacks of cash that he kept in the freezer. It only took but a few minutes and Lanier walked out the back door and back into the rain. He had the duffle bag over his shoulder, a hat pulled down low over his brow, and he didn't run but walked fast in the direction of his car.

PART TWO

CRYSSAL HEARTS

SADIE: English origin, name meaning princess,
also the wife of Abraham and the mother of Isaac.

Sweet Sometime, fly fast to me:
Poor Now-time sits in the Lonesome-tree
And broods as gray as any dove,
And calls, When wilt thou come, O Love?
And pleads across the waste to thee"

—S. Lanier (1842–1881)

16

A light sweat covered the back of her neck. A queer smile lay across her face as she fell in and out of sleep; half awake, she stretched out her legs and her shoes slipped off. She rubbed her pale and slender ankles together. Her toes curled and then relaxed. One little fist was balled near her chin. Her fingers smelled like crayons and construction paper from the church. As she lay on her side, she struggled to pry an eye open, then the other, and watched as Lanier's feet worked the pedals, the air conditioning vents damp with condensation, the radio on a low volume and a tape jutted out of the ejector. She closed her eyes back, the lids heavy like wet sheets, and snuggled her hands to herself and breathed deeply through her nose.

The car came to a stop and she was awake again, but kept her eyes closed. The door clicking quietly open, a spitting wind circling into the car; she could feel the weight shift and then the door closed her in. Rain pelted down along the windows and on the roof. She wished that he had kept driving. She didn't want to go home yet. She wanted the hum of the engine, the warmth of Lanier's side, the wet-breeze whistling, trying to curl in through the cracked-opened window. Sadie expected him to come and open the passenger door and try to carry her to her house. The rain tickled in through the window crevice. She imagined being sent to her room. She imagined her mother upset with how she had acted at church; she might even get the flyswatter, the spoon, the backside of the brush.

I don't need to be carried, I am not a baby, she readied herself to say. She expected to be handed over to her mother and so she began to snore slightly, not too fake, her eyelids closed, still but not tense. She didn't want to be spanked. Then, as she waited hesitantly, he didn't come. She eventually opened her eyes when she heard the sounds of barking dogs, a raspy sound drowned in the rain and thunder tremors, and then sat up for a moment. She looked down the road and could not recognize anything through the rain except for the golden glow that surrounded the streetlamps. Lanier had already slipped away from sight, and it was hard to see through the windshield without the wipers running, so she lied back down and glanced around the sedan. The brown carpets had dark stains and skids; the felt roofing ballooned out at the edges; the steering wheel was dry and cracked and the seats were soft and full and smelled of popcorn, butter and smoke. She rolled over and looked into the backseat where cassette tapes were scattered, empty cassette cases covered the floor. There were regular tapes, and little small tapes and big clunky tapes. The water cascaded down the rear window and she imagined that she was hiding in a waterfall dungeon with a pillowed ceiling. She wriggled her toes towards the ballooned felt and had a curl of hair in her mouth as she puckered for a kiss. And as she did this, she remembered the boy at school who had pinned her against a fence and pecked her again and again, but had missed her lips. She had chased him and hit him, and when he fell on the ground from running backwards she had fallen on top of him.

On her back in Lanier's car, she puckered her lips with her eyes closed, the slick hair fell away, and she made a kissing sound, and then another, until the sounds one after another created the tone of a song, a song she must have heard before but didn't really know, very similar to *Hava Nagila*. Her rain sprinkled toes danced to the song, the same eighteen or so notes over and over.

She decided that when she did get home she would kiss her cats, one after the next. She didn't want to take a bath, and she didn't want to have her hair fussed with. She didn't want to have to change into another dress. She knew that as soon as she got home she would be spanked. It didn't seem fair. She wondered whether other mothers spanked so hard, or if other girls were hit as often as she was. She simply assumed that they were and rolled onto her back and tucked a hand under her head and began to count the flowers that were embroidered into her skirt. She stopped at thirty-two, and then started again but with more strategy, more systematically. She started with one line moving down and then over and up, then over and down, and so on. She got to forty-one before the numbers were too heavy to keep counting, and as they faded away she saw a new world in front of her, a world her mind created, full of wet grass and fog, frogs and kitty cats.

She lied still on her side, and as the key slid in and the latch gave and the creaking springs buoyed the trunk door upwards, her eyes began to move under her closed lids. She was not fully awake and yet not completely asleep. Something heavy was placed into the trunk compartment shifting the balance of the car and someone crept up to the driver's side. She could smell him. He slipped into the car and tossed the hat that he was wearing into the backseat. The hum of the engine resumed and his hand felt for the underside of her wrist. His fingertips were wet and warm, and as two of his fingers seemed to press into her wrist, she did not move. The feel of his hands comforted her. His thin-lipped smile played in her mind. His body sent waves of heat; his clothes carried the odor of fresh smoke; the windshield wipers sloshed the water off of the car; and looking through crossed eyelashes she could partially see a blur of treetops. Lanier's damp hands coursed through her hair and rested on her shoulder. She wondered if they were meeting her mother for dinner. She wouldn't have to change, so she smiled. The jacket he had on now was not for the clubhouse though. Just from the touch, she could tell it was slick like plastic and the old man who stood at the door wouldn't allow it, much like the time she had on her sneakers, or when two boys had to leave because their jackets had grass stains on the elbows. Her stomach set off on a low gurgle. Did he go in and talk to her mother, is that where he went? she wondered. Was there a surprise? She remembered when her friend Tammy had a surprise party and everyone yelled "Happy Birthday!" at her when she had walked through the front door. And when everyone yelled, Tammy started to cry immediately. She kept crying even when everyone huddled around her and her father brought out the biggest present anyone had ever seen. Tammy looked like she had got stung in the butt, Sadie thought.

But it wasn't Sadie's birthday. She could hear Lanier talking under his breath, mumbling, with part of his body shaking against her. She wanted to hold him still, but she kept her eyes closed and her hands to herself. Maybe there's a surprise for someone else, she thought.

Tammy-Tammy, bo-bammy, banana-famma, fo-fammy, fe, fi, fo-ma'ammy, Tammy, she sang in her head. Lanier removed his hand from her side and the spot that it left felt cold. A lighter sparked and seconds later the tinge of burnt paper and tobacco filled the car. The window opened a little more and the wind rushed in the car, spitting and hissing. Lanier's pants were wet from the knees down and not only his hands were shaking, but his entire body gave out in sporadic trembles. She opened her eyes completely for a moment and what she could see was marked by darkness and claps of white light, nothing but the slanting sheets of rain coming from the sky remained. Her eyes closed.

Sadie's hair was wrapped in the fingers of his right hand and he held the wheel with his left knee. He had caressed her cheek, her elbow, her waist as she lay curled on the front seat of his car, gently held her hair rubbing strands between his fingers as she fell in and out of sleep. When she did open her eyes, she read aloud a sign, "Lake Seminole, Paradise Acres," but she soon closed them back and was asleep.

Sadie had not moved, no more than her slowed pulse, until they started driving in the direction of the Gulf where the salt and humidity thickened the air. Lanier had driven her away from the storm, and when the sun finished its heavy descent, the colors melted and mixed in the sky like a child's sherbet. One of her legs stretched out, her mouth slightly opened. The coast lay to their right, too far to see the sand dunes and sea oats, but close enough to taste the lingering salt in the southwinds. Pastures filled out from the highway where low-rolling hills were speckled with hay-rounds, and small congregations of black cows stood ankle deep in murky waterholes.

17

Corey rode out to the new lots, where the boys like to hang out in the houses that were being built. He was drenched by the time he found the others, and when he popped in through a window opening they did not speak to him. It had rained steadily most of the afternoon, and it only grew stronger and darker now. Corey walked through the grey slab cement house, through puddles that were welling under the swollen planks of the roof. Their raincoats dripped to the saw-dusted floor, and the bottoms of their slacks were darkened by mud and water. Considering how wet they all were, Corey could tell that they hadn't been there very long. The others sat on turned over buckets inside the naked dining room, under a roof that someone had tried to install quickly, before the probable hurricane, but it was leaking. Drake shook his head, his mouth pressed white. AJ glared at his brother, and Corey noticed something completely new about his brother, something older. It was not only the way that AJ looked at him—with that newfound anger and resentment, no longer a fearful respect but a sorrowful pity and embarrassment—but it was also in the way he took long pulls as he smoked and let the smoke file out of his nose slowly. Corey was almost proud for a second, proud that his brother had finally learned to smoke right. Fatty was the only one with a smile, a taunting affair with dimples like they were sewn in. Corey walked up to the others and didn't bother trying to find a bucket to sit on. He wanted to ask what the problem was, but he pretty much knew. He wanted to take the pot from them, but he didn't. He stood there and rolled his own joint as they smoked cigarettes after pot and pot after the cigarettes in front of him without passing. Corey broke the silence, a hand at the side of his head, "Man, my ear won't stop ringing. AJ really tagged me good. Check how swolled up it already got."

Nobody moved.

"I wouldn't of hit him so hard if he hadn't gone and bit me like a girl," AJ said to Fatty.

"He b-bit you?" Fatty asked.

"Yeah, he fucking bit me. Sissy probly gave me rabies."

"Well that'll go real good with the herpes AJ got from the old hooker," Corey said towards Drake. Drake kept his head slightly tilted, peripherally looking out of a window frame at the blur of rain. His hair was wet and dirty, and drips lined his face like diluted charcoal.

"I told you not to call her that. Look what happened the last time he called her that."

"What? A hooker? Because that's what she is? Probably a fucking crack whore with AIDS."

"At least sh-she was a wuh-w-woman," Fatty said.

"What's that supposed to mean? Huh Fatty?"

"Nothing," he replied with a shrug of the shoulders, a smirk on his face. "Nothing m-man."

"No, tell me. What is the fuck is that supposed to mean?" Corey demanded.

"You're a fucking faggot, I can't believe my brother is a fag," AJ said to his brother.

"What are you talking about? I'm not a fucking fag?"

"Whatever dude, Drake told us what you did, you fucking dick licker," AJ said just as Fatty burst into choking laughter. "And dad even said that he always thought you was gay. He said that's why you have to talk to a shrink every month."

"You s-s-serious?" said Fatty.

"What the fuck are you talking about AJ?" Corey forced a few short laughs. But Drake stood up to leave. He was grinding his molars, and the vein in his forehead pronounced, a bulging split vein that darkened his entire face.

"It ma-m-makes sense. M-ma-maybe because he la-likes asshole so much, that's why he's s-such an da-dd-dick?" Fatty said.

"Fuck you, fucking fat ass. You're just a fat piece of shit," Corey puffed up.

"You'd pp-paprobably would like t-tt-t-to fuck my fat ass, wuh-wouldn't you?" Fatty put a hand on his hip and a finger to his lip. Drake turned away as AJ fell into a full cackle, and then Corey, livid and red faced, started in towards Fatty. Stumbling backwards to get away, Fatty fell back off of the bucket that he was sitting on and banged his head on a sill behind him, making a knocking, hollow thud.

"I want to get some more of that powder from Lenny," Drake said as he was leaving, his back to the group. He didn't ask, he simply said it, and the laughter fell away. "I want to go with you. I want to meet him," he demanded.

"That ain't a good idea. He'll probably cut me if he knew I told anyone about him." Then he stopped. He noticed that Drake wasn't listening to him anymore. He had already started to pull his raincoat over his head and had one foot on the windowsill ready to leap outside. "Besides, he's usually at church all day on Sundays, sometimes even all night."

"Well you already told *me* so take me over there, or I'll go myself," Drake said.

"When, right now?" Corey asked.

"What do you want it so bad for?" AJ asked as he handed the blunt to Fatty.

"What? I wouldn't m-m-mind doing it again," Fatty dug in his pant pockets for his lighter and evened out the coal.

"I want to ask him what that shit was. I want to be able to get some whenever I want," Drake said and turned partially to the group, both hands bracing the empty window frame.

"And if I don't want to go?"

"I told you. I'll go over there anyway. I'll tell him that you stole a shit load of dope and been telling everybody around."

"Are you fucking serious? What's your fucking problem?" Corey's shoulders sagged and his belly jutted in and out.

"You're a cocksucker." Drake said. "Fucking do it, or don't." They met eye to eye, an exhausted silence.

Corey stood there for a minute and had to look towards the ground. He was ashamed of himself, everything up until last night was gone. The respect and trust he had, the love he had, the friends he had, all gone even though they stood in front of him, they were gone. "Fine—whatever—let's go. You all want to meet Lenny? I don't give a shit, let's go."

Fatty and AJ both looked at each other, and AJ turned back to Corey and said, "I don't really care."

Fatty shook his head as he took short quick pulls on the cigar stub, not letting his lips touch the tobacco skin. "Drake bb-better wuh-watch his ass," Fatty said and took a final slow and whistling pull on the blunt.

Corey lit the joint and zipped up his raincoat and pulled over the hood. He breathed in deep and swallowed, peered around the bare house, and spit on the floor. Drake was already on his bike riding away. Corey took the last few drags and tossed the roach into a rain puddle and hurried after him. He could only see the red reflector under Drake's seat, and then even that vanished as Corey stood up on his bike pedals and rode into the rain as hard as he could.

Drake was already waiting behind Lenny's house, letting the menthol smoke curl up over his upper lip, into his nostrils, and then down to the bottom of his lungs. Corey stepped off of his bike and pulled back his hood and straightened his hat.

"Lights are off," Drake said.

Corey came up to a separation in the hedges, stumbled through and walked up to one of the back windows. He put his hands up to the wet glass like parentheses on either side of his face; he panned across the room. He pulled back and wiped the beads of rainwater from the window with his sleeve and looked in again. "I don't see anyone."

He saw that Drake was right behind him. One arm crossed his midsection while the other cupped his cigarette, his eyes wide as the throat of a cottonmouth. He squinted through holes in the perimeter hedges, towards the neighbors' backyards and verandas with wicker furniture turned over by the tropical winds. Water thudded the roofs and ran over the edges at the corners. A dog whinnied but it was distant, faint. The clouds were dark foam above them, rumbling a bit, rain driving down on them at a slant. Drake came up to the window and looked in as Corey walked around to the backdoor and knocked. No one came to the door, so Corey knocked a little louder. His empty stomach had synched up, tight like a clay-hardened stone.

"Shhh," Drake said. "You're gonna get the neighbors out here."

"So what," Corey said. "Nobody knows what you want." Their voices drowned in the perpetual rain, the slop of water, the tinging and clanking off of the metal gutters.

"Shut up faggot, you never know if someone's listening." Drake pushed

Corey aside and cradled the doorknob under his fingers, tried to turn it but it was locked. "I wonder if he keeps a key out here."

"Fuck you, dick." Corey spit foamy white spittle on the ground, looked at him, and back to the window. "Go around front."

"Fuck you."

"Jesus Christ," Corey said and walked past Drake and came up alongside the house to the front door. He knocked hard and the door gave way to his knuckles. "Anybody home?" He pulled the door closed behind him. He said it again softly as he walked down the hallway. Chairs were overturned, the hallway closet was ripped apart, the kitchen cabinets and the dripping freezer door sat open. Corey walked the extent of the hallway and came to the back door and unlocked it, "He ain't here."

Drake shouldered by and his steps faded down the hallway. "Somebody destroyed this fucking place."

Corey watched Drake head towards the living room, and so he followed dragging his feet on the carpet. Rainwater had soaked through his socks and squished between his softening toes.

Drake picked up a couple of resonated foil squares from the counter and a couple of the straws—then dropped them back where they were. "You think he got raided by the cops?" He dabbed a finger at a small pile of powder on a magazine and put his finger to his mouth.

Corey stood in the hallway while Drake perused the random scatterings of a meth addict, watching the front door and listening for the back door. "I doubt it. I don't think cops would leave all this shit behind." His eyes cut around the room, the sofa sunken in the middle, the window blinds pulled down with a few broken in the middle, the empty bottle and mugs on the splintered coffee table, the wadded clothing on the floor like dead animals. The dim living room light contained them like a yellow flame, his heart beating like locust wings.

Drake picked up a book from the floor, glanced at the sleeve and put it on the table. He followed Corey down the hall. The bedroom door was open and the closet light was on. No one was in the room; no one else was in the house. He showed Drake bags of pot under the desk, walked over to the closet and showed the plants in their cycles.

Corey pulled down shoe boxes from the top shelves filled with knives: pockets and butterflies, butchers and divers, forged steels and full tangs. One box held a small humidor with a Santa Domingo label and two small mason jars half-full of clear, corn-syrupy liquid. "What's this?" Corey asked, an element of disgust in his tone. Something was in the jars, broken down shreds of white and dried brownish pink, like stripped clams. The boys looked inside the humidor, "These look like the dried mushrooms my step-mom buys. Morels, Chanterelles, something like that?"

"I don't fucking care what that shit is. Where's the powder?" Drake asked.

"I don't know, go look for it," he said and then started to put the boxes back together as Drake walked away. Corey had one of the dried pieces from the humidor, and put it between his front teeth and tasted it, "Doesn't taste like a mushroom." He tore off a piece, "Too tough to be a mushroom."

"Then maybe you shouldn't eat it," Drake said from the hallway. "But you'd probably put anything in your mouth," he said.

"Damn that's salty. It's like jerky," Corey said to himself and put the rest of the piece into his pocket. There were three photographs on the floor of the closet. The one on top was weathered but not that old and it was of a little girl with her mother at the beach. The second and third were much older pictures, grainy, to where the black had faded to a dark green and they were both of a man in khaki military attire. As soon as Corey saw the last picture, glass in another room shattered and his chest rattled, his breaths became short and blood rushed up his neck. Corey hollered out with a cracked voice, "What the fuck was that?"

"Nothing," Drake hollered from the bathroom where there was a Bunsen burner and a few glass dishes with yellowed rings and dried, chalky residue pools. Trash was piled in the corner of the bathroom and the exhaust fan whistled out air. Corey came in holding two freezer bags, one of powder in his left hand, one of crystal in his right. Corey saw the broken glass, the clumped residues in the tub. "Dude, what the fuck?"

"It was like this when I came in here."

"I heard something break."

"So, I broke something. Most of this shit was already broken," Drake said and dropped another jagged beaker into the bathtub and watched as it shattered to smaller shards. It had contained no more than a few ounces of liquid, but the liquid was bitter and strong like skunk spray, and it immediately started to react with the other chemical residues lining the tub. Drake took the bag of powder from Corey who was also holding the three pictures in the same hand and they fell to the ground. The crinkled picture of the young girl and her mother at a beach lay on top. Tall alligator reeds swayed in the background. "I wonder if Lenny has a family."

"I don't give a shit. I'm getting out of here." And the two boys left the room as the air became hard to breath. They walked out and down towards the backdoor and the smell lingered out into the hallway after them. Drake opened the bag of powder and tasted a little bit, "I think this is it. I'm just gonna take it."

"What the hell else were you planning on doing?"

"Are you gonna take anything?"

Corey had a couple bags full of pot tucked under his jacket that he lifted to show, his pale belly behind it, and then he pulled a bag of pills and a few different sheathed and clasped knives from his pockets. "You want these pills?"

"What are they?"

"Shit if I know, just a bunch of different pills. I bet some of them got the names on them."

"Might as well take them." Drake grabbed the bag of pills and reached out his skinny fingers and touched the large bag full of crystals that Corey still held in his right hand. "What the hell is that shit?"

"No clue. Could be diamonds for all I know."

Drake opened the bag and pulled out one of the rocks, "Do you think that shit's crack?"

"I've never seen crack before."

Drake looked at the single shard of meth for a second and dropped it to the floor. "Who cares? I'm getting the fuck out of here," and he headed for the backdoor as Corey returned to the bathroom and left the bag of crystals on the floor near the toilet. The smell was unbearable, burning the inside of his nostrils. He had to cover his face and his eyes began to water, so he ran back to where Drake was at the backdoor watching carefully for anyone in the neighboring lots. Then they simply walked out, leaving mud tracks that filled immediately with storm water as they cut through a crease in the hedges and got onto their bikes.

"Hey Drake?"

"What?"

"Man, I'm sorry."

"I don't want to talk about it."

"Dude, it was that shit. I was fucking high. I didn't know what was going on," Corey said. His look was inward, even though it pointed towards the dead leaves on the ground. "Dude, I ain't no fag."

"Just leave me alone, all right."

"Come on, man," Corey said plainly.

"Dude, you're fucking sick," Drake got onto his bike, the bag of powder pouched in the front pocket of his pullover rain coat. He raised his hood.

"What are you gonna go do?" Corey climbed onto his bike. The rain drove through the canopy above them, covered their faces, dripped from their shoulders.

"Not hang out with you." Drake pedaled off in one direction, a middle finger waved goodbye.

18

Sophia had washed off her church make-up and had painted on more sensual tones: soft pinks, deep purples, and a sharp, dark lip-liner. She had already put on her navy dress, white lace peeking out from the bottom, a v-shape that bared her shoulders and the folding bulges of her back. Her sweat and perfume mixed like almonds, sweet mustard, gardenia, and apricot blossoms. She had even lined out what Sadie-baby would wear: her chunky-heeled maryjanes, easter pink socks and skirt, a navy cardigan, and the butterfly jeweled barrettes. Sophia was sure that the Bible group was over. It was past dinnertime when she had first walked over to Lanier's house and knocked on the door, and no one was there. She had no idea why he would go home without bringing Sadie home first, but something in her mind made her go over and check.

Now, she held the telephone receiver in her one hand idly at her side and held her hair back from her face with her other hand, breathing in deeply through her nose. She had called the church, but no one answered. She had called her neighbors with the little boy who was Sadie's age, but he didn't go to the Bible study that evening. She stood in her kitchen, the phone cord keeping her contained to a little circle. Sophia was talking to herself, though it sounded more like a prayer, "It's after nine." She took a few steps, turned and stopped. "God, what if there was an accident?" Her hands came to her mouth. "God, where are they? Oh God." Tears started to line above her bottom eyelids, mixing with mascara. She dabbed with a tissue, trying not to blur her lines, and breathed in deeply through her nose, out through her mouth. Everything's fine. There's nothing to worry about. Calm down, there's always an explanation, she thought. She stepped into her white heels and hung up the phone. She grabbed her purse and keys and hurried out of the kitchen towards the front door. With an umbrella propped over her head, she carefully trotted through the small puddles that spotted the entryway.

Before she got into her car to circle the community, Sophia walked back over to Lanier's house again. It was only a few doors down, and she realized, as if it had not occurred to her before, that she had never been inside. Lanier had always come to her. She rang the doorbell and again there was no answer. She peered through the ovate windows, where only a light that was on at the end of the hallway could be seen, shimmered by the iced glass. She tried the door handle, and it was unlocked.

Sophia passed through the living room, calling out her daughter's name first and then Lanier's with a wavering voice. She looked inside the hall closet, the kitchen, the half-bath. She walked the length of the hall and on into the master bedroom where desk drawers were pulled to the ground, plants were toppled over each other in the closet, and the mixed stench of chemical burn and tobacco stains permeated from every corner and seemed to rise from the ground. A SeaWorld calendar of two years past hung on the wall near a mirror, and crumpled clothes were scattered in clumps on the carpet, holding the sourness of mildew. Slowly, she walked across the room to the desk in the corner. Pills, pipes, papers, maps, knives, powder, marijuana: Sophia looked amongst the trash, dope and filth. She mindlessly fumbled through a few of the letters that were on top of the desk, mostly bills and promos with envelopes that read different names but the same address. She ripped everything off of the countertop and onto the floor; her face went bloodless, bleached and sallow, and she made her way for the bathroom.

After a few dry-heaves, gasps and deep-seated moans, her eyes closed and her lungs began to refill with the tainted air. As her eyes reopened, she saw a bag of white rocks, clumps like sea salt, and the picture on the floor next to it; the picture was of her baby, of her and her baby at the beach. She picked it up, held the photograph to her chest and ran back home.

19

Sadie snored even as Lanier came to Cook's Hammock, turned off the highway and ordered food at a drive-thru. He drove down to a gas mart and bought sodas and snacks, a Styrofoam cooler and ice, and continued down a winding county road surrounded by marshland. Thin trees stood from the stagnant black water, the trunks covered with lichen, dark algae and mushrooms that grew off the sides like little orange elephant ears.

Sadie woke up in the middle of the night. Her eyes opened slowly, then shut for a few minutes, then opened slowly again. Her arms stretched out—her fingers clenched onto the sleeping bag she was in. The bed she was on gave a little under each of her movements. The sleeping shirt she woke up in, the sleeping bag, the pillow under her head, everything was all new, still with the tags, stiff, itchy; even a doll, much like the one she sleeps with at home, was huddled next to her—though this one carried the scent of the cardboard box it came from and the soft plastic face and smelled nothing like hers. Turning her head and looking around the room, she sat up and let her eyes adjust. Sadie's little grey-blue globes glanced from corner to corner as she chewed the inside of her mouth, feeling completely alone. It was a simple, square bunker-cabin with a slate roof, rusted bunks, and torn screens for windows. She was surrounded by the smells of summer camp—the mildewed soft wood, the decaying compost.

"Pretty neat, huh?" Lanier said from a dark corner. "I thought getting this cabin would be more fun than a regular old hotel." Lanier had one eye opened more than the other and streaks of his dark hair cascaded across his brow, leaving a dark shadow.

She let out the air that had compressed inside of her as her eyes adjusted to him. He was sitting on the edge of a sturdy folding chair beside the dim gas lantern light, his elbow resting on his shaking leg, a hat bunched in his hand. He had a dry smile that quickly turned straight-lined and grave, his stare crystal-cut and glazed.

"Are you thirsty?" he asked.

She didn't respond. She didn't understand why there were here, and even where here was, but she wasn't terribly afraid. She wondered where her mother was, but just waking up, she was still rather groggy and tired. She wanted to go back to sleep, and possibly wake up in her own bed, but she did continue to sit up and look at him. He smiled at her again. She liked his smile, but she wouldn't smile back. She was just glad that someone was with her. She wasn't scared of being alone in this dark cabin with Lanier, she was scared of being alone in this dark cabin. She liked Lanier, but she didn't want him to know. She simply turned her face towards the screened flats; darkness and the sounds of darkness surrounded, just beyond them. A shiver took over her. He pulled a bottle of water from the cooler, shook it—and she wondered why he would shake a bottle of water. But she didn't want to talk yet, so she didn't ask. She watched as he wiped away the small pieces of ice and condensation and twisted the cap off for her.

"You have to be thirsty. Are you hungry?"

She didn't answer him again.

He told her that she had to eat something.

She was hungry and stared at the McDonald's bag next to him. Lanier reached into the bag and pulled out a cheeseburger for himself and undid the wrapping. He took half of it in one bite and then held the bag out to her.

The shiver in her wouldn't stop, and she didn't want to uncross her arms to reach for the bag, but she eventually did and was surprised at how many sandwiches were in the bag. She pulled one out and set it on her lap. Sadie rubbed the back of her hand against her cheeks, her knuckles digging at the corners of her eyes, and took in a short yawn.

"Good, 'cause you have to eat something, Sadie."

Sadie watched as he swallowed the other half of his cheeseburger. She took the sandwich from her lap and chewed off a small bite and hesitated to swallow. "It's cold," she said. He didn't say anything, simply looked at her as she ate. Then she stopped. "Where's my mom?" she asked. He just looked at her. There was nothing in the room but her, him, the metal bunks, the bed she slept on and the folding chair that he sat on, and she could only see a part of him by the light of the lamp.

Lanier lit a cigarette and blew the smoke up towards the ceiling, cob-webbed in the corners. He chewed at the side of his fingernails, and spit out little pieces of dead skin. "She's coming to meet us, and then we're all going to SeaWorld."

Sadie swallowed some of the water, her brow slightly wriggled.

Lanier dropped the half-smoked cigarette into a cup. There was a quick fizz and then sizzle. "Your mother decided," he pulled the chair a step closer to her, "that we should all go on a surprise vacation."

"Where's my mom then?" she asked again.

"I just told you, she's gonna meet up with us and we're all going to Orlando."

"Why didn't she come with us?" Sadie's lips turned down at the corners.

"I'm not even supposed to tell you because it was a surprise, but she just said that she had to take care of a few special things for you and that she would probably have to fly down anyway. But, she wanted you to take a drive with me so we could get to know each other better. She thought that maybe we could become friends. And then, when we go back, maybe we can all live together?"

Her chin reddened, crinkled. The creases of her eyes began to pull down.

"What Sadie-baby, what? This is gonna be fun. Now we have a few days and we can do whatever *you* want. So what do *you* want to do? I thought maybe we could do some camping, and we can go swimming." Then he smiled.

"I don't want to!"

"What's wrong?" He spoke from the center of his chest. "Everything is okay. She's flying down, and she's bringing you something really special. We'll all be together in a couple of days. But this time is for you. Anything you want, I want to do for you. Anything at all…" He let out a soft and simple, consoling laugh. "When you start crying you remind me of my little sister when she was your age. You know you look an awful lot like she did?"

Sadie shook her head.

"She wasn't as pretty as you are, but you still remind me of her." Lanier made two fists and set them on each of his knees and began to drum out a song. "I would sing to her. That was the only way she'd stop crying."

Sadie held her sandwich still up to her mouth, almost hiding behind the bun. She looked into his eyes, a calmness coming over her as he sang in a whiny country twang. She sat there, a feeling whole and good, and flustered him with her loose smile that spread over her face. She watched as he wrung his hands together. She turned her head and rubbed her chin on her shoulder, then set her shoulders back a little.

"She was such a little snotnose. You aren't a little snotnose, are you? We can have some fun, right?"

She shook the curls over a smile that she was biting back.

"What? You're not a snotnose, or we can't have any fun?" He leaned back into the chair. Smoothed the wrinkles in his pants. "If you really want to, we can just go back home and not go to SeaWorld."

She raised her eyes with her head bent forward and gave him a quick look, primly tucking her feet beneath herself. She didn't answer for a minute. Then she whispered hoarsely, "What's SeaWorld?"

Lanier pulled his bifold out of his back pocket and unfolded a brochure, worn thin and pressed by the contents of his wallet. He opened it delicately and handed it to her. "Do you like dolphins?"

She nodded.

"SeaWorld is a place where you can pet dolphins and play with sea turtles. They have almost everything that lives in the water and you can get up close and feed them. You probably won't believe this, but some little girls even get to swim with whales and sea lions."

"What's a sea lion?"

"It like a big cat that lives in the water. A water kitty."

"Who's gonna take care of my kitties while we're gone?"

"That's one of the things that your mother is taking care of before she comes down to meet us."

She sat and looked at the brochure, the map, the pictures. A picture of a little boy with his head turned away, his arm extended with a fish in his hand and a dolphin standing half out of the water. A picture of a penguin sliding down an ice shoot, a picture of a shark swimming over a glass-domed walkway. People eating, smiling. Pink birds. She laid the brochure down in front of her.

He pulled off his shirt and hung it on the back of the chair. "You want to see something funny?" he asked.

She watched him as he ran his fingers in his hair and hunched over, sucking his belly in and out in a rolling motion. He flexed his arms out in front of him and the tendons in his neck stood out like elevens. His stomach rolling up and down like water in a tank. "Can you do that?" he asked.

She shook her head, wanting to feel the pouch of his stomach, his protruding ribs. A smile started at the corners of his mouth, his midsection twisting and rolling. She yawned and blinked.

"Have you ever tried? It's pretty easy."

She looked down to where her belly was and shook her head again.

"Try it."

She laid the sandwich down and stood on the bed, steadying herself as the air in the mattress compressed and shifted, and pulled her shirt to her underarms and tried to roll her stomach, but could only suck it in and out. "I can't do it."

"Sure you can. You just have to let it sway. Put your back into it."

She tried again.

He walked over to her and placed one hand on the small of her back and the other on her stomach and she giggled at his touch. "What? Are you ticklish?"

She shook her head, but couldn't contain the laughter as he ran his fingertips along her sides and up into her armpits. She squirmed and scrunched to one side and then the other and finally fell back to the bed. She laughed and pulled at her shirt trying to cover herself, but his hands roamed underneath, tickling up to her armpits and down to her hips.

"You sound like a little monkey. Are you part monkey?"

She shook her head, the laughter rolling out of her mouth, her cheeks red and deep set by her dimples.

"I think you're part monkey." And Lanier gave out a monkey call, scratching at his head with one hand and the other fingering at his own side. He bounced from one foot to the other. "You are a little monkey?"

20

Sadie lied there, occasionally opening her eyes to see him sitting next to her, as he sang to her before she had fallen back asleep. Her breathing became heavy, her eyes flickering behind her closed eyelids. He cleared the hair from her face, her forehead damp with sweat, and gently caressed her cheeks with the back of his hand. He ran his fingers across her lips. He pulled back the blanket and lifted one of her hands up to his mouth and sucked the dirt and salt from her fingertips, nibbled on the base of her palm. Her body unmoved in a dead sleep. He laid her hand on his lap and pulled the knife from his pocket and clicked it open and ran the backside of the blade along her thin arm and down the middle of her chest. He stood the blade on her belly and held the handle with both hands. Her ribs gently rising and falling against the metal point. He raised his hands into the darkness above, the sounds of choking cries circling in his mind. He closed his eyes and could see the smoke and the flames, could smell the burning hair and could feel his pulse beating throughout his body. The knife hanging there, above her, wanting to fall, his arms becoming weak. He didn't know how much longer he could hold them, as if the knife pulled towards her and he held against it. She rolled over on her side and pulled her hand from his lap and rested it under her chin, her other hand sliding under her pillow. She tucked her knees up. She mumbled. He put the knife down on the ground. "What'd you say, Sadie Baby?"

"I'm cold," she mumbled again, her eyes remained closed.

He pulled the blanket up to her shoulders and tucked it down over her arm. "That better?"

She slept.

When she woke up in the morning, Lanier was sitting in the chair with his head lulled back, his eyes opened to the ceiling of the cabin watching a moth trying to pull away from a spider web, one wing flapping desperately.

She sat up in the bed, the lump in his throat moving up and down. She shifted in her sheets and his head snapped up.

"Were you crying?" she asked.

"No," he said. He turned to look out of the screened windows. "Looks like the storm is following us." Black birds on the ground outside kept other birds from the small puddles of rainwater. They hopped a few feet and stopped, then hopped a few more feet. The wind ran through the trees and slapped against the screens carrying the sound of waves crashing on the shore.

"Your eyes are all red," she said.

"Just couldn't sleep very well." Lanier sneezed, breathed in deeply and sneezed twice more.

She drew a curl of hair away from her nose and tucked the blanket around herself. The blank white of lightning piercing through the screens showed dust floating in the air. "Maybe you're 'lergic?"

"Could be," he said. "That's awfully smart. I probably am allergic to something out here."

"I'm 'lergic to cats," she said.

"But you have so many of them."

"I take medicine," she said and stood from the sheets and onto the cold floor of the cabin.

He was angry with himself for not knowing.

She stayed on her toes and came over to him and pulled herself onto his lap and laughed when he winced and let out a guttural breath. He could feel her thin tailbone digging into his thigh; his hand came to rest on her knee. He squeezed with his thumb and forefinger and she squirmed in his lap. He squeezed again, the friction playing with his groin causing a slight pain in his lower abdomen, a pulsing in his flesh.

"You're in a good mood this morning," he said with a rising note.

"Can we get pancakes?" she asked and smiled.

"Whatever *you* want Sadie-baby."

"I don't want to be called baby," Sadie said as she shook her nose at him then rolled her eyes. She slid down from his lap and hurried to the clothes that Lanier had lined out for her. She pulled off the tags before she put them on. Lanier stood from his chair and lit a cigarette. He walked out of the cabin and stood with his back to the door as she put on a tank top and then pulled up some denim shorts that were too big for her. "They're too big," she said.

He turned back to see.

Sadie was holding up the waist of the shorts as she came out to him. "They're too big," she said again. She watched Lanier looking around in the trees and the down in the bushes, as if he was going to find a belt somewhere. She even laughed a little, and then he looked back down to her and she stopped. He put his finger up, told her to stay put, and walked off into the woods. He didn't go very far because she could hear him walking on the twigs and leaves, so she just stayed where she was until he came walking back with a long strand of vine in his hand. He got down on one knee in front of her and began braiding the vine through the belt loops and tied it off.

"Is that better?" he asked.

Sadie nodded.

Lanier walked out ahead of her, and as she followed she lifted her hand up to his, grasping onto his fingers as they followed a windy path of trodden upland flatwoods covered in years of detritus. Lanier lifted her up into his arms and carried her over the saw palmetto and fallen trees and hooked an arm over her head to guard her from low-laying vines that hung down from the pignut trees. The surrounding bush seemed alive, teeming with the shuffling of branches and the quick dash of small animals. He avoided the large spider webs and the ground that seemed to move in front of him. She burrowed her face into the nape of his neck. As he was about to set his foot down, he stopped. She pulled her head out and looked down.

"What is it?" she asked.

"A rhino beetle." The pointy-headed beetle had been flipped onto its domed back, its little legs plucking at the air above. He set her down and stayed bent at the knees.

"Do they bite?" she asked.

"I don't know, probably not."

He pulled out the pocketknife and flicked it open and tapped at the beetle's side. The legs stood still. Sadie went to touch it but pulled her hand back when the little black legs began an open air sprint. Lanier kept prodding with the tip of his knife. "It's pretty gross, huh," he asked.

She nodded. "Are you gonna kill it?"

"We could sacrifice it," he suggested.

"What does that mean?"

"That means you give it back to God."

She didn't understand.

"Either you are grateful or sorry for something, and you show God by sacrificing it to him. Is there anything that you are sorry for doing?"

She shook her head. "I don't know."

"Is there anything that you want to thank God for giving you?"

She shrugged her shoulders.

"Are you thankful for God giving you your kitties?"

"But God didn't give them to me. My ma' did."

"Your ma' only gave them to you because God allowed it."

It took another moment or two and then she nodded her head.

"Then maybe we should sacrifice this beetle to show God that you're thankful. What do you think?"

"So, we're gonna kill it?"

"Yeah, but for a good reason. It's up to you though. If you don't want to say thank you to God, then we won't. But if you don't say thank you, then he might not give you anything else that you want."

"How do we do it?" she asked.

"First we say a short prayer together. You ready? You have to repeat after me."

She nodded.

He bowed his head, peeked out of the corner of his eye to see if she did the same. She did.

"Gathered around the altar of love," he said and waited for her. She followed in a soft whisper.

"May all be united in listening to your word," he said, and she repeated.

"And sharing the one bread and cup," he said, and again she followed along in a soft whisper.

"And become one people, offering one holy sacrifice," he said, she echoed.

"Amen," he said.

"Amen," she said.

She kept her eyes closed as Lanier lifted the knife above the beetle's midsection, writhing desperately to right itself. He pressed down through the hard shell and waited for the legs to stop moving.

"Is that it?" she asked.

"Almost," he said and then gathered a wig of moss dangling from branches above them. He created a small bed, lit it afire with a match, and rested the dead beetle on the flame. They stood there with their hands clasped and watched as the fire burnt out in a crackling cloud of rising smoke. He lifted her back into his arms and stepped over the smoldered pile and said that that was it. "I already feel a little better, do you?"

She shrugged her shoulders, "I guess so."

They finally came to a white shell road that looked the same in both directions—bare, straight, and confined by hardwood hammock. He set her down and she skipped towards the car that was parked on the roadside. And when Lanier began to drive, Sadie watched the chalk rise and spiral up behind them. The road eventually opened onto a cement one that led into a little town, and Sadie peered into the store windows that they passed by. Most of them were boarded or taped over. One had a sign that read *Cajun Smoked Mullet and Boiled P-nuts*, another was lined with the grayed screens of televisions, another with trinkets and toys. One storefront had the windows filled with sun-bleached books and a large circular sign up close to the window that she read aloud: "Change for a Book, Books for a Change". The few people on the sidewalk walked in the same direction. Only two teenage boys with dingy white t-shirts and no shoes seemed to be avoiding that direction cutting in and around the others. One of the boys saw that Sadie was staring at him and he stopped and smiled at her. She waved at him, and Lanier slowed down for a second and then sped up. His skinny back arched over the wheel as he turned to stare at the boy who had continued on his way. His knuckles became pronounced on the steering wheel as his fingers gripped tighter onto the soft patent leather and padding. He snorted back slightly. Sadie then put one hand onto his wrist and pointed to a diner on the other side of the street and the car seemed to follow her finger.

"I bet they got pancakes," she said.

When they parked, the boy was nowhere to be seen. Lanier had his hand in his pocket caressing the wood grain handle of his pocketknife, and as she walked into the diner, followed by Lanier, the same two teenage boys were in a group that sat off in the corner shooting straw wrappers at each other. Sadie followed the hostess to a booth and sat where she could look in their direction. Lanier sat across from her blocking her view. The waitress came to the table smelling of grilled onions, her apron smeared with ketchup. The woman had a laziness to her gape, one eye sort of dawdling. Sadie didn't seem to notice at first, not until she ordered her pancakes and let out a little gasp as she looked up to the eye that awkwardly looked away. The lady finished taking down the order and put the pad into her apron, and Lanier thanked the waitress. Once she left, Sadie tried to peer around him.

"You want to go sit with those boys?" Lanier asked.

"No," Sadie said quickly as if she were offended. She crossed her arms while her face flushed.

"You like one of those boys, don't you?"

"No I don't! I don't like any boys."

"None of them, huh? Not even me."

"Especially not you," she said and stuck a pointed tongue out in his direction.

"Now that's not very nice. 'Cause I like you, I like you a whole lot."

"You don't like me, you like my ma."

"Nope, I like you Sadie. You're the only girl for me."

"Not uh. I seen you kissing my mom."

"That doesn't mean anything. I kiss my own mom, you kiss your mom. Moms kiss their moms. Moms just need to be kissed. It just has to be done."

Sadie sat there for a moment and Lanier could tell that she was thinking about this until the pancakes made their way to the table. Very thin streams of steam streaked out from under the smothering blueberries, her mouth dewing at the corners, her stomach making little squish and squash sounds. Lanier only had a few small bites of toast before he asked for more coffee.

"These are the best pancakes ever," she said as she dredged another bite into the syrup that then dripped onto her chin on the way to her mouth.

He watched her as he blew on the surface of his coffee. She chewed with her mouth opened and licked the fronts of her teeth just as his sister would. He watched and was amazed at the striking resemblance, the thin upper lip, the perked nose, the soft blonde eyebrows. She ate slowly, but took large bites.

"So what do you want to do today?" he asked as she took a bite far too large for her mouth. "We have the whole day and don't really have to keep moving. We can even stay at the cabin if you want."

"Can we go shopping?" She wiped the syrup from her chin with the back of her hand and wiped her hand on the tablecloth.

"It depends on what you want?" Lanier took a fold of cash from his pocket and left money for the waitress as Sadie put down her fork. "Almost ready?" he asked as he dabbed a napkin in his ice water and handed it to her, and she wiped her mouth and hands.

The two of them left the restaurant and walked along the boulevard lined with dried gum, wrappers, and what looked like glitter in the cement. It shimmered in the sunlight and she danced from speck to speck. Lanier followed just a step or two behind. She ran her finger along the glass of the storefronts. Her finger stopped, pointing at a stuffed cat mounted on a surfboard. Sadie turned completely to face the cat, putting both opened palms on the glass. She looked back to Lanier, "Can we get that for my ma'?" and then walked directly inside before he answered her. Lanier trailed in behind her nodding at the counter clerk. Alligator jaws, bins full of sharks teeth and shells, rotating tiers of sunglasses, rows of straw hats and baseball caps all sat in front of the register.

She grabbed the stuffed animal and then put it down so that she could pick up and put on a pair of bug-eyed sunglasses. "If we go swimming, I need a bathing suit," she said and went to the back with the stacks of swimsuits and towels, where surfboards hung on the walls like the big fish in the clubhouse. Sadie found a white suit with pink butterflies and blue peonies, grabbed it and walked into one of the dressing stalls.

After a few minutes he asked if she was okay in there.

The door to the fitting room was a saloon door and she pushed open one side, showing that the bikini she had picked was far too large. She held onto the side.

"Does it fit?" he asked. He had the stuffed animal tucked under his arm.

She smiled, "Nope."

He went back to the other swimsuits and grabbed two smaller ones with the same design.

When she had on the one that fit snug, she pushed the door back open and nodded and pulled at the elastic bands cupping her buttocks.

"Now your sure it fits right?

"Yep," she said.

"And do you like it?"

She nodded. "But ma' won't let me have it."

"Why not?"

"She's says I'm too young for a bikini."

"Well she's not here, is she? Change back to your clothes and then we can get back and go swimming."

"Don't you need a bathing suit?" she asked.

"Nope."

She let the door swing back closed and Lanier stepped back. Standing in front of the mirror inside of the stall, she looked at the butterfly that seemed to be resting on her waist bone. She pulled the bottoms up higher. She turned a bit and laughed at herself in the mirror, the way her butt cheek was peeking out of the side, her little belly half tucked away. She stared at herself for a few moments before she dressed back into her clothes. When she was done, she walked to the front where Lanier was waiting at the counter with the surfing cat, a couple of straw hats, towels and some sunscreen, and he was already wearing a pair of sunglasses with the tag hanging off the side.

"Where are we gonna go swimming," she asked.

"There are a few springs, where the water comes straight out of the ground. Clear and… " Lanier lit a cigarette.

"I never swam in a spring before."

The boy behind the register cleared his throat, and said with trepidation, "Sir, there's no smoking in here." His face and neck were covered in callous pink acne scars, his hair oily and unkempt. He delivered a polite smile as Lanier took a deep drag, handed over money, and began to leave.

"It's no different than the beach or a pool, just water," Lanier said to Sadie.

"Do you think that my ma' is gonna meet us today?"

"I just called her, and she said she'll probably make it tomorrow afternoon or maybe even the next day. She said she was about to book the flight as we spoke."

"I wanted to talk to her."

"I'm sorry Sadie. She said she was really busy trying to get everything ready so she could leave."

"Can we call her later?"

"Only since you're being so good," he said as he put his hand onto the back of her head and walked her out the door.

As they started back towards the car, Sadie asked, "Where is your ma'?" She reached for his hand and held onto three of the fingers.

"Back in Georgia."

"Is she pretty?"

"She's beautiful."

"Does she have curly hair like me?"

"Sort of," Lanier rounded the bend and directed her towards the parking lot of the pancake house. "It's more wavy than curly," Lanier said and glanced back at a shabby, two-pump garage with a cat on the windowsill and a deputy cruiser parked alongside the curb. He pulled her back to his side, and so she tried to look around him and saw the kitty.

"Is she skinny like you?" Sadie said when they got to the car.

Lanier opened the door for her. "Very skinny," he said.

Sadie pulled herself up onto the seat and, with her eyes framed in the rear view mirror, watched as Lanier walked around the back of the car to the driver's side, and she waited for him to turn the car on before she buckled her safety belt. Her eyes ran over his long nose and his lips, teeny beads of sweat sitting on the stubble. "Was your dad skinny?"

"I don't know. I never met him."

"How come?"

"My mom didn't know who he was."

Sadie sat up in her seat and said, "I bet he was skinny too."

21

Over the next two days, Sadie thought that if she didn't say anything about her mother that her mother wouldn't come. Sadie missed her mom, and most of all her cats, but they didn't stay in her mind for long periods of time. When she did think of her mom, she imagined Lanier kissing her. She wished that Lanier was only her friend. In the mornings, the two searched for frogs and snakes to sacrifice, threw rocks at what he called cooter turtles that were perched on waterlogs and watched as they slipped back into the water like drips of black ink. They torched black and yellow banana spiders in their webs, and ate rice-crispy treats and candy bars. They swam in clear water that bubbled up in places, and they ran around the water's edge with sticks, striking at whooping cranes and egrets. In the surrounding woods, they chased scurrying armadillos and searched for wild pigs and white-tailed deer. At night, Lanier made fires as tall as two people and rolled his own cigarettes, one after another, and burnt brown dog ticks off of their legs and arms with matches. He told her stories from the Bible, about evil men who had finally met with the strong hand of the Lord and little girls who didn't obey their Father's wishes. Little orange fire flakes curled out of the burning wood and flew up towards the sky, and he had said that those were the condemned souls trying to escape from hell and sneak into heaven. "If you watch real close, they never make it," he said, her back curled up against his front. The stories had made the unnoticeable hairs on her body stand; she was covered with them. She watched closely as he stripped and whittled sticks to a point with his pocketknife. She was even allowed to hold it, as long as she promised to be careful. He said that he had had a lot of knives, but that this one was his favorite. That he especially liked this one because the handle was made of a man's bone. They had roasted marshmallows on the whittled sticks, and she was afraid of letting the souls get near them for fear of eating one and having something so evil trapped inside of her. When she slept on the inflatable mattress, he had laid himself on the floor right beside her though he never seemed to be asleep when she woke up; this last night she had rested her hand on his slow moving chest as she slept.

In the morning, they had driven back into the little town and Lanier pulled past the diner and on towards a used car lot that had used cars parked at a slant in front of a retention ditch. He drove past the lot and turned down a secluded clay path, abandoned, squeezed by the overgrown brush at its sides. He drove as far down the path as the suffocating woods would allow. He lifted her from the car and carried her on his shoulders back to the lot of cars for sale. When she asked what they were doing, he said that they were getting a new car. When she asked why, he simply said, "Because." When she asked why again, he said that the old car needed to be sacrificed. When she asked why, he said that he had already explained why we sacrifice things, so she simply said, "Okay."

When he set her down, he told her that she could pick whatever car she wanted, and she walked in between the cars that lined the tall metal fence. A mottled brown dog, chained to a pole, was lying in a patch of mud in the center of the lot, its head down between its shoulders. When they got too close, it bared its teeth and set off on a low gurgling growl, the chain clinking around its neck and a row of hair standing on end down the middle of its back. She moved from car to car, standing on her toes to look inside the windows and leaving handprints on the glass. She stopped at an old convertible, the top harnessed to the windshield with alligator ties and wire, a pool of rainwater sinking the canvas in the middle. A man walked down a couple of steps out of a small office that was lifted off of the ground by cinderblocks. He was tucking in his shirt and pulling the waist of his pants up to the bottom round of his stomach that pushed them back down as he took a few more steps. The dog stood for a moment and watched the man walking towards them and sat back down on its tucked tail, wagging under its hind legs. Sadie looked over at him and then back to the car. "I want this one," she said.

"Why this one?"

"It's pretty."

"Is it a good car?" Lanier asked.

"May not look like much, but it'll get you where you need to go," the man said. He spoke as if he had to pull the words from deep in his belly. His chin doubled up and pressed down to his chest. He snorted back and swallowed, lifting at the waist of his pants again. He pulled out a ring of keys and opened the door and Sadie pulled herself up into the driver's seat and put her hands on the steering wheel. "You old enough to drive Shirley Temple?"

Sadie nodded.

"Look just a bit south to me," he said, giving a short laugh. "Well, how does she feel?"

"Who?" Sadie asked.

"The old girl, how's she feel there?"

Sadie looked up at the man who was between her and the opened door. He had his elbow rested on the canvas, a foot on the car's sidestep. She couldn't make sense of what the man was saying, so she turned back to the steering wheel in front of her. She reached up to the top of the wheel and pulled herself up to look out of the windshield and then ran her fingers over the radio knobs and pulled the gear shifter with both hands. It wouldn't budge. Her toes stretched out for the pedals, but couldn't reach even as she slunk back into the seat. She got out of the car and stood behind Lanier's leg, her hand on the small of his back, his shirt damp from perspiration. The two men went back and forth about the car and when they shook hands and headed towards the office, Sadie made a wide arc around the chained dog and hurried back to Lanier's side and took hold of the bottom fingers of his right hand.

The office was cold, the wall unit dripping onto a water-soaked towel on the linoleum. The portly man pulled at his belt line and turned his head toward her suspiciously. She stared back at him as he lit a cigarette and sat down. "You want a soda?" he asked her.

Sadie shrugged her shoulders and nodded.

He sat down at the desk and leaned back in his chair and pulled open the door to a mini fridge behind him, "Is it all right if she has a soda?"

Lanier said that it was.

"Regular, grape, or orange?" he asked.

"Grape," she said, standing there with her ankles crossed.

"That's my favorite," he said to her as he pulled out two cans. "Would you like something to drink, sir?"

Lanier put up his hand and said that he wasn't thirsty.

With the cigarette huddled back between his fore- and middle fingers, the man snapped the cans open one at a time and handed one towards her. She slurped from the can, holding it with both hands and licking the purple line that sat above her lip.

Lanier counted out three piles of money and pushed them across the desk.

When they came back outside, Sadie ran back to their new car and had to use both hands to get the passenger door's lever to give way. She pried the creaking door open and edged herself into the front seat. She hummed a soft melody as she waited for Lanier and the man to get to the car.

"Now, have any trouble with her, just bring her on back. Swap you out no problem. Got my word on that," the man said.

Sadie was still confused as to whom the man was referring to. Was he talking about me, she wondered. She watched the two men as they shook hands again before Lanier got into the driver's seat and once more through the opened window after Lanier sat down and started the car. As they drove out of the lot away from the small town, the man gave a soft wave with one hand as he pulled up at the waistline of his pants with the other. The dog even stood from its mud pit and let out a short howl.

"Who are you going to bring back if you have trouble?" she asked.

Lanier looked over to Sadie, "What are you talking about?"

"That man said if you have any trouble, then you should just bring *her* back. I don't want to go back there."

"He wasn't talking about you, you silly girl. He was talking about the car."

"How can a car be a *her*?"

"Most cars are girls. That's just the way it is."

"How come?"

"I don't know how come. That's just how it is."

"Well, I didn't like that man, and I don't think we should go back there no matter what," she said and crossed her arms.

"Then we won't ever go back there. Don't you worry," Lanier said. "We'll never see that man again."

"Where are we gonna go now?"

"It depends on what you want to do."

"Can we get more pancakes?"

"Again?" Lanier asked.

Sadie laughed and watched Lanier nod as he adjusted the rearview.

"Anything *you* want."

The car stuttered as it changed from gear to gear, a brief rattling, and then smoothed. Lanier sped up and the car seemed to settle and sink as it picked up momentum, the steering wheel bouncing slightly in his hands. She held on to the seatbelt that cut across her waist and looked out of her window into the side mirror and could see thick white gasps of smoke billowing up behind them. She looked back to Lanier as he slowed the car and made a wide circle turn to head back towards the abandoned road where he had left the other car. She sat and watched as Lanier unloaded the old car, the bags from the trunk, the toys that he had brought for her, every cassette. He motioned for her to get out and join him once he had everything loaded in the new car. She pulled at the handle with both hands and forced the door open with her shoulder. They said their prayer, and he doused the seats in what he called holy water, though she knew that it smelled like gasoline. He pulled a pack of matches from his pocket.

Before he struck a match, she asked, "How do you kill the car? You can't just light the fire without killing it first."

"You're right. We'd just be burning her alive, and that's not right, is it?"

She said that it wasn't.

Lanier walked to the front of the car and unlatched the hood. He pulled out the pocketknife and she watched as he cut at the wires and lifted a hunk of metal out. He said, "There's no way a car can live without this," and he dropped it to the ground. "Stand back over near the new car." He unscrewed the gas cap and tossed that on the ground as well. He lit the entire pack of matches and dropped the flame onto the front seat.

They sat in the new car and backed off a ways down the clay road, just enough so that they could watch the flames and smoke rise throughout the car, lifting out of the windows and around the roof and braiding back together.

He asked, "Do you like the new car?"

Sadie smiled, emphatically working her head up and down, "Yeppers. She's a good car." She nibbled at the cuticle of her pinky finger.

"As long as the tape player works, I'm happy. Can you reach in the back and grab a tape?"

She pulled down the armrests that separated the bench seat and leaned over them trying to grab for one of the tapes. She could feel the coarse callousness of Lanier's hand holding her from falling into the backseat.

"Be careful," he said. "Can you reach?"

Sadie popped back up with two tapes in her right hand and pushed one into the tape deck. Lanier turned the volume dial and they could hear the static of the cassette playing over the speakers, then the first notes of a song. Sadie studied the other tape in her hand, the thin clear plastic, the strip of audio film that ran at the bottom. She stuck her finger into one of the reels and turned it tight, then loosened it.

"Those were my sister's tapes. She spent a lot of time making all of those tapes."

"Where is she now?"

Lanier didn't answer her.

"Is she with your ma'?" Sadie watched as his smile vanished, his eyes squeezing to a dark squint. "Can I meet her?"

Lanier didn't answer her as they pulled back into the diner that they had eaten at before. The car idled in the parking spot, the front end of the car trembling. He turned in his seat to face her, his eyes wet-rimmed. She started to ask again, but he shook his head and leaned over her to open her door and then his own and stood out of the car, closing the door behind him. Her seatbelt wouldn't come undone. She called for him, but his back was to her and he didn't turn. She pulled at the clasp, dug her thumb into the release. She writhed and wriggled, but was only able to slide out from under the belt.

She saw how he wiped away the thin line of water balancing on his bottom eyelids before they went inside, and she had never seen a man cry before. She didn't like it, but she knew that she shouldn't say anything, so she simply reached for his fingers as they walked into the diner. They were seated at the same table they had sat at before. As they waited for service, Lanier sat in silence. Even as the waitress came and took Sadie's order, he simply put up a hand when she asked what he would like to have. After Sadie had finished half of her first pancake, he asked for a cup of coffee from an old woman who came up to their table, but she talked about a group of girls at the church who liked to get together around this time—she asked if Sadie would like to join them. The old woman, her shoulders set forward and holding onto one of her thin wrists, rambled on saying over and over again that Sadie was just too precious. "God Bless her heart," the old lady had finally said. Lanier stood up and put out his hand to the lady, gently. He introduced himself as a Pastor and asked if he could get directions from her to this church. She had started to name streets, but then said that it was awful close. "You ain't got to drive even." The woman took Lanier's elbow by the sleeve and walked him to the front of the restaurant, pointing here and there.

Lanier turned back before they left through the front door and motioned for Sadie to stay put, and she did for a few minutes. But Lanier and the lady left the diner and disappeared from her sight. Being left there felt terrible, the people in the diner looking over at her. She kept looking out of the windows, hoping that he would reappear, but he didn't. The worry made her feel sick, growing like weeds twisting inside of her. She pulled herself out of the booth and walked out front, where she looked down the sidewalk of the short strip both ways and didn't see either of them and had started towards the car, panic building in her belly, abandonment rising in her chest. She had walked around the lot, past the car parked next to theirs and then farther and farther until she was in the absolute back, where there weren't any cars. Behind the strip of buildings were stacking crates, broken-down cardboard boxes, and two sets of large dumpsters that she had started to walk towards, looking at them from a distance.

"Sadie!" she heard in the distance behind her. She heard it again. She turned around directly and saw Lanier waving her in, concern riddling his yells, painting his face pink. She dawdled in his direction, then stopped and stooped, the toe of her shoe playing in a black puddle. He started towards her and her eyes came into contact with his, and as he smoothed the agonizing expression from his face she couldn't help but smile.

"What's so funny?" he asked. "What did you run off back here for?"

"I thought you left."

"Sadie, you think I would ever leave you, in the middle of nowhere? You silly little monkey," he said and started to turn back towards the restaurant.

Sadie took his hand. "Are we going to go to that church?" she asked with a dull lull in her voice.

"Only if you want to," Lanier held open the door to the restaurant for her, followed her back to the table and slid in next to her on the booth.

She smiled, drew his hand near her mouth and bit the loose skin near his thumb gently. It was a musk that she had smelled many times, but the taste was much different; she tasted nothing. She left a slobbery imprint, a little pinched-red six-tooth impression.

"Ow! What did you do that for?"

"Because you like me," she said.

"What makes you think that I like you?"

"A hundred reasons."

"Name one?"

"I'm very pretty."

"You're very modest."

"I'm cute too."

"How can you be cute and pretty?"

"It's not easy."

Behind them, this old woman seemed to be approaching another table with two loud, little freckled boys. She had her Bible tucked under her arm, and when she looked back over at Lanier with a curtsy of sorts, Sadie stuck her tongue out at her. Lanier laughed silently, yet at the same time tugged on her shirt to stop her. "My pancakes are cold," Sadie complained.

"Do you want more?" Lanier asked.

"Yes! But I only want one little one, with extra blueberries. And I want it to be really hot, so when I put the butter on it, it melts all at once."

Lanier flagged down the waitress, who was carrying a coffee pot and two sippers of syrup, and he apologized first and then relayed the order just the way she had told him, "...so the butter melts all at once."

From the pancake house, they drove past the gas station where the same patrolman's car was still parked, but now the cat was lying on the hood, basking in the midmorning sun that stole through the surrounding rain clouds.

"Can we stop and pet the kitty?" Sadie pointed towards the striped car.

"No," Lanier said sharply, but he then calmly said, "Don't point, it's rude."

"You're rude," she said and watched as the little town passed by and out of sight.

After Lanier lit his third cigarette, Sadie asked, "Why do you have to smoke all the time?" She had two of the toy dolls in her lap, their hair long braided. She held them so that they stood on her legs.

"I don't know. I just do."

She held one of the dolls up and acted as if it spoke for her, "I don't have to smoke."

"Do you want to?"

"No."

"Well I do," he said and blew the smoke out of the window. "Besides, you've never said anything before, so how was I to know that you didn't like it."

"I didn't say that I didn't like it, she did," she said still holding the doll up.

"Why does it bother *her* all of a sudden?"

"It's stinky," she said.

"Oh," he said and tossed the cigarette out of the window. "Tell her that I am very sorry. Tell her that I won't smoke around her ever again."

Sadie pulled the doll close to her mouth and whispered. Then she turned back to Lanier, "She says, thank you."

He drove for a long time, longer than it took to get to the pancakes.

"Where are we going?"

"Well I guess we ought to make it down to SeaWorld, meet up with your mother."

"But," she stopped herself.

"But what?" he asked.

As she thought of what to say, she straightened her shirt and found a dollop of drying syrup down at the bottom, and she pulled the little stain up to her mouth leaving her belly bare and began to suckle on the hardening sugars that seemed to break free, coating her tongue and the roof of her mouth. It wasn't long before they passed a lone sign, indicating a nearby beach. "Can we go to the beach?" Sadie asked, looking over at him now. When he didn't respond, she reached out with her two pointer fingers and dug into his side making him squirm.

"Quit it. Stop it! That tickles." Lanier couldn't stop from laughing, so much so that the car slowed and pulled over on the shoulder, and he unbuckled his safety belt. Sadie sat still, not sure whether to laugh or yelp. His face read nothing to her, his voice dry and indiscernible. Then he pointed behind her, and she wouldn't turn to look. She looked blankly into his eyes, like hard, cold stones. He pointed again, "Look at that. Oh my God!"

She looked but there was nothing. And then he had her, both hands up under her arms, tickling as she wiggled, jostling her as she cried out in shrieks of joy. "Stop. Please. You're gonna make me pee myself. Stop," she yelped. The dimples on either side of her smile reached their deepest pits and felt tired. He finally stopped for a second, letting her breathe in deeply. She let out a few tremor laughs, and he started back in on her lower ribs, unbuckled her. She lied back, as he continued at her sides, rolling in a curdling laughter. Then he stopped, still holding her close, practically above her. He came down with his lips to her face and she turned away, "Stop!"

"What?" he asked.

"Stop!" she said. "I can't breathe." A sense of alarm rushed over her face; she could feel it as it coursed through her. It was in his eyes, his thin lips, something lay behind them, a look that she could see behind his smile, his soft brown hair hanging over his eyes, behind them was something very angry. His forehead squished together, his hair in strands hanging over her, slightly touching her face. He sat up and looked down the empty state road.

"I need a cigarette after that work out. I'll be right back." He popped open the door and strode out into the woods.

Sadie lied there looking at the goose bumps and feeling the thin hairs that ran down her arms; she lied there for thirteen minutes, and as the clock clicked over to the fourteenth minute she worked the door open and there he was heading back. His hair and face looked wet, and his eyes were open wide and looked scared. He jogged back to the car, and when he sat down, his knee began to shake.

"What happened?"

"Nothing," he said.

"Your eyes look like this," and she tried to mimic his expression by pulling apart her eyelids as wide as possible. She pulled down the vanity mirror and looked at herself and then at him and she laughed louder than when she was being tickled.

"All right, enough," he said and pulled the car back onto the road. "We going to the beach, or what?"

"I don't want to go to the beach no more."

"Why not?"

"I just don't wanna. I'd rather go to the movies."

"And see what?"

"Something funny, something with a beach in it."

"Why don't we just go to the beach and do something funny?"

"Like what," Sadie asked.

"Like tie our ankles together and get into the water and wait and see how long it takes for us to turn into mermaids."

"You can't be a mermaid."

"Why not?"

"Because you're a boy."

"Oh. Well, then I'll turn into a dolphin, or maybe I'll turn into a shark and eat you. What do you think of that?"

"Sharks don't eat mermaids."

"Of course they do. Why do you think there're more sharks than mermaids," Lanier reached into his pocket and pulled out his lighter and pack of cigarettes and in a brief moment had the cigarette embers crackling and the window cracked.

"But you promised?"

"You're right, I forgot," and he pulled hard on the cigarette and flicked it out the window. Lanier tossed the pack of cigarettes up onto the dashboard and tucked his lighter back into his pocket.

"So are we going to the movies?"

"If that's what you want," Lanier said.

"Why are you sweating so much? It's not that hot."

"I'm okay Sadie."

"I changed my mind. I want to go bowling," she said.

Lanier sat for a second, sighed and said, "I can't promise that we are going to find a bowling alley anywhere round here."

"Well, I want to go bowling."

"What happened to the movies and the beach?"

"I don't want to do that anymore."

"*I don't want to do that anymore*," he mimed.

"Stop it."

"*Stop it.*"

"Stop."

"*Stop.*"

"I hate you!" she yelled.

"No, you don't hate me," Lanier rubbed the stubble on his chin, "you love me. *Sadie loves Lenny. Sadie loves Lenny. Sadie loves Lenny.*"

"Shut up. I do not. I hate you. Leave me alone. I hate you!" And then she swore herself to be silent for as long as she could. She wasn't going to say a thing, pursing her lips together and crossing her arms. They passed the sign indicating that it was the last stop for the beach, and still she decided to remain silent, silently hoping that he would turn down the sandy road anyway. He didn't, and it was a long time before they saw another sign.

22

The school bus passed the feed store, the lumber yard, the fenced in rolling green fields of tall wiregrass and scrub trees. Rainwater spread over the road. Flat bed semi-trucks passing in the other direction carried skinned trees and the scent of fresh cut pine and sent sweeping arcs of water against the side of the bus. Many of the children told stories of their Thanksgiving break, what they had shot while hunting, what they had caught while fishing. Stories with trumped up exaggerations. Redfish that filled the bottom of the boat, fall turkeys like feathered beach balls. Corey sat huddled in the back corner looking out of the window. The lanky boy in the seat next to him had his hand under a girl's shirt, and every few minutes she would turn and tell the boy to quit. Trying to ignore it, Corey could still see it all reflecting in the glass inches from his face. She was a chubby girl, her face contorted and round. Two girls in the seat in front squirmed and pointed, blushing, whispering into each other's ears and laughing in unison. The driver occasionally glanced back, her eyes framed in the long mirror. A group of boys in the front were telling jokes about dead babies. What's funnier than a dead baby, how do you make a dead baby float, how many dead babies does it take to paint a house. The air and spits of rain whistled in through cracked windows. Though Corey could hear what the others on the bus were saying, he tried not to listen. Drake didn't come back to school, and Corey wondered what it was going to be like when he finally did and everyone knew what he had done. He replayed that night in his mind without cease, each step to the bed a decision that seemed weighted down like walking through a pool of dead babies. When the bus made the stop in front of Graceville Hills, he was the only one left and didn't move to get off the bus until the driver hollered back to him.

"Move it or lose it," she said.

His forehead pressed against the glass window, he sat still and didn't move until the driver turned in her seat. "Let's go Mr. Leavitt, I'm waitin' for you. Get a move on."

He looked up towards her, her thin hair pulled back, the weight of her cheeks pushing in on her nose. He shouldered his bookbag and walked off the bus apologizing. He always waited at the bus stop for the junior high bus, and he and AJ would smoke on the way home, but there was no waiting today. As he passed the waving guard at the gate, he didn't wave back. Corey pulled the front tire of his bike out of the rack, saddled his leg over the seat and stood on the pedals as he rode down a path, sheltered from the rain by the awning branches of oaks. He eventually stopped, let his bike fall and leaned his back against the trunk of a tree. He pulled his backpack to the front and felt around for a pack of cigarettes and a lighter. He pulled out a joint and lit it, sucking in the smoke until it burned throughout his chest making him cough.

He wanted to talk to someone. Someone who wouldn't talk back. He didn't want to talk to his father. He didn't want to talk to his doctor. He didn't want to talk to his teachers. They would all tell him what he didn't want to hear. He knew what he did wasn't right, but he also knew that there was nothing wrong with him. He thought that God made him a certain way, that God made everyone a certain way for a reason. He thought about going to the church in the community. He had smoked dope behind it, ridden his bike all around it, even spray-painted the side of it with swastikas and upside down crosses, yet he had never been inside before. His father had sent him to a Catholic school before they moved down, but during mass he was told to sit in the corner with the other Jewish children who were not permitted to take communion. He often watched a number of his classmates go into the confessional after the mass every week, one at a time, joking before they went in and coming out with their heads down and their eyes between their ankles. He often imagined that they had been beaten in there, though he knew that couldn't be true. He never had to do anything to be a Jew. He liked that. But he also felt further from God, like he had no relationship or understanding whatsoever. He didn't really understand what being Jewish was. He had never been to a synagogue and he celebrated Christmas, never had a Bar Mitzvah, never took off the holidays that Jews were permitted. He wanted to talk to someone, but just didn't know who it was, and he thought who better than God. He didn't know how it worked. He just knew that he wanted to go to the church.

When he came to the church grounds, he left his bike on the open lawn. Not a soul was around, and when he walked into the main hall he found no one there. He wanted to turn around and leave, but instead he walked down the center aisle towards the pulpit and kept his eyes on the statue of Jesus with his hands out, a Jesus that looked so disappointed out over the open pews. Corey dragged his feet all the way to the first row and sat down, waiting. His teacher had told him that Jesus was a Jew, and his classmates had told him that Jews killed Jesus. He looked into the eyes of the statue, and waited, exactly for what he did not know.

He must have sat there for close to an hour before a janitor came and opened the choir door and walked an industrial carpet cleaner around the organ, yanking a long extension cord that lagged behind him. The man, whistling, walking casually with his dark eyes watching the carpet, did not even notice Corey until he was right upon him. The man looked up from under the loose fit hat sitting atop his head and then plucked at the curls of his sideburns. He looked over at Corey for a few moments before he even turned off the machine. The man's shoulders pointed out, and his fingers, long, thin and dark brown, held the handles of the vacuum. "Can I help you son?"

"Is there a confessional here?" Corey asked.

"Not 'ere. This's a Batist church. They don't do that."

Corey pressed his thumbs together and turned back to the Christ statue and then looked down and away.

The old man turned the vacuum on again, but before he went back to work, he turned it right back off. "Ain't nobody 'til tomorrow evening gone be're."

Corey nodded.

"You in need of some help? Some sorta trouble?"

"No. That's all right."

"Look like you could use some help. Having one of those days, ain't you?" The man let the words hang in the air. He pulled a toothpick from pocket and sucked at his teeth. "I been having one of them days. Late to work cause my other job had me held up. Somebody bounced me a check and so my rent check bounce. And look at this," and the man lifted the back of his foot and showed Corey how the heel of his work shoe had come away and flapped down with every step. "Just gone be one of them days. Nothing you can do 'bout it but wait it out."

"Yeah," Corey said, nodding along and hoping that the man would leave him alone.

"But if you can wait it out, it always blows over. That's the truth, always does. No matter how it seems, always does just that, blows over—even if it feel like it's going to take you along for the ride. Usually end up on your feet and stronger than before though. Least for me."

Corey sat there, his hands together. "Is there a priest or someone I could talk to?"

"No, don't think so. Pastor probably gone on home." The man took off his knit cap and scratched at the crown of hair that circled around the back of his head.

Corey watched his dark eyes lull about, watched him wipe his nose with his sleeve.

"What's going on boy? What's the trouble?"

"Nothing," Corey said and stood to walk back up the aisle.

The man put his hand on Corey's shoulder and pulled him half way around and said, "If I was the pastor, you'd talk to me, huh? Well, what've I am a preacher. Listen 'ere, if I can see you're hurting, so can God. If you don't want to talk to me, that's fine, but God is always listening, even if you don't want him to hear. You understand?"

Corey jerked his shoulder back around and headed back up the aisle. Before he was halfway towards the door, he could feel the soft hum of the vacuum, could hear it running over the carpet, back and forth, back and forth.

Corey walked his bike back to his house and left it on the doorstep and went up to his room. He locked the door. He pulled the knife from his pocket, clicked it open and tested the blade against his forearm, not hard enough to break the skin, just enough to leave an irritated red streak. He did it again and this time a thin, dark seam came to the end of the blade. He put down the knife and wiped the tiny beads of blood from his arm. He looked at the cut, couldn't feel it. He thought about killing himself, but didn't think about death. He thought about the funeral. Who would be there, who would be crying, who would care? The teacher that told him about Jesus being a Jew had just read a play to the class before the break about a salesman that killed himself. He wondered how long it would take for the blood to run out of his arms. He wondered how many pills it would take. If a belt could hold him by the neck? Would he be able to drown himself? What he would write in a note, and he imagined his father reading it, his friends reading it. He wondered if that would make them cry. He wondered all this in front of his mirror, but he couldn't look himself in the eyes or he felt that he would cry.

23

Growing up, he didn't understand why he killed the first three girls, other than they all reminded him of his sister in one way or another, and he was angry with them for that. They were mocking him. The first girl's laugh. The second girl's touch. The third's smell. By the time he found the fourth girl, he had already begun to truly study the word of God. He sought redemption, he sought peace, he sought forgiveness, and so he justified those first three deaths as sacrificing the innocent in an attempt to save his soul for what he had done to his sister. But even after the third girl, he hadn't felt saved. He still didn't feel cleared of his sin.

He did everything by the Book. He figured that they weren't innocent. Not innocent enough.

24

Sadie finally jolted awake at the sound of a loud and long bang. The car was parked with the windows rolled down. A suffocating mugginess covered her, and she was all alone. She was covered with sweat, and the vinyl seats leeched to her skin and left red marks on her cheek. Again, much like the first night in the cabin, she woke up feeling that desperate and abandoned panic course through her. Again, she half expected to wake up in her own bed at home. Only this time, she hoped that Lanier would be waiting there next to her. Instead, she was simply alone in an unfamiliar place. She lifted herself up and looked out of the windshield and saw that a very small home was in front of the car, and to the right were many more in rows. The little homes had cement blocks under them keeping them off of the ground; some of them even had wheels underneath at one end and blocks at the other. Lanier opened the door of one and walked out towards the car, drinking slowly from a green bottle and watching Sadie as she got out of the car. Sadie looked around and saw that there was a swing set, but two of the seats were split completely down the middle. She saw other parts of a playground: a merry-go-round with rusted bars and one side resting on the ground, a spring horse bent over completely with the head busted in, and a splintered seesaw warped in the middle so that both ends sagged. She saw that there were a few boys and a tall girl sitting in the sand of the lot tinkering with something furry, something that looked alive. She opened the door and stepped out of the car but stood there next to it for a long while watching the other children, mostly staring at the one boy who was not wearing a shirt. He was holding a long stick and outlining whatever it was that was on the ground. His little belly rounded out, smeared and scratched red in spots. Where his belly button should have been, it looked like there was a thumb trying to poke out. Sadie meandered over towards the other children, just a few steps at a time, but then sat down on the one good swing so that she could see as to what the children were playing with.

Lanier started towards Sadie on the swing when an older woman came out from the same little home that he had come from.

"You know what that is?" Lanier asked Sadie.

"I think it's a dog. Is it dead?" Sadie questioned back to him and then remembered that she wasn't supposed to speak.

"It's a fox honey, and he ain't dead, just got him good with the trank," the lady said as she walked past and put a hand on one of the boys. The woman looked, from a distance, like the lady at the pancake house, so much so that Sadie felt confused for a moment. But as she came much closer, Sadie could see a scar that ran the length of her face that the pancake lady did not have—it looked soft.

"What's a *trank*?" Sadie asked.

"Somethin'll put'chasleep for a long while," said the boy who was holding the stick. He went on back to poking at the little, red-haired bushy tail. The girl, much taller than Sadie and with a lot of space between her teeth, was smiling and stroking the large, pie-slice shaped ears while the two other boys just sat and watched. Sadie approached the circle of children, stopping shy of the group, not wanting to get too close.

"Well, come on now, he could wake up soon," one of the littlest boys said to her and opened the circle for her to join in.

"It's like a dog, right?" Sadie asked.

"Surta," the oldest boy said.

"No you stupid, it's ain't nuttin' like a dog. Good damn, ain't nobody taught you nothing," the girl said viciously.

"Bet be nice Mary Beth," scolded the older woman.

"But Gramms, it ain't no dog," the girl said.

"May not, but that don't mean you gotta act that sorta way. Understand me?"

Mary Beth nodded, her jaws working.

"She don't look like she belong around here," one of the boys said. "She's pretty, huh Gramms?"

"She stick out like a sore thumb, huh Gramms," said the shirtless boy.

You look like you have a sore thumb sticking out of you, Sadie thought to herself.

"Gramms, where she come from?" asked the boy as he scratched his bare belly.

"Ain't you gone answer for yourself?" the lady asked Sadie, who immediately looked away.

Lanier stepped forward and finished his beer, and as he belched he said, "This here's my little sweetheart."

"But I thought I was?" said Mary Beth. "Uncle Butch, I thought I was? That's not fair."

"No, you're my sugar pie, Mary Beth. This here is my honey bun. Ain't you Sadie?"

Sadie wouldn't look back. Even when Lanier put his hand onto her shoulder and held her close to his side, she didn't care to look up at the others. She went to tugging on the bottom of Lanier's shirt. When he bowed to her, she whispered into his ear, "Why did she call you that?"

"Call me what?" he whispered back

"Uncle Butch."

"Everyone calls me that around here. It's sort of a nickname."

Out of the corner of her eye she could see Mary Beth's ugly smile, smiling up at Lanier, bits of her tongue poking through the gaps. Lanier said that he needed another beer and the lady walked back, and Sadie noticed how the little home shifted as the door opened and closed. When the two adults had their backs turned, Mary Beth spit a few inches from Sadie's flip flops, and Sadie looked up directly towards Mary Beth.

Staring right back with a scrunched nose and one eyebrow lifted, Mary Beth silently mouthed, "Fuck you."

25

Drake had been awake for four days straight. He was sitting in his room with the door locked, watching the local news on a little fifteen-inch television. The reporter noted that two squad cars had been sent to the abductee's house late in the night and were later relieved by two other squad cars of deputies after midnight. It was still early in the morning, and the reporter had large jaw muscles like wads of cotton and a flat white paper smile. Three officers stood in the background of the shot, one of which sipped from a foam cup.

The mother sat on the sofa, the camera keyed on the sorrow in her face. She hadn't even turned towards the shatter of thunder; soft streaks of lightning stole through the window blinds and further illuminated her lined posture, wet and vacant.

The reporter stood slightly out of shot, yet explaining the current situation.

Drake's nose was red-rimmed and dusted. Vessels had popped in and around his clear amber eyes, and even his sallow cheeks seemed bloodshot.

Her voice drifted away on the television, a loitering stare blank in front of the camera.

He averted his eyes from the television and sat in the chilling silence.

The mother brought a handful of tissue to her nose and wept, staring vacantly in front of herself, rocking front to back. "He took her, I know he took her and it's all my fault."

Drake watched as the sketch composite of Lanier was placed on the screen. It looked vaguely like himself, and then a profile and pictures of the girl, Sadie Joelle, came onto the screen one after the next—various ages, of her and a kitten, of her with her mother at church, of her at a birthday blowing out candles. Then they showed the picture of her with her mother at the beach, the one from the house that Corey had found.

Drake dipped a key into the bag of meth powder and dropped a small chalky mound under his tongue. He tapped his fingers against his bouncing knee and rolled his head back from shoulder to shoulder, a tick playing in his neck.

It had now been days since Sadie had been reported missing. With most of the community, especially parents, sitting in at advisory meetings at the clubhouse, the Leavitt boys and Fatty sat at the clubhouse bar with the television on in front of them. AJ leaned back into the corner and watched the heavy rain through the windows, walls of water falling from the roof. Even Fatty chewed the inside of his mouth, not making jokes but merely moving his eyes sedately through the crowded dining area that was stripped of tables and chairs and swarmed in a confusion of voices, confessions, murmurs and delegations. Corey couldn't take his eyes off of the television. Working associates and acquaintances of Lanier's were being interviewed; Pastor Deene broke out on live television and wept like a child about how betrayed he had felt, how unassuming he had been, and how perfectly decent Lanier had seemed. More and more volunteers collected and searched night and day.

A newscaster of mixed ethnicity was speaking about how a couple of detectives had opened the suspect's house for investigation the morning after abduction, and it wasn't but thirty minutes before labeled bags of paraphernalia were seized from the premises and placed in the custody of the local sheriff. What he said was repeated, but this time in Spanish, as video footage was shown of two men placing full, clear plastic bags into their departmental vehicles, packing their trunks and back seats with bagged plants and broken beakers. The same footage played over and over on local and even larger networks nationwide. They showed the pictures of the abducted, Sadie Joelle, cited her stature and disposition: seven years of age, four feet and two inches, sixty-two pounds, dark red hair, freckles. A drawn description of the suspect, along with his height and build flashed on the screen. Fingerprints were said to have been collected and under evaluation.

"I can't believe this shit. All along," Corey said.

"D-d-da-don't you think that you sh-should t-t-t-tell someone?" Fatty asked.

"Are you fucking crazy? I didn't know him hardly at all," Corey stopped himself before he said anything too loudly.

"Yeah, but you d-did kn-nah-know him."

"I didn't know what the fuck was going on, and I don't want anything to do with this," Corey said through clenched teeth. "He's seemed like a nice guy, like everyone else says."

"Yeah, a n-n-nice guy with a shit-lal-load of d-dope and hookers and st-st-steals little girls," Fatty said.

"Would you shut up? Jesus, you're gonna get us all in trouble," AJ said.

"Na-na-n-no one's paying any at-te-t-tention to us," Fatty said. "What the f-fuck do we know?"

"He's right. What the fuck do we know? Nothing," Corey said. "I can't believe this shit."

Corey took off the mohair sweater his father had insisted upon. A slight pressure, a pang in his upper back subsided but left a ripple along the right side of his neck over to his shoulder. He pinched, rubbed at it. The drawn picture of Lanier was on the screen again. It wasn't accurate; his nose was narrower with a slight bend at the bridge—his hair looked right, but then the lips were too full, the cheekbones too wide. The newscaster read out possible aliases as the picture aired. It could have been a thousand different men of a thousand different names, twenty of which in the room adjacent fit the loose descriptions. Then the picture of Sadie came on the screen, the same photo that Corey had held and had shown to Drake; the picture that he had left on Lanier's bathroom floor was shown on the television. "Have any of ya'll talked to Drake?"

"Nope," Fatty said.

AJ didn't turn his head, nor did he care to answer his brother.

Corey could not help but wonder what Drake thought of all this. Had he seen the picture, would he recognize it? Did he even care? "Fucking asshole," Corey said under his breath.

The commotion in the dining area turned into a wave of motion heading towards the door and then it surged back again. Some of the people strained and shushed others trying to hear, and others talked louder in order to hear one another. The boys were too far off in their own little corner to know the specifics of what anyone was all talking about. Corey stood up from his barstool, set the sweater down on his seat and told the other two to stick around. He walked over to the crowd and then merged into it. People were in tighter nooks than it looked from a distance. Most of the men smoked and the desensitizing smell of the cigar tobacco made the air rich and textured. He could feel that smell brush against him, stick to his cheeks, blur his vision. Corey walked around the small crowds and picked up words here and there: *Terrible. Awful. Just a little girl.* The closer he came to the entry way the thicker the smell of the crowd, the sweat, the sour, the sweet, the smell of fear mixed with anxiety like vinegar and cheese. What was said seemed to also have more bearing: *Boxes of knives. Methamphetamines. Pedophile.* He could make out a figure at the front of the crowd, facing the people, an officer of sorts, a billed hat tucked under his arm, the shine of metal on his breast pocket. Corey tried desperately to hear what was being said, and then the crowd at the front started to disperse, mostly following after the man who had been talking.

Corey tried to twist through the tight circles, around the smells and into the voices. The people he passed didn't seem to notice him. The ones that did seemed to look right through him. He pushed on as most of the people washed out through the building. When he stopped, he stopped near a circle of police officers. He caught himself staring at the mirror black shoes. For some reason, he thought about how much it would hurt to be kicked by one. His eyes ran up along the nylon green pants, the black seams, and stopped at the belts—the guns, handcuffs, flashlights—and he worked his eyes up to the brass fixtures on their chests and shoulders. A few of the officers had their backs to him, and as he walked up to one and tapped him on the shoulder, the man didn't even turn. Corey waited a few seconds, but then knocked on his arm like he would a door, with the back of his knuckle. As the officer turned to face Corey, the others kept the conversation going, something about western winds and how some guy hooked a Spanish Mack trolling a soda straw and a hook. The man's sunken eyes looked down his nose, his chin blended above his thick neck. Corey imagined trying to fit both of his hands around that neck if he had to. He imagined choking the officer. He imagined the officer, in turn, choking him. He then imagined all of the officers coming down on his curled up body with those patent leather shoes.

"Yeah?" the officer asked.

Corey just stood there looking at that neck.

"Something I can help you with son?"

Something at the base of the neck beat out, red, like the collar was too tight.

"I think I might know this guy."

"Speak up kid, I didn't hear a word you said."

He spoke a little louder, "I think I know this guy that took the girl."

"Yeah? What do you know?"

"I just…if it was this guy that I know, then I just know him I guess."

"A lot of people say they know him."

Corey nodded.

"You have any idea where he is?"

Corey shook his head.

"You have any idea why he took this girl?"

"No, but…"

"What do you know that we don't already know?"

Corey opened his mouth, but then closed it. He was going to tell him about how he bought pot from Lenny, but wondered if he would get in trouble. He shrugged his shoulders.

The man bent down, so as to be eye to eye, and said, "It sounds like you don't know shit from a chocolate sunday. Go home, kid." The officer turned back and reentered the conversation as if he hadn't missed a word.

26

Lanier was in front of the fire sitting on a halved tree trunk set on its side, half submerged into the ground. He was smoking and the night heat around the RV lot was thick and stagnant like the puddles of muddied rain that pooled in and around soft spots and sinkholes. A few teenage boys had approached from what appeared to be shadows—wet from the waist down, wearing sleeveless flannels that were dripping dry and mesh-backed ballcaps that were bleached with chalky white sweat lines. The boys were carrying ropes over their shoulders, ropes strung with green, whiskered catfish with flat heads like the backsides of coal shovels—the backs of the boys' hands, their knuckles, streaked with diluted blood. The young men dumped their fish-lined ropes at the feet of the old woman who began to inspect the eyes and the gills of each fish—the boys nodding and saying things like "Here go Gramms." The gills must have a deep pinkish-brown, she said to Lanier; the eyes, which were a reflective blue with black centers, "They cain be cloudy," she said. Only one of the fish still had a kick in its fin; then it lay languidly there as she drove a knife down above the eyes, and Sadie gasped.

She pulled on Lanier's pants, and this time he picked her up and set her in his lap. She whispered in his ear that the lady didn't say the prayer. He gave a soft laugh and then whispered back, "That's okay. This is dinner, not a sacrifice." The fish were gutted with the long and thin knife and the body cavities, one by one, were emptied, the flesh stripped from the smooth skin.

An even older woman than Gramms came out of an RV wearing a terry cloth turban covering thin rasps of silvery white hair, and Lanier called out to her, "Be careful now Ma'amMaw, it's real wet out."

She shuffled over to Lanier and gave him a kiss on the forehead. "How's my boy?" she asked, reaching out for Lanier's hand. "It's so good to see 'yer Butchie."

"Doing good Ma'amMaw, doing just fine."

"You know we missed seeing yer. Boy it show good to see 'yer." She kissed his hand before she sat in a folding chair corroded at the hinges and then began to pluck the bones from the fillets with rusted needle-nose pliers. Her face composed an exhausted expression, almost like wadded paper—her skin blotched, cracked, and wrinkled, divided by the lines; her eyes held the only lies of timelessness in her age, and even her eyes, though clear and dark, had been closed in on by the loose, hanging skin above them. Her lips had no color as if they had disappeared or curled back into her mouth. She was draped in a large polka-dotted tablecloth, under that a Princeton sweater and a plaid scarf kept her thoroughly covered from the wet and the mosquitoes. The fillets were cut into mouthful chunks and then dropped into a bowl of curdling buttermilk; the scraps were tossed onto a pile of fish heads left attached to the spine, drying out and covered in a host of greenbottle flies; a group of feral cats gradually came out from under the little homes, huddled, picked apart and cawed over the fresh meal.

Sadie asked who these old ladies were. Lanier pointed to the one he called Ma'amMaw and told Sadie that she was his great grandmother. "So that's your mom's mom's mom?" Sadie whispered back.

"Yep. You got it."

"Who's the other lady then? Is that your grandma?" Sadie whispered into Lanier's ear.

"That's Gramms."

Sadie quietly confirmed, "So that's your grandma."

Lanier nodded and then took a long drink to finish his bottle of beer. He dropped the bottle to the ground and grabbed another one from the cooler.

On the fire was a warped and tarnished pot of oil with large cuts of potato floating at the surface and a tripod of black metal legs standing on the flames, digging directly into the embers and coals. Gramms stood over the vat of browning oil as she held a sliding spoon and dunked in chunks of battered catfish, swirled the oil, and pulled out golden brown knots that flaked apart. Little beads of sweat dripped down from her smudged and worried brow into the vat making the oil jump and cackle, crackle, spit and hiss, and as the oil jumped out in little specs onto her liver spotted arms and neck she didn't even attempt to dodge the popping splash but merely stood there like a bear digging in a honey hive. Sadie and Lanier hadn't eaten anything but sweets for days and the smell of the fish fry bellowed inside of her. One of the older boys said that it was well after midnight, but since she had slept most of the evening in the car, she didn't feel tired, only hungry.

More dirt-faced children seemed to simply appear from the dark corners where the steaming woods blurred out. The smell of the oil—pungent, perfumed by the visceral melding of peppered flour, natural sugars, the salt and water, burning corn meal—it all called people from out of their little homes and into the open. A few of the men came with a hand out to Lanier, shaking his hand or bracing the top round of his shoulder. Many of the overhang lights were now on, showing the muddied cinderblocks stepping up to the RV front doors, doors that were covered in fingerprints dark from oils and mud, clay and blood. These little homes were covered in bugs. Flying bugs were sucked into neon blue lights, sometimes catching in a quick burst of hissing smoke, sparking like a match and dropping to a pile. Bugs incessantly buzzed in and around Sadie's hanging curls, resting on her pale skin and occasionally sinking down into her.

The young children and toddlers were running up and down the blacktop, their feet darkened in soot and grime. They darted about in packs led by one of the youngest boys—whom Sadie thought to be too old for a diaper but was still wearing one—and he ran with lit sparklers in his hands, leading the way like a swarm of elusive fireflies. The children who were Sadie's age and a little older sat in a circle, just far enough from being heard by the adults. And the fox that had been shot with a tranquilizer was still barely conscious and laying down on the ground, now penned in by chicken wire. Sadie looked around trying to take in her surroundings: the homes with wheels, the large fire, the two old ladies—Ma'amMaw and Gramms—the dark, the smell of smoke. For a moment she thought to herself—this isn't a place for a girl like me. The boy was right. The lady who stood at the fire, the one who Lanier and the other children called Gramms, wiped her hands, which were covered up to the wrists in batter. She wiped them directly onto the bottom of her shirt and the front of her denim jeans. She called out for a smoke and Lanier set Sadie down and walked up from behind and held his cigarette up to her mouth. Her cheeks caved in as she sucked deeply from his hand and her face tightened back to her cheekbones and exposed how these two frail bones seemed to hold up her entire body that sagged beneath them.

Sadie stood alone, fifteen feet away from the fire on a stump with her hands together, almost in the dark completely, but she could feel Lanier's eyes glancing at her occasionally, and that comforted her. But when Mary Beth came up to her from behind and dropped a handful of dirt onto her head and ran back to the group, Sadie just stayed still for a few moments before she even tried to shake out the dirt and pebbles. She then walked over to the downtrodden cats and Lanier took her outstretched hand before she was able to touch one of them. Bending over, he pulled her little fist up to his mouth and kissed it and spun her back towards the other kids and nudged her in that direction, but she dug in her heels and crossed her arms.

"You don't want to play with these cats," he said.

"Nothing wrong with them cats," Gramms said.

"Lord Mercy, nothing wrong them cats," said Ma'amMaw. Her knotted, arthritic fingers gripped the pliers that swung through the air as she spoke in a drooling drawl.

Sadie leaned back into his pushing hands with full resistance and turned into his midsection, but Lanier held both of her shoulders and turned her once again towards the others sitting in a circle. Sadie scoffed and began to whine and moan.

"She's got to be hungry," Gramms said. "You want some of this 'ere?"

Sadie was scared to look at either of the women directly. Even with her eyes averted, she still nodded her head and was presented with a plate of the fried nuggets.

"Aw Gramms, how come she get to eat first?" one of the kids hollered, and the others followed with similar complaints.

"Hush up!" Ma'amMaw coughed out, and the kids went silent. The pink, white fish flesh danced in her shaking hand, her other hand cutting through the air with her bone-plucking pliers. "Better be mindful of the company."

"Kids ain't got manners for nothing," said Gramms.

"Good for nothing little shits," said Ma'amMaw.

"Ma'. . ." Gramms said.

"What?"

"Enough ma," said Gramms.

"Don't 'enough' me."

Lanier laughed as the two ladies went back and forth, and Sadie ate the food and watched peripherally as a boy walked up to her. He held out his hand as he approached her, and when she looked over he quickly opened his closed palm. Sadie flinched back, anticipating that the boy was going to throw a frog or lizard at her face. She closed her eyes and turned her head to the side; then she peeked back. The creases in his hands and fingers were black-lined, making the white cloudiness of the milky quartz that he held for her seem so pure and beautiful. As she peered deeper into the rather opaque clump of stones, she could see gold like lace coursing throughout. And when she didn't reach out to take it from him, he grabbed her hand, opened it and gave her the crystal.

After a short rush of silence, he told her that his father digs in the river, that he's the best digger'n'sifter in town. He said that his eyes was good for gold, that they was made for finding gold. He finally said that his father could even see it with his eyes closed. When Sadie asked what the rock was, the boy answered promptly, "Cryssal." He appeared to be confused, either confused or angry. "Ain't you never seen cryssal."

Her sense of belonging felt even more distant, her sense of understanding even more remote. And as she stared into the glossy and yet clouded rock that sat in her opened palm, the boy reached for her other hand and pulled her along. "Come on," he said. He pulled her over to the other children and sat down. When he sat, she remained standing, hovering above the uninviting faces that looked back at her. He still held onto her hand though, and he tugged a couple of times before she decided to sit. It wasn't long before all of the children had eaten their fish nuggets and swollen corn cobs, and they were pulling Sadie this way and that way, trying to show her as much of their world as they could. They first took her to the well where they hid things. They surrounded the rim of the well and looked down into the black depths. One of the older kids, who was probably twelve or thirteen, took out a half-smoked cigarette and dug out a couple of loose bricks. Behind the bricks was a scrap of tarp that he unfolded. There was a gas lighter, a few coins, bullet casings, a small metal pipe and a folded magazine picture of a woman's breasts. He lit the smoke and passed it around. Mary Beth took a long pull that filled her cheeks, didn't breathe in the smoke but blew it right back out towards Sadie's face.

"Ya'll wanna check the bog," one of the boys asked.

"Could," another said.

"Could dig up some nightcrawlers."

The group of them stood around, taking turns glancing at Sadie. She could feel their eyes. The cigarette had burned to the filter and was tossed down the hole Their faces then huddled over the opening, watching the small cherry pit flame swim down and disappear. Two of the boys complained that they didn't get any.

"I got anothern," a boy across the well from her said and held his hand out for the lighter. He put the cigarette in between his lips and lit the end. His volcanic ash eyes above the flame, his fingernails long and lined with resinous dirt. Sadie watched as the tobacco embers curled out like little singed orange worms. He pulled on the cigarette twice and passed it. When it came to Sadie, she ducked her head back and they passed it in front of her, a thin line of smoke coming at her face.

"Could go down to the junk lots and play manhunt?" another asked, but the others shook their heads.

The horizon was a stand of moonlit treetops rolling down a hill, and in the distance a thin tower with blinking lights, power lines sagging from one tall pole to another. They stood listening, their breath, the chirps of insects, the rustling of leaves on thin branches. The boys stood there slumped. The older one with a bandana wrapped around his wrist, smacking mosquitoes off of his bare arms, lit firecrackers and dropped them down the well and they watched the sparkle make its descent and pop a flash of light. Two boys with ratty long hair and filth lines on their foreheads shuffled their feet piling dirt between them. They were thin boys, their cheeks caved and the bones of their wrists and knuckles pronounced through their skin. One boy huddled down with his elbows on the ledge of the well, the magazine picture in front of his face at an angle, another standing behind him looking down over his shoulder.

"What you wanna do?" one of them asked her.

Sadie wanted to say something, but didn't. She couldn't think of anything.

She was scared, but didn't want it to show. She shrugged her shoulders.

"Why ya'll care so much what she likes," Mary Beth said.

"What's the matter Mary Beth, you jealous of this lil'ole girl?" said the boy with the cigarette dangling between his lips, smoke rising up around his nose. He wiped the sweat from his forehead with the bandana.

"Better shut up. I ain't jealous'a no girl."

"What you gone do if I don't?" The boy's smirk rose in the dim light.

Mary Beth smacked her tongue against the roof of her mouth and sighed.

The shirtless boy said something about gigging frogs, and Sadie couldn't even imagine what that must have meant, but all of the other boys settled in on the plan.

"My brother said when they was catfisting, saw Old Boy Turpentine out there," Mary Beth threatened.

Sadie figured that she must not have liked frogs much either.

"Shnot uh," said a red-haired boy with a mouth full of gum. "Ain't no'smore Old Boy Turpentine. Gramms said he dead."

"That's 'cause you're scared," Mary Beth said. "Gramms don't want to hear no crying baby."

"Shnot uh, I ain't escared a no gator."

"Come on then."

Sadie simply followed the kids back to the lots for their flashlights, and many of them grabbed special sticks with three or four sharp points at one end. Then the boy, the one who had given her the stone, again took her hand and pulled her along. It was very dark under the trees, but with the boy's hand she felt as if she knew where she was going even if she could see no better with her eyes closed. A few of the boys' flashlights were on, but the white rays bounced off of the wet ground and from tree to tree, not allowing for Sadie to truly see what they approached. All she could feel other than the boy's clammy palm was the softening of the ground beneath her. It started to give slightly, and the farther they went the more of her flip flop became submerged into the suckling muck. She even had to stop a couple of times to pull it out of the muck and slide it back on her foot. Then the others in front of her stopped. The flashlights became steady as they patrolled over what now became clear to be a rippling black surface of a river, the sound of the wind on the water, the water running over the pebbles slightly lapping at the bank where they stood. The boys split off in groups and every now and then there would be a splash and a holler. Sadie stood there next to the young boy, and when the first group returned with a frog speared and spread eagle, her first reaction was to laugh.

The older boy climbed a tree that curled over the water's edge and from there he pointed them out. Then he whistled to everyone's attention. "Oh shit! You think that's him, over in the middle there. That's a long tail. That's a big gator," he whispered down from the branches, hushing the others. They stood there silently, the eyes sitting on the water glistening back like they were charged. And as Sadie's eyes adjusted, the moon spotlighting the river, she could see the muddy banks lined with lily and the dark bowling pin-like backs of two gators resting above the water's surface.

She now held tight to the boy's hand, and the chill that climbed her spine stayed there, sending shrills of excitement and fear through her body. She could see what appeared to be a pier made of mud that ventured fifteen yards into the river, a set of eyes and a tail waded in the water just beyond. She only counted three sets of eyes, after that it seemed somewhat pointless. Those eyes, like little white candles on the water. She thought it pretty for a moment.

Then, as if a great beast and the gust of wind it created lifted her off of her feet, she was thrust towards the water and before she was even wet she had already started to cry. The river bottom seemed to drop out fast, and when she didn't feel the ground directly beneath her she froze in a paralytic panic. Through water-blurred eyes, she could see many of the kids running off and Mary Beth standing where she was, pointing and laughing. The boy who had been holding Sadie's hand was yelling and hitting Mary Beth, until she pushed him down. Sadie sat in the water, fixed in fear, but she soon began desperately turning her head around, thrashing her arms and legs in the water. Then a sudden bansheed burst erupted from her lungs, and the rest of the children ran off for help assuming that she was being eaten. Only Mary Beth stood at the bank, only four or five feet from where Sadie sat bobbing in the water. She wasn't being eaten, but she had felt something brush against her. She began to swim for the bank when Mary Beth jumped in the water and helped pull her up on the shore. Sadie simply clung to the girl, exhausted. She breathed in deep the air, the cool and moist air that made her lungs ache. Sniveling, wet snot hanging from her nose. Shivering, the cotton clinging to her. Her toes curling in the water and mud that clumped on her sandals. She continued to cry but would not let go of Mary Beth's waist, her hair matted down to the sides of her face, her head under the girl's arm. Her blurred vision could only make out a smoky light off in the woods. They stood there for some time before they started to walk away from the river, but when Sadie turned to look back at the water where the sets of eyes had been glaring back, she noticed that they had all disappeared. "Where did they all go?"

"They ran back to Gramms to tell on me for pushing you in."

"No, not them. Where did all the gators go?" Sadie asked.

"You had to of scared the ever living shit out anything in that river when you screeched like you did. I never heard nothing like that. Like something possessed," Mary Beth laughed a little and Sadie couldn't help but smile too, a shivering, teeth chattering smile.

"Do gators eat people?"

"Well, yeah. It don't happen that often though."

"Then why'd you throw me in the water like that?"

"I don't know. I just felt like it. Tommy did it too, wasn't just me," she explained. "Besides, nothing happened."

Sadie held herself from shivering as she walked alongside Mary Beth, just hoping that Mary Beth wouldn't sprint off, leaving her alone under the trees where it was too dark to see where she was. They walked for a few minutes, but the time seemed to stretch with the silence that grew between them. Then Mary Beth put out a hand in front of Sadie's chest, stopping her from going any farther. "Hold on," she said.

"Please, don't leave me out here," Sadie whined.

"I ain't gone leave you, just hold on." Mary Beth carefully kicked at the ground around them, and then it slithered off, rustling in the bushes.

"What was that?"

"Probly a cottonmouth, don't know?"

"Can we please go back?" Sadie said in a desperate tone.

"Where do you think we're going?"

And sure enough they began to pass by cleared lots of broken down cars, many of them with the hoods up and rusted parts and pieces spread over the ground. Some of them didn't have doors and others had the windows broken. Beyond that were the RV's with their front lights on. When Sadie finally began to hear the voices of the others, she started to walk faster. Mary Beth reached out and grabbed her forearm.

"Let go, please," Sadie pleaded.

"Hold on, I just...I'm sorry. I didn't mean it," Mary Beth slurred her words as she let go of Sadie's arm. "You gonna tell on me too?"

Sadie just looked back at the girl's dirty face, how her eyes were underlined with smeared mud, her cheeks dripped gritty carbon. Blanched and sick with fear. She looked past Mary Beth's eyes and shrugged her shoulders and walked towards the voices. When she noticed that Lanier was approaching her, she began to walk faster. He picked her up, and the water from her clothes seeped into his. He held her tight to himself and began to inspect her for anything that might be amiss. She asked him to stop, but he wouldn't. He carried her into one of the little homes that moved as they moved, and she listened to the hollow sound of the floor giving way under each step. The bowed ceiling was close enough to reach up and touch. He set her down and checked her thoroughly, but only found a slight cut and scrape from being pulled ashore. He wrapped her in a towel and told her to go to the bathroom and rinse off. When she came back to the room, Lanier had fresh clothes and a blanket out on the couch for her. But he was not there. She could hear him though, she could hear his hoarse voice, a deep bellied brass voice hissing, raw and cold. She dressed herself with what lay on top and rushed outside to see Lanier holding Mary Beth down on the ground. She was attempting to cover her own face. When Lanier turned to look back at the sound of Sadie approaching, his appearance was something that startled her, almost frightening enough to make her turn and run. But then Sadie focused on Mary Beth, panicking, bobbing there, crying, desperately turning her head, thrashing about. Sadie watched for a moment, something inside of her wanting to laugh at the girl. And for that brief moment, Sadie thought that the girl deserved it, but it wasn't that Mary Beth was being hurt that scared her, it was Lanier's face that scared her. It was that look on his face. It was the same, Sadie thought, the look in his eyes was the same look he had when he came over her in the car, when she almost peed from being tickled. That look was stuck in her mind, and it was so hard to understand. At first, she thought it was just angry, but it was empty, like he wasn't really there when that look was on his face. It was someone else, she thought.

As he doubled his grip on the girl's wrists, Sadie rushed up to Lanier and tried pulling his arm off of her, but she couldn't. Lanier was holding Mary Beth's lower jaw, squeezing it so that her lips puckered out and her gapped teeth stood apparent.

"Stop," she garbled. "Please."

"Stop," Sadie demanded. "Stop it, it wasn't her fault. Stop it. She helped me. Stop..."

"What's your problem Mary Beth," Lanier's face only inches from Mary Beth's, still holding her mouth open, his fingers digging deep into her cheeks, purpling under his grip.

"I'm sorry. I didn't mean it. Promise, I didn't."

"Stop it, please," Sadie pleaded. She grabbed his lower jaw with both of her hands and tried to turn his head to face her. Her eyes alone asked again the same question.

27

At six-thirty in the morning, Corey woke up and would not try to go back to sleep. A dream he did not want to return to waited for him. So he tried to keep his eyes open, but as they closed gently like fluttering coins in water, he could hear the sound of steps climbing the stairs into the den and down the hallway. He could hear his father's voice, a hollow tone floating between the corridor of rooms, singing a silly song that he hadn't heard since he was little. "Reading, writing and arithmetic, da-da-dada, da-tata-ta-da. Let's go boys, early birds, early birds, da-da-dada, da-tata-ta-da." With his eyes closed, the faces he saw in his dream were still there, people he did not know chattering. He pleaded with them for help and forgiveness, a leprous cry. They called him a thief and a fag, a loser and an addict. Most of them girls, beautiful girls, thin oval faces, a laughing piquancy to their eyes, retrousse noses, Florida skin like creamed coffee, their breasts soft dollops behind white linen. His friends were behind him, but they wouldn't say anything. Their heads were down. His father's singing coming closer. Corey would not let himself fall back into that dream completely and forced himself to sit up, and he picked at the scurfy crust under his eyes before he pulled the sheeting from his legs and set his feet out of the bed. He shuffled into the bathroom and turned on the shower, stood in front of the mirror until a faint white plume from the steam spread around the glass. He pulled down the shorts that he slept in, tugged at his withdrawing penis, stepped into the water and sat down on the cold porcelain and let the water shower over him. When his father knocked on the bathroom door, the water was already cold and pooled up the sides of his legs.

"You're not going to have time for breakfast," he said through the door.

Corey came out with a shiver that he couldn't contain. AJ already had his backpack over his shoulder and his hair parted to the side, headphones in his ears and his head bobbing over his shoulders. They followed their father down the stairs and along the breezeway towards the kitchen where Mr. Leavitt had already squeezed a glass jug of fresh orange juice and buttered some toast. Corey watched as AJ smeared jam on a slice and ate it in three large bites, then turned to his father holding a mug of coffee up to his nose, blowing the steam from the surface. A newspaper lay on the table in front of him.

AJ pulled down one of the earphones and asked, "Are you taking us to school today?"

Their father nodded.

"How come?"

Mr. Leavitt sipped from the coffee and looked up from the newspaper. "Because."

"'Cause why?"

"Just because."

"You gonna pick us up after school, too?"

He nodded. "Finish your juice," he said and spooned sugar into his coffee, swirled the spoon, and tapped it against the mug's rim. "Corey, eat something."

AJ finished his juice and poured another half glass and finished that too. Corey rubbed at his eyes with his knuckles and shouldered his backpack. They followed their father into the garage and squinted at the light that crept in from under the rising door.

Corey walked to homeroom, sat at his desk with his head down on his folded arms and listened to the other kids, their voices, sounds bouncing between the four walls. To his right, a boy spitting dip juice into a cup, a softened sound like toes pressing down inside wet shoes. Girls whispering behind him. The teacher at the front of the room sitting on the desk edge, her shoe hanging from her toes, clapping at the bottom of her foot. The pop of gum. The scratch of pencil. Fingernails tacking on a desk. The murmur of voices over voices. When the students were asked to stand the noises fell away, blanketed. He stood and held his hand over his heart and mumbled the pledge of allegiance with the rest of the class. He questioned the unison, the collective voice, how the words left his body without any meaning. He looked away from the sagging flag and studied the faces of his classmates, the blank stares, the repetition like trained dogs. They sat when they were told to sit.

After second period, he felt a bit relieved that Drake still hadn't returned to school and so he asked for a pass to the infirmary. Corey walked out into the yard behind the school and then onto the coarse gravel bed lot of faculty cars, past the sun blistered track, coppered and sunken with rain puddles. Past the wooden bleachers, warped, the paint coming away in scabrous patches. He came to a waist-high fence, crawled between the cross planks and walked out into the field of wiregrass. He looked back, making sure that he wasn't leaving a trail, not flattening the tufts, and saw no one following him. He hunkered between beautyberry bushes, his back against a live oak, and set his bag on the ground between his legs. The school's roof sat over the fields in front of him. He plucked clusters of the shiny, lavender berries from the long, arching branches and tossed them to the ground. He shaved the bark off dead limbs that were scattered at the base of the tree. He thumbed the wheel of his lighter. He did anything to occupy his mind, but nothing seemed to work. He smoked and watched his white breath rise above him, but didn't think that it could be seen from the school. He told himself that he didn't care if it could. As he sat there, the same dream seemed to be waiting for him to fall back to sleep. He could only resist for so long before those girls were there again, laughing at him, pointing. He didn't know what they were pointing at. He looked down, but couldn't see his body there below him. They simply laughed, the laughs becoming softer, distanced. Then a new dream began, a violent dream.

Mr. Leavitt had pulled alongside the curb waiting outside of the school for him, AJ already in the seat behind his father, his head turning from person to person in the small crowd that came out of the high school entrance. Corey lagged behind the exiting herd, his head down and his hands in his pockets. They drove for thirty minutes down 231, one side of the road filled with long, unending pasture, the other sparsely lined with large colonial houses of sunburnt brick, white cornices and columns, bargeboard moldings, red clay driveways. They drove until they were just outside of downtown Marianna. Mr. Leavitt passed the long graveyard on Watford and then pulled directly into the parking lot of a white-washed one story building. He drove under the awning and told the boys to go in while he found a parking spot.

"What is this place?" AJ asked.

"The health clinic."

"Do we have to go in there?"

"Yes, you have to go in there."

"But I feel fine."

"It doesn't matter."

"But."

"Enough buts, just go sign in. Corey take your brother inside."

A set of automatic, tinted black glass doors opened to a reception area, another door with double-paned, chickenwired windows looked into the waiting room. All the chairs in the waiting room faced one way like at a theatre, but the suspense contained behind those doors was much more personal, much more intimate than any film.

"Name and reason for coming." The attendant at the desk said this without turning away from a handful of files. A thick slab glass partition separated her from the boys, but the sound of her thin, gold bracelets clinked and jingled through the opened slide where papers could be passed through.

Corey spoke first, "Corey Leavitt. I need to be checked out."

"Fill this out and bring it to the desk clerk in the next room." She looked up and jutted her neck and pointed her chin towards the door leading to the waiting room. "Next. Name and reason for coming?"

"Abe Leavitt. My brother thinks I need to be checked out, but I feel fine."

"Fill this out and bring it to the desk clerk in the next room."

Mr. Leavitt walked into the clinic, pocketing his keys and checking the pager that was clipped on his belt, following his two boys into the waiting room. The chairs faced another door with a wall clock centered above it. A few women sat rows apart and were the only people waiting. Corey eyed one who was pregnant—her tight, dirty white tank-style undershirt, scarred skin like an orange peel, her nipples stretched and dark through the fabric. Across the room sat a group of children, one lighter than the others, and they crowded in the corner over a bin of toys of snap blocks and ratty dolls. Corey sat down in an empty row, then his father, then his brother. The two boys began filling out the information sheets, the pens pressing hard onto the paper.

"What's my social security number?"

"What kind of insurance do we have?"

"When it says citizenship, what does naturalized mean?"

"What's secondary education?"

"Who should be contacted in case of an emergency?"

"Do we have a history of family illness?"

"What's jaundice?"

Their father eventually took the forms and finished filling them out for them, and they walked them to the desk clerk who spoke with a thick molasses, patois creole voice, "Hey dare, shuggas. How yuh'll doing today?" A gloss to her pocked skin. Her hair in standing waves like black icing. Her backside cascading over the seat she sat on. The cold air rolling out over their arms carrying the smell of grape chewing gum and latex. "Two check-ups for me little studs, huh? Breddas, huh? Can't keep yuh little stance in yuh pants, hey bwais? Well I cain't blame yuh'now."

The boys didn't say anything, but they didn't walk away. They stood there hesitantly with forced smiles.

"Ma'ama Jean'll love yuh no madda. Yuh feel me?"

AJ blushed.

"Yuh two bwais are some 'andsome devils, ain't yuh'nuh? Well, let us see if me can get ya'in and out," she said.

Before the boys were called back together, Corey turned to look at his father who had the pager off of his belt and was putting his glasses on to try and read the number.

"Unnu can come wid me."

As he turned back, he noticed the uncertainty flickering in AJ's eyes like a dying flashlight, but he still didn't speak to his brother to question it. Ma'ama Jean walked them down a hallway to a room that smelled of ammonia, four walls bleached by the white light. She opened cabinets and gathered a few materials from a metal dispenser and put on plastic medical gloves. She drew blood from their arms. AJ let the needle slide in, but Corey jerked at the pressure and watched as the blood drove out of his own arm into the little red-capped tube, how it coated the glass, its thick, syrupy composition. A spell of lightheadedness rushed through him, and when he shook his head trying to remedy the faint, in one swift movement she popped the needle and full tube from his arm and covered the puncture with gauze and a cartoon bandage.

"Now, who's gwaan be first? No volunteer?"

Corey raised his hand from his pocket and said that he would be first.

"Gwaan den youth, stand outside which yuhself. I'll send yuh bredda for ya'inna minute." Once AJ closed the door behind him, she said, "Drop'pem." She then sat down in a rolling chair.

Corey wanted to tell her that he was a virgin, but he didn't, his stare blank and pale.

She repeated herself, "Yuh slacks. Gwaan now. No need for nah trouble. I seen'tall afore." He unbuttoned, unzipped and dropped his pants. "Yuh bottoms too, now." He stared straight ahead and pulled down his boxers. Her fingers, the plastic warmth cradled the undercarriage of his flaccid penis, lifted to inspect the underbelly, examined the base and both sides, and let it fall. She snapped off the gloves, pulling one off onto the other, and threw them in the basket and reached into a few of the cabinets. She pulled out a box of stick-swabs and a little container of liquid and set them down on the thin plate metal workstation. She put on a new pair of med gloves, took a q-tip and dunked it in the liquid and stuck it into Corey's urethra and twisted. He curled away from the initial pressure, his mouth opened and he didn't breathe for a few seconds. She put the swab into a labeled bag and penned the label. "Yuh done leave a contact number on deh form already now?"

Corey nodded.

"Well, we be calling a'soon as the results in. Go on and send yuh bredda in'ere."

Corey stood outside of the door in the hallway and waited for his brother to go through the same ritual. He could hear her soft voice muffled by the closed door. He ran his shoe over snags in the carpet and didn't want to look at the poster of the male's genitalia on the wall in front of him. He didn't want to. He crossed the hallway and put his back to that wall and waited for his brother.

When they walked back into the waiting room, their father stopped pacing and went straight to Corey and grabbed him by the flesh of his upper arm and pulled him out of the consecutive sets of doors. "What? What did I do? What? That hurts. Stop! Jesus Christ! What are you doing?" Corey said in a sharp whisper. AJ followed timidly behind, looked at the reactions of the people in the building who seemed to notice nothing. Corey was pulled all the way to the car and then shoved into the front seat. Mr. Leavitt left black rubber stains from his tires in the parking lot. Walking down the street, people turned and watched him yelling through the closed windows.

"The police...the police are at the house waiting for you. My wife was taken from her tennis lesson, practically swarmed by the damn police. How do you explain that?" He slammed his hand down on the horn, and then darted around the car in front of him. "They're at the house waiting for me to bring you to them. What did you do? Tell me now, and tell me the truth, or it'll be even worse."

"I don't know what I did. What the fuck did I do? I didn't do anything," Corey pleaded.

"You must have done something. They said that they have the painter's kid, Francis Drake; he's at the house and said he told them everything."

"It's probably nothing," Corey said inwardly.

"Corey, cops don't swarm people for nothing."

"But I haven't done anything wrong," he complained.

The rest of the drive home seemed long, quiet, the tension hot like the breath of a panting dog. He imagined what Drake must have told the cops.

As they pulled down their street, neighbors stood on their doorsteps or near their mailboxes and watched what they could of the three cruisers pulled into the driveway and the one alongside the curb out front. Inside, the police stood around Mrs. Leavitt in the kitchen, taking from a box of assorted Danishes. Drake was at the kitchen table sitting down with his face in his hands. Corey walked in behind his father and AJ followed. Drake didn't look up, but everyone else's attention turned towards the doorway. Corey stared at the top of his friend's head, the hair between his fingers, his thin wrists. A few of the deputies sauntered over; one of the officers came up to Mr. Leavitt. He wasn't the oldest, but looked assertive enough to be in charge, Corey thought. There were those shined shoes, and his flocked black hat removed and tucked under his left arm. He put a hand on Corey's shoulder, then asked questions about the man who took the girl.

"I demand to know what the hell is going on." Mr. Leavitt had a fear in his throat, soft and broken, and yet still forceful.

Corey said that he didn't know anything. Drake said that Corey knew, said that he was lying. Corey told Drake to shut the fuck up.

The officer reprimanded him for the language and asked Corey about the drugs, but he wouldn't say anything. Again, Drake said that he was lying. The officer said Corey's entire name and spun him around. He padded down pockets and the boy's chest, under his beltline, between his thighs and inside the tops of his socks. He spun the boy back around and cuffed Corey's wrists in front.

"Now is this necessary? I do happen to know my rights, and the rights of my family. You have to release my son," Mr. Leavitt demanded.

"Can't do that. You see your son…your son and Mr. Drake's son there are now accessories after the fact in an abduction that happened at some point this past Sunday, around three in the afternoon."

"I don't understand. He's fifteen years old for crying out loud. What the hell are you guys thinking?"

"Mr. Leavitt, I'm gonna have to ask you to try and stay composed. Calm."

"No! What do you think? You think that he took somebody. Where do you think he put a person? Under his bead, in his closet. He's just a kid for chrissake. He doesn't even have a car."

"We do have plenty of reason to believe that they are involved, or know about a kidnapping of a seven-year-old girl who lived in this community. Now, her mother is two sips from a nervous wreck. I can't tell you what this must be like for her. And as of right now, we're going off of evidence that these two boys are gonna have to sum up or they could be in for a heap of trouble. Until they can clear theirselves, they are withholding pertinent information, which is a felony in a case of this magnitude."

Mr. Leavitt was already finding the number of his attorney. He fidgeted with his little black book, closed it and went for the kitchen phone.

"Who are you trying to call?" his wife asked.

Mr. Leavitt rifled through his rolodex.

"Are you trying to call Gerald? If you're trying to call Gerald, he's already on his way," she said and he slashed the phone back in its cradle.

"My attorney should be here. You have to at least wait until he gets here so that I can know what I have to do."

"We can wait, that's no problem, but you gonna have to understand that your son is coming with us no matter, at least for a little while. And to tell you the truth I won't be able to tell your lawyer no more than I've ready told you. Not until we're able to fully question these two boys."

They sat Corey down across from Drake, and he wanted to lurch across the table and rip into his friend's thin neck. He imagined it over and over before he shook the thought from his mind. Corey looked over to AJ and could see the worry crack between his brother's bushy eyebrows, the glazed whites of his eyes, the flare in his nostrils. He started clinching his fists, his chest muscles worked tighter, his molars grinding.

"What are you gonna do with my brother?" AJ blurted. "You can't take him, he didn't do anything. He didn't do anything!"

"AJ, go upstairs."

"No, I'm not letting them take him, dad! He hasn't done anything wrong."

Mr. Leavitt kicked one of his cabinet doors and the wood split down the middle, "AJ! God damn it! Go upstairs. I can't handle all this."

"But…"

"Please!" he kicked it again and it snapped in half. AJ lowered his head and walked towards his brother.

Corey raised his cuffed hands up, over his brother who bent down and rested his forehead on Corey's shoulder. "It's all right," Corey said. "Don't worry, I didn't do nothing, and I don't know what the hell they're talking about." And he pressed his lips against the top of his brother's head, and it occurred to him that he had never done such a thing before.

AJ swallowed the lump that was sitting in his throat and wiped at his eyes with the shoulder of his shirt.

"Just go on," Corey told him, and AJ walked out of the kitchen and down the breezeway towards the guesthouse just as the family attorney, Gerald, chimed at the front door.

28

Outside the RV, puddles were widening, giving way to small trenches and little levies of rainwater burrowing through the soft sand. Lanier wasn't watching her when she woke up from her nap but instead was hunched over the sink looking out of the opened window. With his shirt off she could see how long and thin his back was and she stared at the scarred sections of skin that puffed out in stretched blotches like bubble gum. The rain drops that hit the screen in front of him broke into water fragments that spit over his shoulders and chest. She heard the click of his lighter and saw a thick curl of smoke crawl around his face as he sucked in long and hard, his lungs expanding the width of his back. He did it again, and then crumpled up whatever he was holding in front of him and put the lighter in his pocket. She could tell when he turned around that he was surprised to see her staring back at him, with how his eyes worked and how the muscles around his neck tightened. He pulled back out his lighter and grabbed the pack of cigarettes off the countertop and lit one, puffing fresh tobacco smoke into the air.

He had not been shaving and the stubble now stood out from his face, thick at the cheeks and the chin, thin above the lip. His hair was clumped and the oils glistened.

"You see those trees out there?" he asked.

Sadie stood up and came over to him. He lifted her onto the counter.

"You see them?"

She nodded.

"You see those leaves that cover those trees, completely cover them up and down?"

"Yes."

"Those leaves, they aren't a part of those trees."

"They're not?"

"It's a vine, a vine that's killing those trees, did you know that?"

"No."

He sucked on the cigarette, flicked the ashes into the sink basin and blew the smoke out of the side of his mouth away from her. Both of them stared out of the window. He filled a plastic cup with water and gave it to her. She took a long drink from it. He finished what was left in the cup and set it before him. He lifted his head, his small dark eyes intent, and leaned towards the window. He breathed out deeply, the breath like burnt leaves. She yawned, her arms stretched over her head, her fingers netted together. "Do you know where you live Sadie?"

Sadie nodded.

"Where do you live?"

Sadie shrugged her shoulders.

"You know where you live. Tell me," he said.

"Graceville."

"You heard of Chipley, the town next to us?"

Sadie nodded.

"A long time ago, a lady from Chipley thought these leaves where really pretty, so she took them from where they came from and brought them home with her." Lanier cleared his throat and drowned the coal of his cigarette in a bowl of standing water in the sink. A quick hiss. "We never used to have these vines around here."

"Where do they come from?"

"From a far away place, a place much different from here."

"Why did she take them?"

"She didn't think about what would happen, she just wanted to always have these leaves. But then the leaves took over, and she couldn't stop them. She tried to kill them, but they spread like a disease. Do you understand what I mean by disease?"

"I think so," she said.

"Well those leaves spread like a disease without a cure. Over poles, trees, buildings for miles and miles. They even came into her house through her windows, crawled in under the door. They can cover something your size in one night. They hug onto anything they can, loving it, smothering it with love."

"Does it hurt?"

"No, I don't think so."

"Then how does it kill those trees?"

"It kills them with love. Suffocates the life out of them. It doesn't allow whatever it's hugging to breathe or get what it needs to survive."

"Did they kill the lady?"

"No, they didn't kill the lady, just everything she loved around her."

Gramms came up to the RV and opened the door quietly, first looking over to see if Sadie was still sleeping. As the door creaked open, Sadie dropped down from the counter and held onto Lanier's hand. Gramms held something, and Lanier removed his hand from hers and grabbed a towel and followed the lady outside. He told Saide to stay put, so she climbed onto the bed and watched him through the window. He sat in a rusted lawn chair and caped the towel around his neck, covering his chest, shoulders, and back. The lady took her time to bend over and dig out the end of an extension cord from a utility bin, bracing herself with a hand just above her backside. She plugged in whatever she was holding and an audible buzz could be heard. Sadie squinted through the tattered blinds and the grime streaked window as Gramms ran her fingers through Lanier's hair, dropping handfuls at a time.

Sadie slipped on her flip flops and came outside. With a shaved head and a scruffy beard, Lanier appeared much older. His crooked nose looked longer and more crooked without the strands of hair falling down and around his face. He turned to look back at her and Gramms flipped off the switch and dusted off the clipper blades.

"You next, sweetheart?" she asked.

"Uh-uh," Sadie said as she held on to her hair.

"You sure?" she asked and the words lingered in cigarette smoke. "I'm just pulling your yarn, I wouldn't dare lay a hand on that hair. Other than to maybe warsh it. You look like you could use a good clean," and Gramms came over and began to comb through Sadie's curls with a long blade cover and then rubbed at her cheeks with licked fingers that were very rough.

Sadie tried to squirm away, the smell of the spit on her fingers was terrible, but Lanier came up and told her that there was no use fighting it, "She's gonna get you clean."

Gramms walked back into the little home and returned with a towel and washcloth folded over her arm. She reached down and held onto one of Sadie's hands and pulled her along. Sadie initially resisted but then resigned to follow, more interested in watching how this lady walked, as if one leg was just a little longer than the other. Her knees went outwards, and her buttocks were long and flat under her jeans. The ground gave beneath them to muck, and by the time they came to the stall showers, they were both already soaked from the rain. They left on their sandals and rinsed their legs up to the ankles under a spigot.

"What's that?" Sadie pointed towards the lady's right leg.

"What's what?"

"That," and Sadie pointed again, reaching down to touch the soft and colored skin.

"That, I got that when I was very young," Gramms said, looking down at the blurred and blotched remnants of a tattoo. "It was a rose. I must had been sixteen. It's so old now, you can't hardly tell what it is anymore, can you?"

"I think it's pretty."

"Thank you darling, that's very sweet. Now go on and get stripped while I warm up the water." The tiled room was open and empty, gray limed grime in the grouts, a series of shower heads, a lingering odor.

"What's that smell?" Sadie asked and pinched her nose.

"I don't smell nothing."

"It's stinky," Sadie said and peered about to make sure that no one was around. She walked back to the entryway and looked around as well. She heard and saw no one. All she could see were the footprints they had just left being filled with muddy water and washed away in the trail they followed from the little homes in the distance. She turned back and pulled her shirt over her head and removed the sleeping shorts that she had on, leaving on her underwear and crossing her arms over herself. The back of the old lady's hand was under the thin streams of water, the other adjusting the virescent metal handles. The woman's taut grin, lips drained of color, "It ain't gonna stay warm for long."

Sadie bounced on her toes under the threaded stream, her arms still wrapped in front of herself and her eyes closed. The water sat in her hair and then ran over her shoulders and down her back, spattering on the tiles and gurgling down the drain. The hard bar soap and washcloth mixed like lemon rind and dryer sheets. She stayed on her toes, tramping on the tiles, using the cloth to scrub her arms and stomach. Gramms lathered up more soap and bunched up Sadie's curls and began to work the suds throughout. Sadie sucked air in through her clenched teeth when her hair was pulled or tangled in the gold rings on the woman's hands. As she squirmed and tried to get away, Gramms held her firmly by the hair.

"I can do it," Sadie said.

"I just want to make sure you get clean."

"Let me do it." And she could feel the lady's hands pull out of her hair and Sadie let the water dilute the soap until it was gone. She could feel the lady looking at her and was afraid to turn. When Sadie finally turned, a dark-stained beach towel was waiting for her. While she wrapped herself in the towel, two young boys standing on crates stacked four high and staring through the slated vents came crashing to the ground. The noise was enough for Sadie to freeze, terrified, and Gramms hurried outside with a sandal hefted in one hand. The boys were too quick, already forty feet down the trail. Sadie had her clothes on in a matter of seconds, damp patches in the cotton shirt, her wet underwear bleeding through her shorts, and when Gramms came back laughing, saying, "Boys are gone be boys," Sadie wasn't sure if she wanted to cry or smile. The lady took the towel and wrapped it around Sadie's head, squeezing the water from her hair, laughing, and eventually Sadie too began to laugh. "They must think you're awful special, them boys." Sadie simply looked down at the rusted water drain, a dimple set deep beside a half smile.

When she returned to the camp with Gramms, a few of the older boys were already taking bags out of the trunk of Lanier's car and packing up the blanket and the bed and Sadie's other belongings. Lanier came out of one home with Mary Beth and Ma'amMaw following. Ma'amMaw had a long, thin cigarette hanging limply from her lips, a quilt wrapped over her shoulders. Mary Beth reached out for Lanier's hand, but Lanier walked up to Gramms and kissed her scarred cheek, and Sadie grabbed a hold of Lanier's hand before Mary Beth got close enough, looking at the gangly girl mockingly, her tongue between her teeth, her stare direct. Lanier picked up Sadie and swung her around and put her back down. "You ready to keep moving?"

"Where are we going?"

Gramms reached out for Lanier's arm. She held on to his elbow, tightly. "Be careful, I want to see you again."

"I'll be careful grandma, promise."

Ma'amMaw waddled over, small and bent, shrunken mucus blue eyes in the sunlight. She leaned towards Lanier and held her hands out, thin flaps of loose skin hung down from her wrists to her elbows. "Let go of my boy," she said to Gramms. "You know it's real good to see 'yer Butchie. We tend to miss good boys round here. And when you talk to your momma, bet be sure to tell her to come on home."

Sadie held close to Lanier's leg and watched as the adults spoke, wondering when she would see her own mother. It had to be soon. How long had it already been? she wondered.

29

"Wuh-what's g-gonna happen?"

AJ didn't answer.

"Should we-we do any th-th-thing?"

AJ, mute as a cold statue, opened and closed one of his brother's pocketknives. He studied the blade—the broken tip, the shallow bellying arc, the six serrated teeth above the stamped ricasso—and ran the flat of his thumb across the edge and tried to shave the hairs on the back of his knuckle, but the knife was too dull. Standing at the window, he pressed his forehead against the glass, he could hardly see the hedges and rosebushes that ran around the backside of the guesthouse because the rain pattering on the spanish tiles came down in a falling wash in front of him. AJ could hear the shifts of wind in tearing plumes. He closed the knife and ran his fingers over the gloss of the wooden handle. Thin, bare around the rivets. He turned and walked to his bed post and emptied his bookbag on the floor. Papers, pens, sheets of loose leaf and a couple of folders littered down in a flat pile. He pulled the drawers of his bureau open and grabbed a couple of shirts and some socks, some fresh boxers and crammed it all down to the bottom. He tossed in the knife and began to peer around the room. He grabbed two packs of cigarettes and a couple of lighters.

"What are y-ya-you d-dd-doing?"

AJ went to digging around the closet, under shoes and boxes, throwing action figures and stuffed animals aside. He changed into a tattered and ratty pair of sneakers and Fatty followed him out of the room.

The rain continued, an unyielding black sponge in the sky. The breezeway had been under an inch of water for the last three days. As AJ walked into the main house, he put up his hand and motioned for Fatty to stay where he was and to be quiet. He could hear his father yelling. He took off his shoes and glided silently along the tiled floors in his socks, climbed the stairs trying to keep the wood from groaning under his weight. As he passed by the partially opened door of his father's room, he could see his stepmother standing in front of a mirror curling out her hair where it fell to her shoulders, and AJ could see the noncommittal look in her eyes, vacant and unsympathetic. When he came back downstairs, he had the bookbag over his shoulder and was folding a handgun in a shirt.

"Come on."

"Wh-wah-where we going?"

AJ didn't explain. He put the folded shirt into the bookbag, zipped it back up and put it back over his shoulder and dug his feet back into his shoes. Fatty asked again but still did not get a reply. The two boys had on their raincoats and went out the back and got on their bikes. As they were about to pedal away, Fatty stopped and asked a third time, "What the f-f-fuck? Where we g-g-going?"

"I don't know. We're just going."

"I'm a little too old to be r-r-running away."

"We're not running away." AJ stood off of his pedals. "Where do you think he went?"

"Who?"

"Lenny."

"How the f-f-fuck should I kn-know? He could've g-g-gone anywhere."

"How can we find out?"

"I da-d-don't know. If the p-p-police don't know, how are w-w-we sa-sa-supposed to figure it out?"

"If we had to?" AJ turned his bike around and stared into Fatty's face. It was a blank, yet animated face he looked at, as if Fatty didn't understand the thoughts that ran through his own mind, and what he did understand he didn't agree with or want to entertain. The face was soft, simple. The beads of rain sitting on his cheeks. A wet redlined roll of fat around the base of his neck. "What if we talked to Crystal?" AJ said and started back towards the guesthouse.

Fatty hollered after him, "You're nah-nanot t-talking about that ha-hook-kek-ker?"

AJ let his bike fall and jogged back up to the guesthouse and when he came back outside with the number that she had given him, Fatty was huddled against the trunk of the domed magnolia, the elastic strings of his hood pulled and cinched, the oval of his face turned away from the wet wind. AJ pedaled hard through the rain that spit into his eyes, blurring what he could see, the wind parachuting the back of his raincoat and Fatty struggled to keep up. They pulled back their hoods as they came to the canopied walkway that was behind Lenny's house, slowed, could see the front end of a police car out front, the windshield wipers on a slow speed, and stood off of their seats and rode their bikes along the back trails all the way to Fatty's house, driving hard through the puddles and lifting the front tires of their bikes over the gnarled branches fallen along the path. They pushed under the trumpet vines and in between the privet hedges, and AJ could see the paired chimneys and low-pitched roof of Fatty's house. They idled down the slight slope of grass and AJ lifted his leg over and ran alongside the bike before he let go of the handles, the front wheel still spinning as the frame teetered on the pedal digging down into Fatty's backyard. AJ leaped the two steps onto the spindlework trimmed porch, took off his backpack and his raincoat and set them on the seat of one of the rocking chairs, and waited for Fatty to open the back door.

Fatty's mother called out, "That you Jarvis?"

"Yes m-m-ma'am."

"Take off your shoes," she hollered down the stairs.

"O-k-kay."

"Did you hear me? I said take off your shoes."

"I h-h-heard you," he hollered back.

The boys pulled off their shoes and walked across the living room into the foyer where the oil luster of a tall family portrait hung in the yellow chandelier light. AJ could hear her coming down the stairs and he walked out from behind Fatty and forced a smile as she appeared, her hand bracing the curving banister. She stopped at the middle of the flight. "Oh, hello Abraham." The way she always called him by his full name made him feel unwanted, like when people called their mothers, mother, instead of mom. It was a cold distance. She held tight the lapels of the dark robe, embroidered, and had a towel turbaned around her hair, the scent of her perfume spilled down the stairs like gin, a mix of cloves and juniper berries. "Jarivs, I've told you a hundred time, you need to let me know if you plan to have your little friends over," she said, and then stopped abruptly. "Nevermind, it doesn't matter. I don't have time for this. You're gonna have to order dinner if you're staying here. Your father and I are meeting with the Lafferty's tonight."

"O-k-kay," he said.

"You're welcome to come," she said as she started back up the stairs, holding the front of her robe closed.

"No th-thanks," he crossed the hall into his room, a room that jutted out of the side of the house with three windows, one facing the cul-de-sac in the front, one out to the side, and one facing the backyard. AJ sat down on the edge of the bed and rolled up the wet ends of his jeans and watched Fatty open his closet door and change into a different shirt. Stretchmarks spread out near his underarms and around his waist, like poorly stitched torn skin. He looked away when Fatty turned to him. A Georgia Bulldogs poster on the back of the door. Model airplanes on floating gallery shelves. A signed, wooden baseball bat in the corner. He looked back to Fatty and told him to fill a bag for a night. Fatty put in rolling papers and a bag of dope, a couple of chocolate bars and packs of licorice, and then put in some dry clothes. AJ pulled the paper with the number out of his pocket and held it in his hand and began to read it aloud. He held onto Fatty's phone and started to dial. As the first beeps sounded, he punched in the return number and then listened for the confirmation beeps. Fatty rolled a joint and they sat in his room with the side window open, the rain coming down at a slant, the sound of thunder off in the murky distance. It took twenty minutes before the phone rang, and they sat there staring at it for a moment.

"What are you g-g-gonna say?"

"I don't know?"

Then the phone stopped ringing. It was only a few moments before it rang again, and this time Fatty swallowed hard and answered it, "Hullo?"

"Somebody paged me," the voice was raspy, humid.

"Give me the phone," AJ said as he pulled it away from Fatty's ear. "Is this Crystal?" he asked.

"Who is this?"

"This is AJ. I met you the other night."

"This the little rich boy? Already looking for more?"

"I need to see you."

"I don't have a ride and I'm a ways off."

"I can meet you somewheres."

"How much do you have?"

"How much?" AJ pulled the phone down to his chest and asked Fatty how much money he had. Fatty shook his head. AJ put the phone back to his mouth and said, "Got a little more than a hundred."

"Take the bus to the station in Dothan. Page me when you get there."

AJ hung up the phone and looked at Fatty. "We need to get some money."

Fatty was taking the last few pulls off of the joint and choking it back with a worried brow. "I du-don't have any m-m-money."

"You could swipe some from your parents."

"I don't n-n-know about this, AJ."

"Come on. We got to do something."

"S-ss-still, how are wha-w-we ss-supposed to do something?"

"It's easy. We find Crystal and she can tell us where Lenny is. Then we tell the police and then they'll let Corey go."

"How do you kna-know they'll let K-kek-Corey go? Besides, how d-d-do you know she's even ga-gonna t-t-ell us where La-lenny is? What if she d-d-doesn't na-n-know?"

"I don't know. But we gotta try."

"But…"

"Fuck man, what else are we gonna do?"

"I d-d-don't know."

"Please, just do this with me?"

AJ and Fatty walked out of the room and down the hallway into the kitchen. His mother's purse was on the counter, the mouth of it opened like scallop shells. AJ stood with his eyes on the bottom of the staircase as Fatty undid the clasp of her wallet and pocketed the cash he could find. "I'll b-be b-b-back later," Fatty called up the stairs towards the hum of a hairdryer. They walked to the back porch and stepped into their shoes, and the two boys got back on their bikes and headed for the bus stop outside of the community. Thunder clapped all around them, making their heads sink between their shoulders. The man at the gate sat in the office with his feet up on the desk, his hat pulled down over his eyes. AJ's bookbag bounced on his back as he took his bike up into the snakeweeds, pedaling hard at a half stand through the murky mud-fogged prairie. Dozens of long-winged pasture grasshoppers leapt into the air around them, blurs of green, some yellow with black stripes, some with red markings. When AJ came to the sheltered bus stop, one had clung onto the shoulder of his raincoat, and he had to pull it away by pinching together both hind legs at the bend. The banded wings fluttered against his fingers. He tossed it against the glass back wall and watched it fall to the ground. It righted itself and hopped back into the glass.

When the bus driver pulled into the station, they stepped off the bus with their backpacks hanging at their sides and unhooked their bikes from the front of the bus and walked them up onto the sidewalk. AJ left his bike with Fatty and walked inside the station. He looked around the creamed pink cinderblock walls, at the two water fountains between the bathroom doors, the smell of stale air coming down from a ceiling vent. He asked for change from the woman who stood behind the counter, and then he used the payphone to page Crystal. He sat in one of the linked honeycomb seats and waited for the call. Fatty eventually rested the bikes against the glass doors where they could see them from inside and came and sat next to AJ and pulled out one of his chocolate bars.

"Wh-what t-t-time is it?"

"Little after seven."

"I'm hu-hungry."

"You're always hungry."

The rain clouds had already been here, and the cars ran through the puddles that lay at the side of the road sending arcs of water up onto the sidewalk. They sat by the phone for close to an hour before it rang and when AJ picked it up, it was a man calling for another man. AJ just hung up the phone and paged Crystal again. It only took another ten minutes for them to get the call.

"Crystal?" he asked as he put the phone to his ear.

"Who's this?"

"It's AJ again. I'm down here at the station. Where are you at?"

"I can't be down there for an hour or two."

There was a pause, and he could hear the scratch of cotton and a spell of buckling coughs.

"Tell you what, there's an old motel in Midland City just outside of Dothan. By bus, should only take you ten, fifteen minutes. I can meet you at the church near the bus stop and we can go down to the motel. I'll be there around nine, or later." She hung up the phone.

AJ didn't speak, he simply held the phone to his ear until the tone went and the recorded operator asked him to hang up and try again. He cradled the phone back into the receiver and walked back to the counter and asked when they could get a bus to Midland City. The lady said that it would be cheaper if they went down a little ways to Foster Street and followed that into downtown and got on the city bus, said that one came every half hour until about nine.

"How do I get to Foster Street?" he asked.

"Got to go down to Dutch Street, which curves into Duke Street, take a right on Selma and a right on Foster."

"Dutch, Duke, Selma and Foster?"

The lady nodded.

The two pedaled on down the road and Fatty turned off at the first fast food restaurant they came to and Corey skidded his back tire to a sliding stop, lifted the front of his bike around and came back. They both laid their bikes where they could see them and walked inside. The door chimed as they entered. No one was inside the restaurant besides the staff behind the counter, two women bagging food and a young boy cradling a basket of fries into the oil.

"Can I take your order?" One of the girls said after she handed a bag of food out of the drive-thru window and came to the register. She had a long patch of white tipped pimples on her dark skinned forehead, framed by long, thin s's of black hair pressed flat along her temples and in front of her ears.

"I'll have a ch-cheeseburger and a large fa-fr-fry."

"Anything to drink?"

"Large orange s-sa-ssoda."

"For you?"

"The same," AJ said.

"Can I also g-g-get a c-couple of ch-cheeseburgers to go?"

"How many?"

"How m-many you th-think AJ?"

"I don't know, whatever man? Get what you want."

"Th-three. No f-ff-four."

"That all?"

"Yeah." Fatty straightened out the money for the food and placed it on the counter as she turned back and filled the soda cups.

AJ stood with his arms crossed, leaning against the counter's edge, and watched an old man outside, his back bent like the crook of a finger. The old man stood near the bikes but was turned away from them. His clothes like rags, patched together, the creaselines on the back of his sun-leathered neck filled with coal black soot. AJ went outside with his soda and stood over the bikes and smoked a cigarette.

The man raised his eyes and turned to him, "You got anothern of those?" Tucked under the crook of his arm was a folded sheet of cardboard, torn ragged around the edges.

AJ lifted his head towards the voice, looked at him for a moment weighing the man in his mind, and held out the opened pack.

The man was missing a finger, the others flat-tipped and slightly shaking as he reached for a cigarette from the pack and lifted it to his mouth, the tip of his nose shifting right and then left above his neglected and filthy beard. He looked scared and AJ wondered if that was how he got people to give him things. He wondered if that was how this man was still alive.

"Got a light?"

AJ sparked the lighter for him and put the pack back into the pocket of his bookbag.

"Ain't you a lit young to be smoking these things?"

AJ didn't say anything, he just smoked his cigarette and sipped from his drink until Fatty came out with a few fries poking out of his mouth and a paper bag of burgers in one hand, his soda in the other. Fatty sat down on the curb next to his bike and pulled out a burger and handed it to AJ. He stubbed his smoke and sat down next to him. The old man turned every few moments and watched the boys eating their food, AJ eyeing him as he did so.

"You guys got any spare?"

"F-fuck off old ma-m-man."

AJ laughed.

The old man sucked the cigarette down to the filter and rubbed it out on the concrete. He lifted a plastic grocery bag and his cardboard sign that read, Jesus loves you, and looked over at Fatty eating a second burger before he walked on down to the corner of an intersection and stood there with the sign held over his sunken midsection. Fatty finished AJ's fries and tucked the last few burgers into his backpack and they both shared a cigarette before they straddled the bikes. "So, what's the d-ddeal?"

"We're gonna meet her in an hour or so down at this old church."

"A cha-ch-ch-chruch? That's a little ff-fafucked up, don't you think?"

"Whatever."

"Where's the ch-church?"

"She said Midland City."

The boys mounted their bikes and glided the declining sidewalk along Foster Street into downtown. When they stopped at Main Street, they could see the bus leaving and they had to wait another half hour for the next one to come. A woman with a baby curled up at her shoulder sat on the bench in front of the bus sign, and AJ asked if this was where they needed to catch the bus to Midland City. She nodded, without taking her eyes off of the infant's sleeping face.

The bus stopped a quarter mile down from the church. From the distance, AJ could see the steeple, the dark brick, the length of the building. Either a statue or a man standing outside. As the boys rode on past, AJ could see that it was a man who wore a clerical collar and black clergy shirt with short sleeves. His hand braced the middle of his back, the stone grey eyebrows above dark slits following them along the road. The man raised his other hand and Fatty waved back to him and AJ kept pedaling. The boys let their bikes down in the tall weeds before a retention ditch and jumped across and walked up to a wire fence that lined the road. There wasn't anything else along the road. Endlessly rolling pasture, kneehigh beggar's tick and yellow wildflowers, the solid dark of pines in the distance. They tossed their packs over the fence and squeezed between the barbed wire and held up in an open lot and waited.

"You th-think it's s-safe to light up here?"

"Probably."

Fatty pulled out his bag of dope and crumbled pot into his palm and then rolled up an emptied cigar and they sat on their backpacks, their feet on the ground, and passed it back and forth until it was gone. The clouds overhead darkened as they waited. They were surrounded by the chirping creaks of crickets.

"Wah-what do you th-th-think Drake and Ke-ke-Corey are doing right n-now?"

"I don't know."

"You th-think they're all r-ra-right?"

"I don't know."

"They're pa-probably d-d-doing okay, d-don't you tha-think?"

"How would you be doing if you were arrested?"

"I'd pa-p-probably b-be p-pretty scared." Fatty went to rolling another. "What if she d-d-doesn't ke-come? Then what d-do we d-d-do?"

"I don't know."

"We ke-ke-can't just st-t-stay out here."

"She'll come."

"She m-may not."

"She will."

Fatty swallowed hard and said, "All right."

AJ looked at his watch and it was close to nine and if what the woman at the bus station said was true there wouldn't be many more buses coming along. "She'll come."

"What d-do you tha-think it's like in j-j-jail."

"It probably fucking sucks. It's a cage. I'd probably rather die than be stuck in a cage. I bet you can't do nothing. Just sit there. If you do something wrong, they probably beat you up. And if you fight back, it's just got to make it worse."

"You tha-think anyone's b-b-beat up Corey or D-dd-drake?"

"Probably."

"Corey b-better not try to b-b-bite anyone in there like he bit you."

AJ looked over and smiled. They both laughed. Even after AJ stopped laughing, Fatty continued to laugh, and then he stopped for a second and then laughed even more.

"What's so funny?" AJ asked.

"N-nnothing."

"Why are you laughing so hard?"

"You won't tha-think it's f-f-funny."

"What?"

"I don't know. You tha-think men really have s-ss-sex with each other in j-jail?"

"I don't know."

"If Corey really is g-gay, then he may never want to la-l-leave."

"That ain't fucking funny," AJ said, but he did laugh.

"I told you you wouldn't tha-think it was f-ffunny."

When a cab pulled out front of the church, the boys stood to watch who would get out. It was her, wearing the same raincoat she had on the other night. They could see her looking around, her hand on the opened door of the cab. When she noticed the boys coming, waving to her, she closed the door and put her hand up.

The boys stuffed their bags and stacked their bikes in the trunk and the cabbie bungeed the trunk door down. They drove down the road until it forked and they kept on, heading towards a strip town lined with light posts. They first passed a gas station, the windows boarded with plywood. The words KEEP OUT! were spray painted on each of the planks. They passed a Dollar General convenience store with old black men sitting on folding chairs out front. The cab pulled into the lot of the motel and up to the center office.

Crystal turned in the front seat and faced the boys, "You got money for the cab?"

AJ looked at Fatty. He gave the driver the money and pocketed the change.

"You're supposed to tip him," she said.

"How m-m-much?"

"A couple of dollars."

He reached back into his pocket and held a couple of dollars over the man's shoulder. "S-ss-sorry."

The cabbie nodded and stepped out of the car and unloaded the trunk.

"You boys are gonna have to pay for the room, too."

"How m-much?" Fatty asked.

"Don't know, imagine no more than forty."

Fatty pulled out two twenties and handed them to Crystal, and they waited for her to come back out with the key to the room. They headed down to the end of the flat, street-side motel. The lights on the sign only lit up a few of the letters. Only one car sat in the lot and it looked as if it hadn't moved in weeks. As they walked by it, AJ could see that oil had puddled under the car and stained the rainwater and one of the side mirrors hung by string.

As they entered the room, a musk of mildew and smoke sat in the air and Crystal went straight to unzipping her coat and pulling back the thin hair on her head. Her black gums stood out as she smiled towards them.

"I wanted to ask you something," AJ said.

She took off her sports bra and her breasts pointed down at the corners. She pulled off the jeans she was wearing and then the underwear. She stood in front of them for a few moments waiting and then walked into the bathroom and turned on the shower.

"I need to talk to the guy who set you up with us. You know how I could get a hold of him? Where he might be?" AJ asked through the half-shut bathroom door.

"Be out in a minute, honey."

He could hear a lighter sparking in the bathroom, but as he tried to look in at the mirror, it was fogged so that he could only make out the dull glow of the flame coming and going and the smeared outline of her frame. The boys sat on the edge of the bed and waited for her to get out of the shower, and when she did, she still didn't cover herself, but simply rubbed the towel at sections of her body and went to standing there naked drying her hair. "Now, what did you ask me?"

"I need to see Lenny."

"I don't know any Lenny," she said.

"Goddammit AJ," Fatty blurted.

"Lenny is the guy that set us up with you."

"Oh, Lenny, okay. That Lenny," she said and then dropped the towel to the floor. "What for?"

"My brother, he's in trouble and I needed to talk with Lenny. See what he could do."

"If *Lenny* ain't around, then there ain't no telling where he is."

"M-mman, f-ffuck, what are we g-ggonna do now?"

"There's nowhere you might think we can find him?" AJ asked.

"Is this what you guys called me out here for? To talk?" she asked.

"I just wanted..." AJ started.

"Well, it's your money. It's all the same to me." The small scars that lined her belly were soft pink and the hair that came up from between her legs dripped beaded water onto the ground.

Fatty watched with a vigorous intent, "I cc-could f-ffuck you ag-ggain."

"Listen," AJ said, "we just need to know where we can find him, that's all."

"I told you, there's no telling."

AJ went to his backpack, both hands buried within, and started to unfold the shirt, one hand cradling the handle of the gun. Crystal watched out of the corner of her eye and AJ hesitated. "Either you tell us or we call the police on you."

"I told you already."

AJ looked into his bag and held the gun's handle, ready to pull it out. He imagined how much trouble he could get into for pointing a gun at someone, but then he wondered if he would really get in that much trouble since she was just a hooker, and again he hesitated as Fatty edged closer to Crystal's leg.

"How much money you got?" she asked.

"Not much."

"I gg-got s-some."

"How much you got sugar," she asked with a pouted smile towards Fatty.

"About a h-hunnerd."

"I'll tell you what. You give me fifty and I'll tell you where you might be able to find him. How's that? There's no guarantee that he'll be there, but he might."

"F-for that, do I get to f-ffuck you too?"

"Can't see why not."

AJ put down his bag and stepped out of the room and kneeled alongside his bike, watching the lightning section the sky off in the distance. The light posts that lined the road flickered and nothing or no one came or went. He smoked two cigarettes while he waited, practicing pulling the smoke from his mouth through his nostrils before he inhaled. His brother had told him that was how the French did it. Even without Corey there, AJ was still intent on impressing his brother. As soon as he took care of this mess and his brother was home, he was going to show him what he could do.

When AJ did come back inside, Fatty was in the bathroom, and Crystal was rolling a joint from their bag. "So where can we go to find him?" he asked.

"I told you, he might not be around," she said and then went to the bed stand and started to write down some directions on the pad that lay by the phone. "There are two places that you can go looking for him. But you ain't gonna be able to get there on a bike."

Crystal sat and smoked and when the joint was half gone, she spit in her hand and put it out and put what was left in a change purse. A cab had pulled out front and honked twice, and she left the room with the boys sitting on the bed.

"We g-g-gonna stay here to-n-night? It's alr-r-ready pr-pre-pretty late."

"Might as well."

"Why d-d-didn't you wah-want to f-f-fuck her?"

"Just didn't."

"You ain't tah-turning g-g-gay like you br-brother, are you?"

"Shut the fuck up?" AJ yelled and grabbed Fatty's collar, a poised clenched fist.

"D-dude, what the f-fuck? I was j-just ka-k-kidding."

"It's not funny."

"I kna-kn-know, but still. For ff-fafuck's sake dude."

AJ let go, dropping his fist to his side.

"I don't e-even kna-know what L-La-Lenny l-looks like, do you?"

"I've seen him before. I'd be able to recognize him."

Fatty slumped down on the floor, the bag of dope and a plastic-sleeved cigar on his lap. AJ went to the window to open the blinds and look around, and came back to the television in the center of room, but all of the channels were either lined or fuzzed. He stood to fiddle with the antenna, but nothing came to. He turned the set back off and sat on the foot of the bed.

PART THREE

A HOLE OF NO BEGINNING OR END

30

Lanier had traded out cars again before they left, this time with one of his cousins whom he had given most of the meth. He sat in the car and looked over at Sadie. She didn't look like his sister anymore. He kept looking at her. He didn't know what he saw. It was something he had never seen before. It scared him. He was looking at God. He was sure of it.

"What's wrong?" she asked.

He hadn't said anything in hours. He could feel the last of the crystal wearing thin in his veins, and he was becoming very tired, the kind of tired that sits in every joint and ligament, the tired that pulls down on your forehead and sores your throat. He couldn't remember when he had slept last, really slept. Even when he pulled to the side of the road and put the car in park, he sat there in his seat with his hands holding the wheel and his head bobbing and drooping with sleep. He couldn't look at her. A pressure was building in him, a suffocating pressure that he didn't know how long he could handle. He kept thinking about the sacrifice, and when he thought about how he would kill her, the muscles in his back would tighten. He was starting to truly believe that nothing could save him. The scent of her filled his nose and sat on the back of his tongue. He closed his eyes, the cries of his little sister panged between his ears.

"I need to go to the bathroom," she said.

He didn't respond.

"Are we gonna get some food?" she asked.

He didn't answer. He simply stared ahead, his eyes wanting to close.

She asked again with her arms crossed.

He was chewing on his bottom lip.

"I want to call my mom," she said.

"She's not home."

"I don't care. I want to try."

"There's no way."

Sadie was kicking out her feet against the door of the glove compartment. He paid no attention at first, so she began kicking harder.

"Quit it," he said.

"No."

"I said, quit."

"I want my mom."

"You'll be with her soon."

"How soon?"

"Soon enough."

"I don't want to sit in the car anymore."

"There's not much further, so please stop whining and stop kicking." The veins in his hands were showing, the reddening of his palms against the steering wheel. "Do you want to get out here? I'll let you out here…"

Sadie stopped still, her curls dancing down in front of her face, her eyes tucked under her forehead.

When they eventually drove off, she turned to look out of the window at her side and the tall grass and the road became a blur, the sound of the engine humming and vibrating the car. They drove for a while before a loud pop sounded and the car began to slow and wobble, and Lanier pulled the car back to the shoulder. Sadie sat very still as Lanier breathed deeply and banged the steering wheel with his fists. He pulled himself out of the car and opened the trunk and grabbed the duffel and as he came to her side he kicked the side panel. He opened her door and undid her seatbelt, pulling her out. Lanier reached for her hand and held it tightly in his. He got down on his knees in front of her. He looked into her eyes. The eyes of God, he thought. He could tell the eyes held fear—but not a fear of him, more of a fear for him. He begged for forgiveness. "Please," he pleaded. "I'm sorry. God I am so sorry."

She asked what was wrong with him.

"I'm just aggravated, so aggravated." He stopped and looked down the road. "I'm sorry. I know that…" No one was coming from either direction. "I'm just so aggravated. Everything seems to be falling apart. Nothing is going right. I'm sorry. Don't be scared. God, I'm gonna make this right. I'm gonna fix this. I just…"

She hugged him. A soft and warm embrace. Both of her little hands holding his shoulder blades.

He picked her up and put her on his shoulders, and walked along the side of the road. It was at least a mile before the first car passed, and Lanier waved it on. He decided to leave the road and cross into a field—towards a long waist high fence lined with barbs and honeysuckle. In the distance, there were cows and even further was the shiny tin roof of a tall house, and banisters of a wrap around porch, and the closer they got, Lanier could eventually see the red brick and white columns.

She asked why there were so many fences.

He said that people tried to protect what they believed was theirs. "But people don't own this," he said. He kicked at the ground. "You know who owns this?" he asked.

"Who?" she asked, looking down at the passing ground.

"You do. This is all yours," he said.

He kept in that direction, looking back every few moments, and she watched as well, but no one was coming. They could no longer see the road behind them. Birds perched waiting for night, squirrels darted through dead leaves with acorn husks, mosquitoes buzzed around their bodies and the looming humidity was like wading through low-laying clouds. When they reached the house, Lanier had sweat through his shirt and sweat lined his face, dripped from his short, patchy beard and glistened on his arms. He knelt down and set her on her feet. He found a spigot at the side of the house and began to drink from it, still holding her hand in his.

"Stay here, and I'll go see if anyone's home. See if you can use the bathroom. See if we can get some food. Maybe call your mom…maybe get some help for the car."

There was a new pick-up around the side of the house, a chicken roosted on the hood. The white picket fence strode out along the hills into the distance. There was nothing but tilled ground, hills, and tall pines in all directions. Lanier had his hands in his pockets as he came up to the back door. He knocked softly, then tried the knob. It was unlocked, but the door creaked at the hinges as he slowly opened it and an elderly man was already making his way towards him. He was a broad shouldered man with thick-rimmed glasses, the glasses a yellowed tint. His thumbs lined the suspenders he wore, and his slacks had fresh creased pleats. Lanier stopped under the door frame.

"Can I help you young man?"

"God, I hope so." Lanier continued inside and closed the door behind him.

"You shouldn't just waltz into someone's home like that without asking first."

"I know, I'm sorry, but it is a bit of an emergency."

"What's the trouble, son?"

"Our car broke down, and my little girl is awfully hungry and needs to go to the bathroom. Well, it's getting late and I was hoping that we could stay here the night and get the car taken care of in the morning and be on our way. I have money." Lanier began to pull out his wallet.

"We don't need your money," he said; then the man called up the stairs to his wife. There was no answer. He called again, much louder. She came to the head of the stairs and looked down at the two men, her husband and Lanier looking up to her. The way her eyes widened and her mouth opened, Lanier knew something was wrong.

"Mother," he said to his wife. "We gonna have company tonight. Can you make up a room for this young gentleman and his daughter?"

Her eyes were fixed on Lanier.

The man grasped onto the railing of the stairs and started to make his way up. He looked back to Lanier and told him that she was a bit hard of hearing. He took his time, and Lanier watched as he braced himself up each stair, leaning heavily on the rail, his left leg bending awkwardly out with each step up. Lanier watched the old man take the final step and leaned in to speak to his wife.

She spoke very loudly, even with her husband right next to her.

"Doesn't he look awful familiar?" she said.

"Not to me," he said softly back.

"I known him, Father. Not sure from where, but I seen this man before." She spoke so loudly to her husband that Lanier could hear her perfectly.

Lanier started up the stairs. He had his hands in his pockets, one holding the pocketknife.

"That's him. Oh dear, dear God."

"Who's him?" he asked, his back turned to Lanier.

She studied him as he came up the stairs. "Charles, that's the man on the news, I'm sure of it," she said and turned away from the stairs in panic.

Lanier clicked open his knife and cradled it against the old man's neck.

"Now son," the man said, walking carefully in front, "just calm down. There's no reason to do something you'll regret."

"Regret. Regret! Poor choice of words *father*. I live in regret. I am the embodiment of regret. I am regret incarnate." Lanier moved the man into one of the rooms with the woman. He was terrified that they would scream and Sadie would hear and either run in the house or run away. But they must have been too afraid or too exhausted, because they just sat there, together. He was so tired that even the knife felt heavy. The man held onto his wife's hand. They said that they had money, that they were old, that they were sorry. Then they began to pray.

"Why are you sorry?" Lanier asked them. "I'm the one who's going to hell. I'm the one who should be sorry. And I am, I am sorry."

When he popped his head out the front door, he told Sadie that no one was home and to come inside. She was sitting in the tall grass, plucking the petals off of daisies that grew in wild patches. She came up the porch steps and he held out his hand for her and she took it. He walked her around the bottom floor until they found the bathroom and when she was done, she followed him into the kitchen. He began to go through the pantries and the icebox. He pulled out meat, jarred peaches and green beans. He said that there was ice cream. He lifted her up onto the counter and set the frozen meat under the running tap.

"Whose house is it?" she asked.

"This is God's house," he said.

"Do you think He'll mind that we're taking His food?"

"What do you think?"

"I don't think He'll mind."

"Then He probably won't mind."

"What about the people who live in God's house?"

"What do you mean?"

"Do you think they'll be mad if they come home?"

"I don't think so," he said.

Before and after dinner, Lanier said a prayer and Sadie bowed her head and held her hands together. They ate fried steaks and green beans, and peaches with ice cream. Lanier hadn't eaten that much in quite some time, so he knew that the drugs were leaving his system. When he brought Sadie upstairs, he walked her down the hall, away from the room with the bodies. He warned her not to go in that first room. "There's something evil in that room. Something no little girl should ever see."

"What?" she asked, both scared and enticed.

But he couldn't think of what would scare her enough to not go in there. He was going to say a dead cat, or an elderly couple with their throats cut, or that behind that door was hell. He was going to tell her the story of Adam and Eve, or the story of Hansel and Gretel. He brought her all the way down the hallway and told her that there was a long, dark hole with no bottom in that first room. It was a hole that lured little girls with chocolate and flowers, kittens and magical fairies, with princess promises and lost puppy dogs. He said that the hole knew what would bring the little girls closest, and once they were too close the hole would swallow them. The hole would be so deep that no girl could ever get out, and no one could help them once the hole had them. He said that he had only heard of these holes before, but this was the first one that he had ever seen with his own eyes.

She followed him into one of the other rooms and asked, "How did you know what it was when you saw it."

"Because the same kind of hole took my sister when we were kids."

"If you never seen one, how do you know that it took your sister?"

"When I walked in that room, it said that it had my little sister. It said that I could never have her back." He walked her to the tub, and he filled it for her.

"What did you do?"

"I started to climb down the hole, but it became cold and slippery and very dark. And the farther I went the more that I knew I would never be able to get back out and be with you."

"Then what did you do?"

"I prayed, and God told me to get out now while I still could. And that's what I did."

"It didn't swallow you because you're not a girl?"

"I think so."

As she bathed, he lay in the bed and it wasn't long before all that tired took over.

31

She sat in the tub until her fingers wilted, until the water was cool. She imagined what was in that room. She imagined the large hole where little girls fell through and couldn't get out. But she knew that it was just a story. She knew there was no such hole. She knew it, but had to see. She could hear Lanier breathing deeply, a slight snore coming from outside of the bathroom. Through the cracked door, she could see his feet crossed on the bed. She climbed out of the tub and dried herself off, then quietly put on the same clothes that she had had on before.

She stood next to Lanier, watching him sleep. Something told her to curl up next to him, but something else pulled her towards that first room. Maybe it was real, she thought. She leaned into him, the beating of his heart like something trying to break free. She placed the small of her hand onto his chest and took a fistful of his shirt, burying her face between his arm and ribs. She could feel his heart kissing her cheek over and over, slow and steady. He didn't move from his sleep. There were no voices, only the sounds of raindrops beginning again, tinkering on the tin roof.

She walked softly out of the room and down the hallway. There were photos framed along the wall. Fancy frames of dark red wood. An old man and a woman sitting in front of him, his hands on her shoulders. There was a picture of a young boy with his hair parted. A picture of two young men holding a long fish together. A picture of a woman in a long white gown. She was cutting into a tall cake. A man in uniform, a fancy hat slightly cocked to one side. Sadie followed the pictures, past the stand with the white doily, past the staircase. She stood with her hand on the doorknob of that first room. Something pulled her, something told her to go inside. Maybe it was real, she thought.

She opened the door. She saw what she was not supposed to see. Their gaping necks, the blood like aprons down their shirts, them sitting in their dark pools. At first, she thought that she should go tell Lanier, but then she realized that he must have known; then she saw his pocketknife sitting on the bed, the bone handle, the blood smeared on the sheets. Once she was outside in the rain, in the dark, the tall wiregrass like black hair, she ran. She ran, and when she fell on her hands and knees and her shoe came off, she left it and continued to run. The rain had soaked her clothes, the mud splash covered her, spit on her face as she splashed through muck. She wouldn't look back. She came to the first fence and crawled through the crossplanks. The fear dizzied through her, kept her pulsing forward. The next fence was barbed, and as she struggled through, it snagged a wet curl of her hair, scraped her along her forearm and across her ankle. Once she was free, there was another fence and she didn't know how long she could run, but she knew that was what she should do. Run.

32

Corey sat in an office and watched the clock. The office had stacks of paper on the desk and file cabinets lined the wall. A corkboard on the wall behind the desk held various pictures, notes, and a calendar marked with red pen. He had been sitting there long enough to watch the little hand on the clock move almost halfway around the circle, his foot digging into the carpet, his hands in his lap. A camera was positioned in the ceiling corner and he didn't care to look into it. He just sat there, glancing from the clock to the carpet to the corkboard to the desk to the door—as if the pattern was uncontrollable—to where his neck began to ache. When the door finally opened and a man in a dark blue button down and grey slacks walked in, he only saw the cold glimmer of the badge positioned on his belt. The man walked around behind Corey and came up and squatted in front of his hands.

"You going to do anything stupid if I take these cuffs off?"

Corey shook his head. "No."

"No, what?"

"No, I'm not gonna do anything stupid."

"No, I'm not going to do anything stupid, what?"

"No, sir," Corey said with his eyes looking at his wrists.

The officer pulled keys from his pocket and unlocked the cuffs and held them in his hand and sat on the edge of the desk. "Now, your friend already told us his side of the story and he's already on his way home. If you cooperate, you'll be in the same boat as him. If you don't cooperate, and your story is different, then you could be here for a while. It's up to you."

Corey nodded.

The man drooped his head down and caught Corey in the eyes. "Do you understand?"

"Yes," Corey said. "Sir."

"You might as well start at the beginning. Tell me how well you knew this man. Tell me everything you know about him. When did you meet him first? How did you contact him? How often did you see him? Everything, understand?"

Corey nodded, "Yes, sir."

The officer sat on the edge of the desk, his hands together on his lap. "Go ahead then."

He had sun-burned cheeks and skin on his nose had begun to peel away. He was a handsome man, Corey thought. The tall, muscular country kind of boy that the girls at his school preferred. Corey hated him for that, and he hated himself for noticing. He swallowed hard and tried to think of what to say, what to start off with. He was thirsty, but didn't want to ask for a drink and appear weak. His backside was sore from the stiff chair, but didn't want to reposition himself and appear nervous. But he was nervous, and he was weak, and he wasn't sure if he could hide these things. He imagined they were obvious. That a true country boy could smell this kind of fear and anxiety. Like rotten chicken to a gator. "The drawings of him that I've seen on TV don't really look like him. You guys made his face too round, or wide or something. I'm not really sure." Corey kept his eyes down, briefly glancing up to the officer, recognizing an element of pity, an element of disgust, an element of hatred, an element of compassion, mixed like a cocktail in his eyes. Corey lifted his shoulders, "And when I would hang out with him, he was a little strange, but he was always nice to me."

"How was he strange?"

"Dunno, he just was, sir. I guess I thought it was strange that he spent so much time at church but also had a lot of dope. I didn't think that made sense. He also collected knives. But I didn't think that was really weird at all, I thought they were pretty cool."

"You didn't think that you should tell someone?"

"No sir. I mean, he was the guy who gave me pot. I wasn't gonna tell anyone about him. He made me promise not to tell anyone about him. I mean, people collect all sorts of things anyways. I have a teacher that collects postcards that've already been used, from people he doesn't even know. He's got stacks of them, but I wouldn't think he was crazy for it. I know some kid that collects lizard tales, you know he catches a lizard and pulls the tail off and keeps them in little baggies. Another kid keeps all of the bubble gum he chews and clumps it into one big ball."

The officer nodded along.

"Am I gonna get in trouble for telling you about the pot?"

The officer waved at the concern. "Don't worry about that right now. Tell me about when you first met him."

Corey sat up in the chair, shifting his weight to the other side. "It was during the summer. The one before last."

"Do you know exactly when?"

"We had pretty much just moved up here, so it had to be the end of July. I was just walking home at night and there he was. It was either a Friday or Saturday 'cause I was coming home from a party. He sorta popped out of nowhere. He asked me if I smoked and I was like, sure. So we went back to his place and smoked some pot. Just like everybody who knew him said, he was real nice. You know? I remember us talking, really about nothing. You know movies, music. We talked about getting high and how Graceville was sorta lame. But then, I can't remember how it came up, but I told him about my mom. She had passed the year before. And he didn't say nothing. Usually people are all like, I'm sorry for your loss. Something like that. I remember, he just nodded. Then, you know what was a bit strange, he started talking about, what was it? It wasn't DisneyWorld, but it was one of those places in Orlando. SeaWorld. It was SeaWorld. He was all about SeaWorld. He asked me if I had ever been. I thought that was weird."

"What else?"

"I dunno, sir. I think he was a nurse at one of the hospitals in Dothan. I thought that was pretty weird, a guy nurse. I think that's where he got all of the pills he always had. I think he said one time that he wrote his own prescriptions. Don't know though, for sure. I would see him probably once or twice a week over at his house, pick up some pot, maybe hang out for a little while. That was about it. He gave me a couple of his knives, I don't know if you guys need those. I mean, you can have them if that helps." When Corey looked up, he could tell that he hadn't said enough by the way the officer looked, and he searched for whatever else he could say. "What else? The last time I saw him, we asked him if he could get us a hooker. It was a stupid idea. I didn't even do it, you know, with her. But I know that I can get her number if you guys need that. Maybe she knew him better."

The officer nodded along, his face now unsympathetic, his eyes like cold sheet metal.

33

The two boys woke up to a knock at the motel door. It was early in the morning, where the light of the sky had just peaked out and broke through the slant pines that stood behind the motel. Hordes of ivy seemed to clothe the smaller trees. AJ turned to Fatty, who was already sitting erect, and his face was marked with worry.

"It's all good," AJ whispered. "Get all of our stuff together."

AJ came to the door and looked through the peephole at a man with a beard that went from black to grey, a rounded nose above the beard and dark eyebrows that spread out to his temples. The knock sounded again and AJ shrunk away from the door.

"Who is it?" AJ called out.

"Open up."

AJ looked out through the peephole again and peered around the man to see if there was anyone else out there. "What for?"

"Open up, or I'll open it up for you."

They could hear a handful of meddling keys, and Fatty was standing behind AJ with both of their bags as AJ cracked open the door as far as the chain lock would allow.

"Where's the woman that checked in last night?"

"She's not here."

"Where's she at?"

"She left."

"Well, it's time for you to go," the man said as he tried to look into the room.

"We paid for the night."

"The night's up. It's time for you to move on."

"W-we ain't in tra-trouble are we?"

"Not yet, not unless you're looking for it."

AJ closed the door and slid off the chain lock and opened the door completely.

The man walked into the room past the boys and looked around the bathroom. "I can't be having no minors holding up. It's the law," he called back from across the room. "Where's the key at?"

"It's on the tat-table th-threre."

"We haven't done nothing wrong," AJ said.

"I don't care. It's time for you to go."

AJ looked around the room for anything they might have left laying around. "Fine. We'll leave."

"That's right you'll leave."

"What's your fucking problem?"

"What'd you say, son?"

"I said, what's your problem."

"First off, it smells like grass in here, and I don't need no punk kids smoking dope in my rooms."

"We ain't smoked shit in here."

"Better check that tone boy. I ain't your daddy, but I'll tan your hide up right here, right now."

"I'd like to see you try that shit," AJ said.

"What'd you say?"

"I said I'd like to see you try that shit, old man."

The man started towards the two boys, and Fatty began to back out towards the opened door and let AJ's bag fall to the floor.

"Whah-what the f-f-uck AJ? Come on. Wa-what are you du-doing?"

The man stood where he was, looking down at the revolver sitting right inside the mouth of the bag. "Better listen to your buddy there."

"Shut up," AJ's voice quivered as he reached down for his bag and the pistol. He tried to steady it, but he could feel the shakes starting and working their way throughout his entire body as he picked up the bag.

"Listen boy, you putting yourself in more trouble than it's worth now. Why don't you just move on?"

"D-da-dude, wah-what the fuck are you d-doing?"

AJ walked over to the bed stand, all the while keeping his eyes on the man, and grabbed the sheet of paper with the addresses that Crystal had written down.

Fatty walked out of the room backwards, and stumbled over the door jam, caught himself with the frame.

"Boy, you must be in some sort of trouble to be carrying round that piece."

AJ didn't say anything.

"Listen here, you do something with that there and you're gonna be arrested. No ifs, ands, or buts. You don't think as soon as you leave that I won't call the sheriff and tell'm what happened."

"Not if I shoot you, you won't," AJ said, but even he didn't believe what he said. Tears started to line his eyes and he struggled to stay strong. He wanted to fall to the bed and curl up, cry like the child he was. He held the gun up and backed out of the room, the put the pistol in the pocket of his raincoat. He lifted his bike and straddled the frame.

"AJ, I w-want to g-ga g-ga-go h-home."

"Get your bike."

As they started to ride off, AJ turned back and saw that the man came out of the room and watched with his arms crossed. There was a smirk on his face, and he didn't look to be in a hurry to call anyone. He just looked content that they were gone.

"We da-don't even kna-know where we're at. We da-don't kna-know where we are ga-ga-going."

"The first bus stop we come to, we'll get on. You can go home if you want, but I'm going to get Lenny."

They rode until the sun was directly above them. They hadn't seen another car on the backroad they had been traveling. His entire body shook. He stared out into the Cancerweeds and Basswoods. A retention trench three quarters full with dark rainwater lay at the side. AJ told Fatty to stop as they crossed over a swollen river. The passing water was clay-brown, unmoving, and two long-necked white ibis were plucking at each other on the banks, leaping into the air with wings spread, pecking and plucking, their thin legs piercing back into the water without a splash. It was a vicious dance, long white feathers falling to the water's edge. AJ stood off of his bike and looked down the road as far as he could and then walked up to the concrete balusters, reached in the bag and threw the gun. It hit the dead water and disappeared.

The first town they came to was covered in dust and a soft green film, everything from the cars to the windows and windowsills of the buildings was covered in rain-streaked pollen. Brick buildings lined the road. It was late in the morning and they followed a city bus to the first stop that it made. Three black boys stood at the corner across the street from them, and AJ glanced from them to Fatty and then kept his eyes on the ground as they headed towards the bus stop.

At the stop was another woman, this one with long fingers and thin bones that protruded from her thin, brown skin. She had on a shirt without sleeves and her arms hung down like tired limbs on a weathered tree. When she stood to get on the bus, she took very small steps. AJ asked if she needed any help, but she seemed not to hear him and continued with her languid approach to the bus doors. She sat in the first seat, right behind the driver, who greeted her by her first name, and then AJ took two steps onto the bus and asked how far it was to the nearest bus station, and how long it would take to get there.

"Need to cross the street, go up 'bout half a mile, and wait on the thirteen, and it'll take you fifteen, twenty minutes to get there."

AJ nodded and stepped back off of the bus and Fatty followed him across the street.

When they reached the station, they stood outside and looked at the people who loitered out front. There were more than ten people with their backsides leaning against the front of the building. One man had a cane, another held a few grocery bags and was eating from a bag of green grapes. Another man scratched at the back of his neck and would stop, look at his fingers, and continue to scratch. Neither Fatty nor AJ made eye contact and both carried their backpacks into the station as if they had taken the wrong school bus and ended up on the other side of town. They kept their eyes on the ground and AJ could feel the people's stares, could feel the eyes moving from his soft hair to his jeans to his sneakers with a little mud splatter dried to the laces and along the sidewall of his right foot.

"I'm ga-going home, AJ. I ain't da-d-doing this a-any ma-m-more."

"That's fine."

"How ma-much do you tha-think it'll ca-kek-cost?"

"How much do you have left?"

Fatty dug deep into his pockets and pulled out fifty-two dollars and a couple of coins and showed it to AJ. "How m-m-much do you ha-have?"

AJ pulled out the paper with the directions and a couple of twenties from his pocket and took their money and headed towards the ticket counter. He paid for one ticket to Graceville and handed it back to Fatty, and turned back to the ticket counter and showed the attendant the directions that he had. "I'm supposed to get to these two places. Can you tell me how far they are and how I can get to them by bus?"

The attendant pulled the glasses out of his shirt pocket and rested them on the bottom of his nose and held the paper out at arm's length. He studied what was written down and began to type into a green-screened computer. "This first one ain't on the map. Couldn't tell you where it is." He looked over his glasses at AJ, pulled out a kerchief and wiped at his nose, then continued to type. "This second is clear down and cross into Orlando. By bus, it'll take you half the day to get down there."

"How much will it cost to get there?"

"Let me see." And the man clicked into his keyboard—the reflection of the screen blinking off of his glasses—and he tallied up an amount with a pencil, licking the tip before he wrote. "You'd have to take, let me see here, three buses. Cross from here to Jacksonville, transfer in Jacksonville, take it down to Daytona, and cross back from Daytona to Orlando. Now, to get you to Jacksonville, it'll cost you a little less than thirty dollars one way, take you about three hours. From there be about another five or six hours, and the whole trup'll cost you bout seventy-five total."

AJ bought the ticket and the two boys sat in the waiting area. It was cold in the station and AJ held his bag close to his body, half to keep warm and half afraid someone was going to come up and take it from him. Outside of the glass door was a dancing man, old and small. He wore all white, slacks, shirt, a tie, and a sailor's hat with the name Dave embroidered on the front. He was a dancing man: his black wing-tips had holes on the midsoles. The old man raised his eyes, tugged on the sharp curls of his white beard, dancing his jig, a crippled sort of dance. He saw the boys watching him. He finished with a spin and came inside. He sat a tattered bag next to the boys and did a quick two-step.

He said, "What yaw folk doing roun'ere?"

AJ looked up into his honey-glazed eyes, at his yellowed nails pulling the thin curls of his beard straight. "Just on our way home."

"Now'where that?"

"Florida."

"Where'bouts?"

"Ga-gg-Grace-vav-ville."

"I got folk down rounder, yessir," he said and braced himself down into the seat right next to the boys. He looked about the room with difficulty, his neck stiff. "It's hod out there. Load, it's hod. Been walking, ain't got no truck, just walking. Thumbin' places. It's hod. Tired and hod," he said and pulled the hat down and wiped his brow with it. "What yaw name?"

"Abraham," said AJ.

"Mister Abraham. Fine name, from the good book. Yessir, a fine name, Mister Abraham."

"Ja-jj-Jarvis," Fatty said.

"Mister Jarvis," he said with a sturdy nod. "Show do like some white folk. I love yaw. Some good white folk." He started an anxious tapping on the floor with his heels. "I was raised by some white folk, you know..."

AJ looked over at Fatty, who just shrugged his shoulders.

"Well'sirs, name is Dave. Everyone round, they all calls me, Dancin' Dave."

The boys nodded.

"Do love some white folk. Probably more than the colored," he whispered. "Show do love yaw. Some good white folk." He wiped at his brow again and then straightened his shirt. "Load, it's hod." Dave began to fan himself with his brimmed hat. "Down from round Slocomb. Yaw know Slocomb?"

The boys shook their heads.

"Don't know Slocomb?" he said and reached down and pulled a Wiregrass brochure from his bag. He flipped it open. "Been all over, but always findin'back'ere. Ole Dancin' Dave, yessirs," he said and showed the boys a picture of himself in the brochure. "Ole Dancin' Dave."

The boys smiled.

Dave smiled back. "No need to be afraid of Dancin' Dave. I love er'buddy. People love me too, I think. I do think they do. Sometimes, people ride me from place to place, other times I thumb where I need to get. But I always gettin' where I goin'. Show do." Dave sat for a minute, looked over to the boys, and then pointed to the holes in his shoes. "It show hod though."

AJ nodded.

"Yaw folk in trub? Doin' round these parts, hope yaw ain't in no trub. Never been in trub myself. Old sheriff love Dancin' Dave. Never done no'bud'no'harm. Never been in county. Don't drink. Never drank no beer. No sirs. I'm good people. Just do like the good book say. I'm good people. Like some white folk, good people. Raised by some white folk."

"Wah-where you a sa-sslave?"

AJ jabbed Fatty in the side with his elbow, a dry, uncertainty on his face.

"Lode no, Mister Jarvis, no sir. Dancin' Dave wunt no slave. Eighty-two yares ole," he said and tugged on the front of his round cap. He laughed a dry, tired laugh. Soft like lemon pucker. "I worked some farms though, wunt no slave. I 'member when all this was peanus. Wunt none of this'ere, just peanus crop and pinewoods. Boy things change, but ole Dancin' Dave gone always be Dancin' Dave. People always saying, got to change with times. Well, I ain't gone change nothing. Dancin' Dave just Dancin' Dave. Little touched or not."

"What's pa-p-penis crop?"

"No sir, Pea-*nuts*, pea-*nuts* crop. Boil peanus, roast peanus, yaw'know, peanus butter."

A bus pulled up to the awning, the brakes loud and piercing, the gears grinding into park. The boys watched and waited for people to exit the bus, but no one came except for the driver who walked down and around front and lit a cigarette.

Dave tucked his bag between his feet and tapped his shoes on the ground, a quick little seated dance.

The boys smiled.

"Why yaw find yourself round'ere?"

"We came looking for someone," AJ said.

"Mister Abraham came looking for someone, huh? Yessir. Find'em?" he asked.

"Not really."

"Either did or didn't, Mister Abraham. Cain't sorta something like 'at."

"I guess not."

"But yaw headed back home now? Good white folk like yaw shouldn't be stayin' round all these colored folk. No sirs. That's why I come sit'ere. No bud gone bother you with Dancin' Dave'ere. Some colored folk, they just don't care for the likes of yaw, not like me."

"Th-tha-thank you."

"Some do awful thangs to good people, Mister Abraham, Mister Jarvis. Yessir, they do. I seen plenty awful thangs. Plenty...I 'member the night some colored folk came and got my pap. Come and took'em. I'se just a yute. Youngern yaw. But I was gone find them people, get my folk back. But didn't know place to look. No sirs. But I went. Full of pis'n'vinegar, I went for those boys. Ended up lost, and sure as shootfire, yessir, sure as shootfire, when I found back'ere, my pap had been back and laid to rest. God rest'him soul. He been back, and I missed. Some people do some awful thangs. Show do..."

As Dave continued, AJ was having a hard time following along, his mind starting to wander. He began wondering about how much money he had left; he didn't want to pull it all out and count it; he was afraid of someone coming and taking it from him; he knew that he didn't have much anyways; he wondered if Corey was back home; maybe they already let him go; he wondered what he would say to Lenny if he found him; he wondered how he was going to find one person in a state full of people; if he could even trust the hooker; wondered if she was just sending him off to nowhere. He was tired. He wanted to be back home. He asked his passed mother, in his mind, what he should do. He heard nothing. He tried to imagine what she would do. He didn't know. He looked over at Dancin' Dave for an answer in his thin smile, then down to the holes in his black shoes where a circle of dark and cracked skin peeked through. AJ stood and set his bag down on his seat. He walked to the counter with the ticket in his hand. He asked for a refund and said he needed the same ticket as his friend, a one-way to Graceville.

The attendant printed the new ticket and gave AJ the change, then pointed out to the bus under the awning and said, "Well that's your guy's bus out there. It's bound to leave any minute now. You boys better go get loaded up."

AJ came back to Fatty and Dancin' Dave. "That's our bus," he said.

"*Our* bus?" Fatty questioned.

AJ nodded and presented the old man with the leftover money that they had.

"What's that?" he asked, still tugging at his beard.

"Just some money," AJ said.

"Lode no sir, I don't need yaw money, just pleasure talking to some good folk is all. I can tell yaw some good, decent white folk. Can I shake yaw hand, Mister Abraham?"

AJ put the money back in his pocket. The man put out his hand and AJ took it, softly, like he was being handed something precious, bones like dead twigs. He was afraid to squeeze too hard.

"Mister Jarvis?"

Fatty shook the hand.

34

Once he was released, Corey liked the idea of having stayed in jail for the night. It made him feel hardened, tougher than any other fifteen year old boy. No one he knew had been in jail before, no other than Drake. He even wanted to keep the wash-faded black and white stripes they made him wear, the slip-on shoes, so that he could prove this newfound toughness. Yet, he knew this was a façade, it wasn't the truth. He knew that they only kept him there to scare him into talking. Scared, he was. During the night, every metallic sound in the little jailhouse terrified him to tears. The clank of the cell door, the tack of the shoes against the cement floors, the creak of the metal bed that he couldn't sleep on. He had just sat there, the whole night through. The hanging fluorescents in the corridor flickering, the electric hum seemed to sit in his stomach. He had kept himself from crying, though that was all he had wanted to do. He had sworn to himself, to his dead mother, to God, that he would stop using drugs, that he would throw away the movies under his bed, that he would stop cursing out his stepmother, that he would stop doing all of the things that he knew were wrong. He also promised that he would study harder, that he would do anything if he didn't have to stay there any longer. But the night continued, slow like the incessant drip of water in the tin sink.

But once released and at home, he closed his door and found his pot and cigarettes. He opened his window and blew the smoke out into the rain. He didn't know where his brother was, nor did he know where anyone was. His stepmother had to come and pick him up from the jail. And when she had told him that he needed to *straighten out*, he told her to shut the fuck up, but then apologized. He apologized for everything. The way he always acted, the way he spoke to her. He had told her that he wasn't really ever mad at her. He said that *in all honesty* he liked her, but that he was mad at his dad for getting married again so soon. That it wasn't fair to his mother. His stepmother said that she had understood, but that she loved his father very much. He didn't really believe her, but it was enough that she said it. He knew that what she really loved was that his father was able to provide for her. She loved the security, the money, the house, the clothes, the jewelry, the privileges that the money provided. But it was enough for now that she said it anyway.

He smoked until his throat burned, until he couldn't stop coughing. Coughing so hard he thought he would suffocate. He fell back onto his bed and looked around his room. When he opened his eyes again, it was late and his brother was standing next to him. He sat up and put his hand on his brother's shoulder and squeezed. The rain had breathed in through the opened window and puddled on the hardwood floor.

"They didn't beat you up?" AJ asked.

"Who?"

"The people in jail."

"No, nobody beat me up."

"What was it like?"

"It fucking sucked. Just sitting there."

"What did you do?"

"I just sat there."

"All night?"

Corey sighed. "Yep, all night. It sucked, but it wasn't that bad." Corey stood and closed the window, then brought a towel and laid it over the water sitting on the ground.

"We went looking for Lenny." AJ said, his hands digging in his pockets.

"You did what?"

"Went looking for Lenny. Me and Fatty. Took a bus up to Dothan and talked to the hooker, Crystal, and asked if she knew where we could find him. I thought that if I could find him, then they would have to let you go."

Corey smiled back to his brother. "So now she's a hooker?"

AJ nodded.

"But you couldn't find him?"

AJ shook his head. "She gave me an address down in Orlando, and I was scared to go all that way by myself, that I wouldn't have had enough money to get back home."

"So you came back home?"

AJ nodded. "Are you in trouble still?"

"No. I told them everything that I knew and they had to let me go."

"What about Drake?"

"Dunno. Don't much care. They said that they'd sent him home."

AJ sat down on the bed next to his brother. "I'm sorry," he said.

"For what?"

"Everything, I guess. Hitting you. I shouldn't'a done that."

Corey put his arm around his brother's shoulder, "It's all done with. Just forget about it." He pulled his brother in, rough, his hair brushing against his cheek. "It didn't even hurt. You hit like a little bitch," Corey said and then laughed.

"Fuck that. I got you good."

The rain just would not stop. It tried to wash away the guilt, the dirt, it tried to wash away the hot, the tired mess. It filled the black lake, over the reeds and cattails and even flooded the tennis courts. It tried to wash away the pain, the defeat. It tried to wash away the hope. But what the rain tried to wash away, it was. It was all of those things.

35

Sadie didn't know how far she ran, but she was far enough so that she couldn't see the house. She was too afraid to go into the woods, so she kept in the pastures, but she was too tired to keep running, but not tired enough to stop moving forward. It was dark all around her, and a wet chill covered her like a thin sheet. When she finally came to a barnhouse, she entered through a crawlspace and huddled inside, against the weather-worn paneling swollen with rainwater. She wiped her face with her wet shirt and sat there with her knees tucked up to her chest. She shook with the cold, she shook with fear. "I want my mom," she cried to herself. "I want to go home." But then the thought seemed to settle into a dark pit, a core of her, and she could feel it growing. She didn't move; she hardly listened to the sounds around her; she only concentrated on this expanding pressure in the pit of herself. That she couldn't find home. That she was lost, that she was alone. She knew that she couldn't stay where she was, knew that she had to keep moving away from what she saw. She could still see their faces, their heads lulled back. Her hand in his. She imagined Lanier with the knife. She imagined Lanier coming for her. She couldn't fall asleep there. She was afraid of the daylight, when it would come and what it would show her of this place that she sat in. She looked down at her one shoe and then to her bare foot. She crawled back out, her hands and knees deep in the mud, the heavy rain showering over her. She picked herself up, wiped at her stinging eyes with the back of her hand. She couldn't run any longer. Her one foot hurt with every step, but she kept forward through the endless field of tall grass, the blur of rain. Lightning splintered the dark sky and would show her the black palings of trees off in the distance and then only further darkness. She was most afraid that she would end up where she started. Whenever she did hear anything she would drop down into the grass, let it swallow her. She would lay in the murk on her belly, bite the skin at the base of her thumb, and keep still. Then she would eventually continue, stumbling and falling through the tall grass. Stopping, then continuing long into the night.

When the sun started to break through the night and show the rain still falling all around her, she could see a pathway, and even further a clay road. She came to the road, but was too afraid to walk it. She hunkered down in a shack, overgrown with ivy and kudzu, covered in pine needles. When she became too afraid and wanted to cry, she would dig into her pocket and pull out the crystal that the young boy had given her and would rub at the jagged edges. She would clench her fist around it. She would pray with it. Then she would put it back into her pocket. She stayed in the shack along the side of that clay road for two nights, and when she slept, she dreamt of being in that long and dark hole. Unable to get out. Feeling around at the walls, wet, ungiving. She could hear Lanier's voice echoing down to her. Calling her. Begging her to climb out.

And on the third morning, the rain had stopped. She walked to the road and continued down—weak with hunger, tired with pain—away from where she came. The crystal in her hand. Her stomach tight. And when the sore on her foot opened, she simply couldn't go any farther. She sat on the side of the road.

PART FOUR

A PRELUDE TO CONFESSION

"HICKEY" HIBBENS: Gaelic Origin, meaning descendant of a healer

36

*F*ather Hibbens is chewing on ice from his drink. The last man had left with the collar of his jacket raised. Voices of a few women are laughing and cussing in a room upstairs directly above Hibbens. A train of colorful women start down the stairs and he does not turn, budge, or even flinch. The women have thick coats on over their dresses, purses tucked under their arms, and they are talking about a certain John that many of them have shared over the last few months. Patty is the last to walk downstairs, her hair pulled back tight peeking out from under her blond wig. She notices the back of him, the only man left in the waiting room. His head is down between his shoulders, a pronounced knot in his neck.

"Hey Hickey," she skips down the last few steps as he turns to her with one arm out. She is tall in heels, dark and beautiful compared to this white and worn father. She cuddles into his arm and gives a kiss on his cheek, then wipes the lipstick off with a bar napkin. "I see you found my cigarettes." She lifts the pack from the bar, "There're only four left. Just helped yourself, didn't you? I didn't think you smoked no more."

"Anymore, baby, it's anymore." His pupils gaze at her through slits fighting to stay open, fraught with exhaustion.

"Anymore. You drunk as a skunk, now ain't you? Well, what you doing down here?"

"Just wanted to see my girl is all." Hibbens burps with his mouth closed, excusing this with a flat palm in the air.

"But it's late. You don't need to be down here with all this mess."

"I don't get to see you enough anymore."

"I still see you, Hickey. What are you talking about?" Still under the weight of one of his arms she pulls him away from the bar. Hibbens drops a loose wad of bills on the counter and lets her gentle pull haul him outside like an undertow he's willing to succumb to.

"You better of held on to some of that," she said with a laugh.

They walk the few blocks to her apartment and mount the four flights of stairs up to her flat. The hallway smells of incense, burnt tires and toasted cumin seed. She opens her door, is followed inside and goes straight to her bedroom and removes the wig and the nylon dress. She covers herself in a loose rayon buttoned shirt and sits down, tucking one foot under herself, smiling, the both of them, and she turns on the television and flips through the channels.

Hibbens sits with a sigh. His white hair is yellow in the fluorescents. His wry, drunken, one-sided smile and a long, aged dimple emerge. His eyes, blue surrounded by glossy white, are covered by rectangular glasses that obscure them. He stares at her. Her arms are long, fingers long and slender, her eyes dark, her hair black with little puffs that frame her forehead and temples. Her cheekbones are high, her face triangular and pointy. Her hand on his.

"So Hickey, what's going on?"

"Nothing's going on. I told you. I just needed to see you."

"Bullshit. There's something going on. You ain't got to tell me, but you cane lie to me neither." She turns from the television to face him, "You just ain't any good at it."

"Never mind it then. How you been doing? You went to church last night?"

"Yeah, I got up to the church, and on Wednesday and on Friday. I started singing again. That choir's something awful."

"You know I love to hear you singing."

"You know, I know."

"Well, what else? How's the work?" he says hesitantly.

"You don't worry yourself with my work."

"Just asking is all," he says.

"Well, people always still trying to talk me into working the candy-bar instead, like those over there in Atlanta. Say that's where the good, safe money is." Patty sits up and lights a Doral, picks up an ashtray and rests it on her knee. She is looking towards the television.

The bourbon makes his eyelids flitter, but he tries to focus, looking towards her profile.

She asks him if he needs a drink then asks if the smoke bothers him. Before he answers her, she stands up and opens a window and pours him a finger of cheap scotch. Her room is cluttered with a kitchenette in the corner and a bar overhang, one bedroom, one bath, one sofa, one poster, one phone, one dead plant. She walks to her kitchen-side and when she comes back with a bowl of cereal, Father Hibbens is holding a letter in his hand. He watches her eat for a few moments. The milk dribbles down from the spoon, a white droplet slowly driving down her chin.

"There was a man, young man about your age, came into confession and read me this letter he wrote."

"What about?" Patty garbles with her mouth full.

"Himself mostly, about being a drug addict and thief. I never heard anything like it. Kept saying he was decent. Said something about giving diseases to my daughters."

She does not reply, but she stops chewing.

"I am just so grateful for you baby, so damn grateful," he says to her.

She puts down her bowl of cereal and kisses the side of his head, holding his bottom jaw in her hands.

"That's my girl."

Patty takes the letter from Father Hibbens and begins to read from it. It has been neatly written and folded, consists of only three paragraphs. She reads slowly. "Is it a prayer? He keeps asking for forgiveness."

"Darling, I just don't know what it is."

"Well, did you forgive him?"

"No, guess I didn't. Just froze up at his voice, how calm it was. I don't think there was much I could have done anyhow."

"You think you should give this to the law?"

"Not sure. I'm guessing as much."

"I'm guessing you ought to."

"First thing in the morning, sweetheart."

She kisses his forehead, loosening his collar. She nibbles his ear, and trails down his neck where the small gray and black curls twist and taper out.

37

When he had finally woken up, he wasn't sure how long he had been asleep. The first thing that he knew was that Sadie was gone. The silence in the house told him that. It was a silence that he couldn't remember. Like nothing had ever happened. He felt a cool rush come over him. He felt the grace of God, he thought. He stood in the first room, the door was left open. He took the knife from the bed and washed the dried blood from the handle and the blade in the bathroom. He closed the knife and put it in his pocket. He looked into the mirror above the sink, the diluted blood streaking towards the drain. He looked into his own eyes; his jaundiced, thin skin; the decay of his front teeth. Many were chipped, the gum lines worn down, some of the roots exposed with small mounds of plaque. One tooth was missing, and he wondered if he had swallowed it while sleeping. As he came back out of the bathroom, he looked at the old couple on the floor, their hands still together, probably hardened that way, unable to come free. He wasn't sure if he should take the bodies out, lay them in the ground. He didn't. He thought of burning the house, but realized that that would draw too much attention. He left the room and came downstairs. He found paper and a pencil and sat at a desk that looked out over the fields. He began to write: *"I am a liar and a thief, but otherwise I strive to be decent..."*

As Lanier drove northwest on the stretch of country road, back into the storm, he rolled his own cigarette, sprinkling his last pinch of crystal at the head, his knees holding the wheel. Though Lanier had remained closely associated with churches throughout his life, he had not confessed since he was a child, when he would sneak his little sister into various denominations for the grape juice, croutons, milk, or cookies, and ultimately make confessions for his mother's sins. As a very young boy, he would pray as his sister finger painted bright yellow Jesus figures and listened to the fables of cursed and tortured men who were stripped bare and martyred. Lanier held the cigarette vertically, puffing down the flame, so the little pieces of meth would catch, crackle and mix with the tobacco. He decided that was what he needed to do. He needed to confess. He pushed in the cassette that jutted out of the tape deck, and the reel to reel tightened and played static for a few seconds before the drums started.

"Young girl, get out of my mind," Lanier sang out as he exhaled a thin cloud of bitter sweet, almost blue chemical smoke. "My love for you is way out of line..." The smoke slowly filtered through the car, and the static from the tape crackled through the speakers, backed by the "dun-da-de-da-de-ta, dun, ta-dun-da-de-dun" of the drums. "Better run, girl..." he sang with passion, driven not only by the amphetamines, but also in the voice that crawled inside of him, a young girl's cry, that same piercing, smoky cry that was all too familiar. "You're much too young, girl." Tears welled in his bottom lids as he sang—the song dictating his emotions and the drugs exaggerating them. He turns the knob up as the trumpets start in. "So hurry home to your ma'ama, I'm sure she wonders where you are. Get out of here, before I have the time to change my mind. 'Cause I'm afraid we'll go too far. Whoa, young girl..." When the song ended, he ejected the tape and tossed it to the side, reaching for another from the backseat. He was able to grab three of them: the plastic hard and thin, the labels soft and worn through, the little reels protected. All of the cassettes were home recorded and appeared the same, only the numbers 1984 were written on the labels; still, Lanier knew each of his cassettes individually and played songs methodically, fast forwarding and rewinding with precision.

38 _____

When cars came, Sadie had tried to hide herself. But the time came when she was only half conscious, draped at the side of the road. And when a gentleman pulled over to inspect what he had seen, the lady who was also in the truck stayed in her seat. Sadie could hardly open her eyes, but when she saw through thin slits that a shadowy man was hunched over her, she tried to scream. She tried to hold her arms out, to cover herself, but she couldn't. The man called back to the truck. Her hair was entangled with pine needles, her mouth dry and cracked. Her scrapes infected. In her mind, she knew that Lanier had found her and could do nothing but allow herself to be carried from where she lay. That the drive would continue.

The woman's voice was there now.

Sadie's head was cradled on the soft fullness of the woman's arm.

The movement of the car.

The smell of perfume.

The cool of the air.

"How long do you think she was there?" the woman asked.

Sadie wanted to speak, but her throat seemed to close around any word that came from below.

"Couldn't tell you. Smells like she soiled herself," the man said.

Again, she wanted to explain, but couldn't.

The woman, with a flat palm, smoothed over Sadie's tangled curls, pulling out the dead leaves and pine needles. Wiping away the smudge on her face with a wet thumb. "She's got a fever," the lady said.

"Ma," Sadie breathed out.

"We'll get you to her, don't worry. We'll get you to your Ma."

She went limp in her arms as the woman carried her to the truck and placed her in the cab. The drive continued. The rain wanted to stop, but it wouldn't; she could hear the rumble of it in the darkened distance. A cross pendant on a thin gold chain hung from the rearview mirror, twisting and dangling in the open-window breeze. She flinched as the man set the back of his hand on her forehead. She turned and buried her face into the woman's blouse. He said that he wasn't going to harm her. He called her darling. She shivered. The lady held her close and said a short prayer. "Lord, don't let this little girl die in my arms."

The drive continued. The road rough. A salty thickness to the air. A saggy-eyed dog stood in the truck bed and looked in the cabin window at her. Barking. Ears flapping in the wind. Drool gliding out. It wasn't a mean bark. It was playful. She wanted to know the dog's name, but couldn't ask. She wanted to know where she was, but couldn't ask. She wanted to know where she was going. She wanted to know how long it would take to get to her mother. But the comfort she had there in the woman's arms was enough. It warmed her, the feel of the woman's hand holding the back of her head. The other arm wrapped around her shoulders, holding her close.

When Sadie closed her eyes, she could see that hole. The hole that had tried to swallow her was closing.

www.ingramcontent.com/pod-product-compliance
Lightning Source LLC
Chambersburg PA
CBHW031947010726
47493CB00007B/2115